BLOODY HARVEST

BLOODY HARVEST

GRAHAME WOODS

McClelland and Stewart

0-7710-9049-8

The Canadian Publishers
McClelland and Stewart Limited
25 Hollinger Road, Toronto

Canadian Cataloguing in Publication Data

Woods, Grahame, 1934-
  Bloody harvest

ISBN 0-7710-9049-8

I. Title.

PS8595.0538B66   C813'.5'4   C77-001364-3
PR9199.3.W665B66

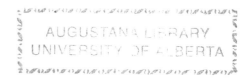

For Glorya
and for
Jayne and Guy

It was one of those strange evenings. The sun, a misty, fiery ball that seemed to hang over the trees, floating on the haze, threw hardly any shadows across the field in front of me. Usually I can get a rough idea of the time by it, dividing the field into zones so that when the shadows reach Zone Two, which runs right across three groundhog holes and a scrub bush, I know that it's around eight o'clock, and by the time they reach the fence line it's getting on for eight-thirty. None of this really matters, of course, because I have a watch, but I like to see how close I can get in my guessing, and anyway, it helps to pass the time.

I had settled down on the front step to enjoy a cigarette and wait for the pain to go when the French Canadian came running toward me, babbling away in French and pointing over to his place.

It had been a hell of a day. Probably the worst I'd known. And I've been coming here for eight years. With the heatwave into its third day it was already eighty-two degrees when we got up, twenty-eight if you understand that Celsius stuff, and it was due to go as high as ninety-five with humidity to match. Around noon my head had started to ache and by the time we'd finished the day's work the pain was stabbing through my eyes from the back of my head and bursting out of my temples. Driving back the light seemed to get brighter, burning up my pupils as it met the pain coming out from the other side, until I wanted to bang my head against the metal of the truck.

I even lay on the bed for a while, twisting around trying to find a position that would relieve the agony, soaking the mattress in sweat while I waited for the 222's to work. They helped a little and for a while I dozed, drifting in and out while the flies moved around like squadrons of Spitfires, using me as a landing strip for their circuits and bumps, and the smell of pork and beans cooking hung over me. Finally, almost out of my mind, I staggered to the woods and threw up, leaning against a tree, holding onto the trunk not caring about the mosquitoes.

Now the French Canadian was going to ruin the peace and quiet.

"*Monsieur! Monsieur! Venez. Venez vite! C'est urgent!*"

I didn't know what the hell he was talking about but I got the word "urgent" and he seemed scared stiff, so I went, half running, while he continued to babble away, almost in tears. We could hear her crying and moaning as we turned the corner of the barn.

The wall of heat that hit us when he opened the door of the old storage shed, a wall of heavy, stinking air mixed in with the smells of cooking, stale sweat and damp, trapped air that had been breathed a thousand times, made my stomach start to heave again.

She was lying at the end of the gloomy room on a metal cot, her hair stringy and matted, tears running down her grey cheeks, sobbing and gulping down air one moment and

8

groaning the next, her face, twisted in pain, caught on one side by the last of the sun glinting through a tiny window covered in flyshit. All she was wearing was a sweat-soaked, grime-covered blouse. She was gripping the sides of the cot, her legs wide apart, sheltering the blood and mess that was to have been her next child.

At the other end of the shed her two children, about eight or nine years old, stood in a dark corner, frightened and staring, their pale faces almost blending into the white-washed boards of the walls, transfixed by her stomach smeared with thick, crimson streaks from her hands, the black pubic hair clotted with blood that had erupted like a volcano, spewing onto the mattress and down her legs. In fact, for a moment we were all transfixed, then suddenly her husband came to life, alternately jabbering at me, then at her, but she didn't seem to hear. My first thought was to get the kids out, but then what difference did it make?

"Towels . . . a blanket!"

"Pardon?"

I said it louder, hoping he might understand. I'd had experience with injured people and knew some of the basic things to do. Sweat pouring down, I rummaged around in the stifling heat until I found a blanket and put it over her. Her forehead was cold and tacky. Hanging on the wall over the cot was a crucifix and a white plastic Mary. Neither of them looked overly concerned with what was going on.

"Doctor! Hospital!" I snapped it out.

"*Oui*. Doc-tor. 'ospital." He moved closer to the cot and took her hand, talking to her quietly but excitedly. In the corner the two children hadn't moved.

For a moment outside I felt cold, even in that heat. Then I ran to Al Rochford's house and explained what had happened.

Al Rochford's wife wrapped her apron around the woman's waist to protect her modesty and we lifted her into the cab of Rochford's pickup. Blood seeped through the apron onto the vinyl seat and trickled down her legs until it dropped into the fine dust and dirt on the floor mats, rolling into tiny balls. The French Canadian climbed in beside her, the kids in the box at the back, and Rochford's wife drove them off to the hospital while we stood watching in silence. Then Rochford shook his head and spat ten feet toward the fence post.

"Sonofabitch, eh?" There was some blood on his hands. He wiped them on the grass, making a face.

"Yeah."

"Think they'd know better. Well, not much we can do now."

"No."

"Had one of the boys clean out the truck just this mornin'. Sonofabitch." He tore the cellophane wrapping off a Colt cigar, chewed the plastic tip for a moment, then lit it with his Zippo, holding it high so that the flame didn't singe him.

When his father was alive, Al and his wife and kid lived in the white frame house his father had built for them when they got married, just down from the main, large, redbrick house that they say was put up over a hundred years ago.

He looked at me for a moment, scratching the back of his crewcut head, as though he'd just realized who he'd been talking to, and I could see the thought turning over in his mind.

"Why the hell would they come and ask you for help, Harris?" Without waiting for an answer he spat again, hitting the second strand of the eight, and walked off toward his house. Only then did I realize that my headache had gone, and in its place was a free, light, floating feeling.

10

"You'dve never known it to look at her."

"Known what?"

"That she was pregnant."

"No."

"They've already got a bunch of kids back in Quebec."

"Yeah?"

"So I heard. It's criminal."

Connie, who since well before we were married always said we'd never have more than three children, was sitting on the step with me, talking quietly so that Janice could get some sleep inside. It was one of the few times of the day that we had any time together, any privacy, and that's one of the problems. Usually, after three or four weeks of long days in the fields and long nights living in these cramped quarters, Connie and me are always bickering at each other, so sometimes we take a walk in the woods. It's not my idea of romance, especially when the mosquitoes are out, and I get the feeling that she goes along with it to keep me happy and doesn't enjoy it, which really makes a guy feel great. But it's peaceful and quiet and when we get back, Janice, if she's awake, pretends not to have noticed. One of the best things about it is that we get away from Janice's radio. Dear Jesus, that radio. We gave it to her for her fourteenth birthday two years ago and ever since it's been like it was grafted to her ear. Tonight I think we got the complete Top Thirty, with some guy in between yelling about air conditioners while they lasted over at some store in Chatham. That and the news that the heatwave was good for another three days at least.

It used to be worse when our two oldest kids came with us and we had to share a converted barn with five other families, but the place we've had for the past couple of years is an old implement shed that's been what Al Rochford calls adapted, by having a floor put in and the steps outside. It's about fourteen by twelve, with one window, the door and enough room for a small table, a couple of chairs, our bed and Janice's bunk bed that has the top bunk converted into a cupboard. The crazy thing is that we have a house up in Black Rapids with a fridge and a stove, a washroom – all the things you need in life, more or less.

"Feel like a walk?"

She looked at me for a moment as though she'd been expecting it, made a face, then almost playfully, making it sound as though she'd really like to and would have any other time, she gave my arm a squeeze.

"Not tonight, Eldon. Right now I feel comfortable. This heat won't last for ever."

"How about down by the stream – then we can cool off after?"

"No. I don't think so. We should be getting to sleep."

"Yeah." Just as I expected. "I think I'll go and cool off anyway."

"Why don't you? I'll probably be in bed when you get back." I got up and lit a cigarette, listening to the crickets, and Connie turned to go inside, stopping at the door. "It's terrible about that woman."

"Yeah."

At the stream I stripped down, waded out to my usual spot where I could lie down using a small, smooth boulder as a headrest, and let the cool water run over me. It was as close to heaven as you could get in southern Ontario.

I thought of the French Canadian woman, wondering what they were doing for her, how the kids must have felt and how long it would take to get over something like that. And Rochford worrying about his goddamned truck, Connie expecting my question and whether next time I'd come out and ask her or just forget about it.

I remember when I was a kid up in Black Rapids going for skinny dips at night, and, when we got more daring, in broad daylight; a bunch of ten-year-olds looking at each other pretending we weren't chicken. And when we were thirteen and wouldn't be caught dead talking to a girl, hiding up in the trees over the river waiting for them to come and swim. My mind was really working overtime tonight. The picture of that woman kept coming back and the crucifix over the bed reminded me of Muriel Lobraico. Jesus, imagine that. All these years – what, thirty-five? – and I still think of her.

When I was in school I thought the sun rose and set on Muriel, except whenever I came face to face with her I could feel myself redden and when I went to say something, nothing came out. Once I was hiding in a tree and Muriel and a friend came down to swim and all I could think of was her catching me spying on them and the shame that would go with it. Not to mention the fact that whatever chance I had of ever going out with her would be lost.

Barely breathing, I looked down on them as they took off their clothes – I say "them," I didn't really see the other girl, my attention was riveted on Muriel – and for a moment I caught a glimpse of her body before she stepped into her swimsuit and jumped into the water, the sun gleaming off her cross and chain. They were in for over an hour and it was all I could do to hang on.

Finally they came out, laughing and talking, looked around to see if anyone was watching, and then peeled off their suits and started to dry themselves.

13

Well, they talk about visions and stuff like that in church, but this was the vision to end visions. Muriel stood there glistening, her hair wet and hanging to her shoulders, the sun lighting it like she had a halo. Her breasts – in those days they were tits, nothing more nor less – stood out like, well, at that time they reminded me of a picture I'd seen in a library book of some statue over in Europe or somewhere, white and made of marble, only it didn't have any arms. Even from where I was rapidly losing the battle to hang on, I could see the goosebumps on her skin, her nipples standing out like two ripe raspberries, and below her stomach, a small but darkening patch.

She was the most beautiful thing I had ever seen, and as she slipped into her blouse she looked right up at me. My heart stopped for a moment, then took off, banging in my head, and I was sure I was going to fall. She had to have seen me, but just as quickly as she looked up she turned away and said something to the other girl, laughing. Then they ran off.

Never before had I seen a naked girl, and the fact that it was Muriel was like a prayer being answered, only I never prayed. Not even in church. I just pretended and stared down at my boots with my hands over my eyes and thought about hockey or baseball. But had I prayed that was what I'dve liked to have asked for, to see Muriel naked, only I figured He wouldn't go for things like that because kids weren't supposed to think of, well, bare naked girls, especially her a Catholic. Now I'd never be able to face her.

14

A loud snapping sound pulled me out of a groggy, heavy sleep, and I sat up confused, breathing hard.

Silence. Then a scraping sound, followed by more silence. In the corner of the room I heard Janice stir.

"You there, dad?"

"Yeah. It was only a rat. Go back to sleep."

"You sure it's dead?"

"Positive. See you in the morning."

I wasn't sure, but it would be by the time we got up. Maybe. I lay back down and looked at my watch. I'd been in my bed for twenty minutes and had to be up in five hours.

The morning sun caught me right in the eyes, flickering as it filtered through the leaves of an apple tree, striking softly at first, then harshly as the leaves moved out of its path. I felt awful. My head was heavy from lack of sleep and my body sticky against the damp bedding. Beside me Connie moved and stretched and I pulled a cover over her where her nightgown had ridden up, clinging to the outline of her body. Over in the corner Janice was sprawled like a rag doll, her radio waiting at arm's length for that reflex action she has of rolling over, grabbing it, and switching it on as soon as she wakes up. God help us if the batteries should ever fail. The heavens would open and the world come crashing down. Which on some days didn't seem like a bad idea.

I hauled myself out of bed and dressed, taking a brief look in Connie's make-up mirror. It didn't look good. My eyes were red and the lines underneath them seemed more pronounced than usual. My hair needed cutting badly and the grey parts seemed to be spreading, but with the dark, sunburned skin, it didn't look too bad. Alex once said my hair made me look like Beethoven and when I got back to Black Rapids that year I borrowed a book about his life from the library. He was quite a guy and if I looked like him it wasn't so bad. In fact, I kind of liked the idea. I even bought a record to see what his music sounded like. The kids thought I was crazy and assured me it wouldn't make the Top Thirty, but I liked it, sort of. All in all I wasn't in bad shape for a guy pushing fifty.

This morning we had three traps out of six, all neat and clean across the neck. Some of them can be messy if they're still alive. I keep a rock outside for those occasions and try to do it as quietly as possible before the others wake up. It's a great way to start the day.

We've developed a sort of routine in the mornings. Before I leave for the stream I put the kettle on and then wake Connie and Janice. While I'm gone, they dress, make the coffee and toast and take the bedding outside to air. It takes me about twenty minutes to wash and shave and I allow a bit more time to give Janice a bit of privacy, something she seems more conscious of these days, now that she's, well, more mature you might say. Everyone says she looks eighteen, though I can't see it. Oh, she's pretty and well-developed and all that, but if anything I'd say she was young for her age. Either way Connie worries about her being here for the summer and not spending it back in B.R. like the other kids. But this is going to be the last year so it's not that bad, and anyway, it's good for kids to see what life's all about.

There were sixteen of us in the back of the truck taking us to the Shantz farm where we were to work for the day, bouncing along the narrow concession road leaving a trail of dust that caught up with us every time we slowed down or stopped. Squeezed in beside the tailgate – we each seemed to have our own reserved position – I watched the fading dust drift up into the trees. On top of a dead elm was a redtail, its back to us. As we clattered past it launched itself into a graceful glide to a quieter spot. We were a strange bunch, all staring into space, lost in our own thoughts of escape, enjoying the extra room left by the French Canadians not showing up, which wasn't surprising. Wonder how she is? It was insane, bringing a woman to work in that condition. Thank God Rochford had his truck handy. Our old station wagon was up on blocks waiting for the heatwave to pass so I could finish fixing the brakes. There's always something.

In the middle of the truck was the Jamaican family. They don't speak much, mainly because no one seems to speak to them, or hardly ever. They're on the Rochford

farm too, only they live in the white house. They're imported, paid at an hourly rate, and the Government makes sure
they're treated all right. From their place the land slopes
down a bit to the storage shed where the French Canadians
live, then there's the barn which used to house over thirty
people in the Old Man's days but Al Rochford didn't like so
many people so close to his place so he stored his tractors
and things in there instead. Then there's us, down from the
barn a couple of hundred feet, and I think we have the best
place, apart from the white house. We've got the woods
close by and the stream about a quarter of a mile further
down, which no one else uses late at night.

It seems that everyone comes from somewhere else ex-
The Jamaicans seem nice enough and I like to listen to
them when they talk to each other with that soft, singing
way they have, especially her. She sounds like that airline
commercial they used to have on the radio that says something about airline stewardesses making you feel good all
over. Well, I wouldn't mind being made to feel good all
over by her. She's about Connie's age and they've got three
kids about fifteen to nineteen and Janice thinks the older
boy is cool, whatever that means.

It seems that everyone comes from somewhere else except Alex sitting opposite me. He just floats around, is the
way he puts it, always on the move but always coming back
for the picking season. He's about my age but slightly heavier and not an ounce of fat. To see him move through those
tomato fields is something else, agile and fast and by far the
best picker I've ever seen. He's something of a legend
around here, so much so that he calls himself the King of
the Tomato Pickers. He averages over 200 baskets a day –
his own personal record is 310 which he hopes to beat once
the weather breaks.

He's been everywhere. Vancouver, California, Mexico,

18

carrying a tent and supplies, goes regularly into Chatham to drink till closing time and manages to survive on four hours sleep a night. Sometimes he talks about the women he meets in Chatham, but whenever I've been there they don't seem to have been any great hell, and sometimes I wonder how much of it is bullshit. He says that he likes at least one piece of ass and a square meal every week and he gets it, free of charge.

But who am I to doubt a guy who can pick over four and a half tons of tomatoes in one day?

We moved up the endless rows of plants like crippled robots, stooped over and aching, sun hats flopping, clothes clinging, breathing in the sweet, sickening smell of the tomatoes.

Someone said it was seventy-nine already, going up to ninety, and we moved on, each working to his own familiar pattern. For me it's legs astride the plants, basket to the left between the rows, pick with the right, transfer to the left, which tosses it into the basket as the right picks off another.

Pick, transfer, toss, pick, transfer, toss, pull the basket up one more plant, pick, transfer, toss . . . keep on moving . . . pick, transfer, toss . . . Jesus, I'd love a gallon of ice-cold orange juice, a whole, beautiful gallon to myself . . . pick, transfer, toss . . . eight o'clock and it must be over eighty already . . . pick, transfer, toss, move the basket up . . . thirty-five cents a basket, ten baskets three-fifty . . . change the pattern, pick, toss, pick, toss . . . Connie was right, Janice shouldn't have to be here. None of us should be here . . . pick, toss, pick, toss . . . eyes blurring from the sweat, salty taste . . . don't, for Chrissakes, wipe your eyes with your hands . . . toss, pick, toss, move the basket up . . . this must be the hottest place on earth . . . sun burning . . . heat coming back off the earth . . . pick, toss, pick, toss . . . the Equator's the hottest place on earth. I remember that. Pick, toss, pick, toss . . .

"Harris – what do you know about the Equator?"

"The Equator is an imaginary line that goes around the middle of the earth. The middle of the world."

"What else?"

"Well . . . it's hot there?"

"It's the hottest place on earth, Harris."

"Yes, sir."

Dear Jesus, I've got to stop . . . rest . . . stand up. That's when I really feel my age, easing myself into an upright position. Sometimes my head swims slightly – I suppose it has something to do with the blood or oxygen. Can't be any good for you, all that blood rushing to your head like that. I looked around and lit up a cigarette stub. Connie was three rows over and slightly behind me, Janice four rows over, both stooped and moving like windup toys, their hats hiding their faces.

"Hey, Eldon! Move your ass!"

Alex's voice roared across the field, followed by his deep, bellowing laugh. He's the only person I've seen who was happy picking tomatoes. For him it was a challenge and nothing bothered him – heat, mosquitoes, deer flies, rashes, nothing. I bent over slowly and started to pick, building up my speed. Maybe two grand by the end of the season . . . pick, toss . . . move the basket up . . .

"Where was the highest temperature in the world recorded, Harris?"

"Me?"

"How many Harrises have we got in this class?"

"Well . . . the Equator . . . sir?"

"You haven't been listening, have you. Muriel?"

I hadn't been listening. I'd been looking out of the window watching the snow which had been falling all day and wondering if it would stop in time to clear the ice for the game – and watching Muriel. She sat one seat down and one desk over so I was able to watch her without her knowing. Now she was standing up, turned slightly toward me, giving me the chance to look at the smooth skin of her cheeks, the slightly turned-up nose and the graceful shape of her arms. If only she knew.

Her voice was firm and confident. "The highest temperature ever recorded was 136.4 degrees Fahrenheit at Al Aziziyah in Libya in 1922."

Shit, I knew that. He just caught me off guard.

I was doing pretty good at school. I mean, I was no Einstein, but then who the hell is, especially in Black Rapids? My math wasn't so hot but I read a lot, Jack London, Robert Louis Stevenson, things like that from the library, and *The Sun Also Rises* which belonged to my mother. I also memorized as much as I could of *Health, Sex and Marriage,* which went around the class for a quarter (a kid named Burns borrowed it from his father's closet) but I had to take it down the river to read so that I wouldn't get caught. Also there was a waiting list and the quarter only got you two days, so I pored over the diagrams and confirmed some of the things I already knew as well as learning other stuff – and all the time I was reading, sitting high in a tree where I wouldn't be seen, I was in agony, with what seemed like a permanent erection. I mean, hell, how often is it you get the chance to look at pictures like that and see what it really looks like up close and get a description of how you really do it? Burns must have made ten bucks from that book.

"Harris! I'm talking to you."
Jesus, he's always picking on me. "I didn't hear you . . . sir."
"I said, give us the relative position of Black Rapids." Goodhead seemed to have days like this when he'd pick on someone and really let him have it, and this was my day. I stood up, trying to remember how I'd written it down in my book. Might as well give him the works and shut him up.
"Er – Black Rapids is situated in Northern Ontario just north of Cochrane and east of Smooth Rock Falls, just below the 50th parallel in line with Mongolia and on a longitude of 81 degrees and . . . something minutes, which is in line with the most southern tip of Florida and Keystone, West Virginia." Now shove that up your ass.
I sat down, pleased with myself, even though I wondered who could give a good goddamn where Black Rapids is, except perhaps the people who live there. And they're stuck with it.

The thing I really excelled at was hockey (though my best mark in school was always for my essays, specially one I did on wheat production in Australia) and my ambition was to play for the Toronto Maple Leafs some day, but in the meantime I was the top scorer for the Black Rapids Midgets and aiming for the Junior club that played in a league with Cochrane, Timmins, Kirkland Lake and Rouyn-Noranda.

In these parts a good hockey player is someone around town, and if you're good enough to make the Junior club, let alone the Maple Leafs, you're a celebrity, a hero.

If you make the NHL you get to leave and go south and make something of your life.

My father came up here from Toronto in the early twenties to stake claims and make his fortune, and wound up working in the yard at the Black Rapids Lumber Company when he ran out of money. It was a good deal, he said. The company eventually provided a house for him when he got married and he paid for it with deductions taken from his weekly pay, and during the depression they deferred payment. He was in so deep to the company he was doomed to Black Rapids for the rest of his life.

He was a big, strong man with a quick temper, and fast with the back of his hand. My mother was scared of him and would do anything to keep the peace. I hated to see her making up to him to get back in his favour.

When I got the offer to try out for the Junior club, even though I was only just sixteen, I had to wait a week for my father to be in the right mood to ask him. We were having dinner and he'd been laughing about Caulfield Sr., who owned the lumber company and was about the richest man in town, slipping on the ice getting out of his Packard at the yard, and I knew that I'd never have a better opportunity.

"Dad?"

"What now?"

"Mr. Brelsford has asked me to try out for the Raiders. He figures I'm good enough to make the team."

My mother smiled proudly at me, and then to my father.

"Isn't it marvellous, dear?" She removed his dinner plate and gave him some jello. His laughter faded off and the light that had been briefly in his eyes dimmed as he leaned forward and placed his spoon on the table, looking at me very steadily, his face hardening.

"He said what?"

"That he thinks I could make the team and he wants me to try out."

There was a long silence while he rolled a cigarette and my mother stared at her jello as though she'd never seen it before. Finally he struck a match under the table, lit the cigarette, and blew smoke up toward the ceiling.

"Where d'you think that'll get you?"

"Maybe the NHL."

"Horseshit! You'd never make the NHL in a month of Sundays."

"How d'you know? You never come and see me play. Last year I got forty-one goals and thirty assists and everyone says that – "

"Everyone says that you're shit-hot and you believe them." He got up and started pacing the kitchen, relit his cigarette and turned, his back to the window. This was his favourite position for delivering a lecture and my mother, sensing it, got up and started to clear away the dishes.

He would start with, "Listen to me, my boy," and then pace to the door leading to the living room, stabbing the air with his finger while he inhaled his cigarette with a hissing sound, sucking air through his teeth.

"Listen, my boy. I don't want you gettin' any big ideas about makin' your livin' playin' hockey. There's no future in it and it's damned near time you started thinking about your future and payin' for your keep. There's opportunity down at the yard for people who're willin' to learn. Willin' to get their hands dirty. A hard day's work never hurt no one, and don't you forget that. A bit of sweat is good for the

25

soul, my father used to say – and I'm not talkin' about chasin' a bit of rubber up and down the ice. There are far more important things in life and any man who works hard, goes to church regular and provides a roof over the heads of his family, like I have . . . ," he let it hang there so's we could think about it and nod gratefully, then sat down and continued quietly, "– has somethin' to be proud of." He looked across at my mother, who was at the sink with her back to us. "Isn't that right, Fran?"

She took her hands from the water, wiped them on her apron and turned to us, not sure.

"Well . . . yes. I mean, everyone likes security and that, but, well, hockey players do get to be famous. Get their names in the paper and on the radio and I suppose they get paid good." He stood up quickly, cutting her off.

"I spose you're on his side? Tell me this! What happens if he breaks a leg or turns out not to be as good as he thought he was? What happens then? I'll tell you what happens, he's finished, good for nothin'." He looked at me for a long time, his mouth moving as he rechewed some meat from his teeth. "Well?"

I gave a weak shrug, knowing that I was losing. "So maybe I won't make the NHL. But right now I just want to play for the Raiders. I could work at the yard and pay for my room and board. It'll be no different than now, just another team."

"Sure. I read about these hockey players. That year Timmins won the cup. Everyone getting drunk and things . . . " I wasn't sure what he meant by that, but I'd heard stories about a big party the cops raided where they caught some of the team with no clothes on. And girls too, naked as when they were born. But it got hushed up and nothing happened.

26

"I don't want my son mixed up with a crowd like that. And!" He stopped. His best argument had just struck him. "And what about when you're through as a player? Eh? You'll be skilled for nothin'. Then whata you do?"

"All I want to do is try. That's all."

There was another long silence. He leaned back in his chair, pulled out his watch from his overalls and wound it, put it back and stuffed his hands into his pockets.

"All right. You go ahead. But–" he swung forward at me, stabbing his finger at my face with every word, "you stay outa trouble and don't come runnin' to me when you realize you've made a mistake. You understand? I've warned you! You get nothin' outa this life except by hard work." He opened his hands in front of me and turned them, showing the hard flesh, darkened by years of grime, the blunted nails and the scars running like rivers on a map. "I got no time for anyone, an' that goes for you too, who's afraid to use his hands." He looked at me for a moment and stood up. "But I spose you figure you know better."

At the north end of the field there is a wooded area and at the noon break everyone headed in that direction to relieve themselves. The women go in first, then the men, and I stood waiting, looking at my hands, and laughed. The sonofabitch didn't know what hard work was, and as for getting nothing out of life without working for it, he didn't know much about that either.

"Be nice to have a real holiday one day." Janice always waited until everyone else had been to the woods before she went in. There was no way she was going to pee in front of a whole bunch of old women, she told us the first year she came, and she's never changed.

"Yeah, it would. Maybe next year, if we can afford it."

"Sure."

My mother had always talked of how she and dad were going to take a trip one day. She'd get out the atlas and we'd pore over it, daydreaming about London, Paris or New York one time and all the romantic islands in the Pacific the next, all the time knowing they'd be lucky to get to Fort William.

She pointed out the red parts on the map that made up the British Empire and told me how when she was a young girl she was taken to see the Prince of Wales at the Canadian National Exhibition in Toronto after the First World War. I got along much better with her than I did my father and she was always interested in what I was doing, including coming along to watch me play hockey. She was a heavy reader, and on my eighth birthday she took me down to the Black Rapids library to get my first card. She was always telling me that reading was the key to life, and even though we lived way out in the sticks there was no excuse for being ignorant.

"Reading, Eldon, is like giving the brain food. That and listening to the radio."

So from that time on I read about three books a month, at least in the winter, and listened to the CBC on the radio that was on a table next to my mother's chair in the living room. We would spend our evenings listening to *Woodhouse and Hawkins* and mum's favourite, *Theatre of Freedom,* which required absolute silence in the house – if I so much as uttered a sound I was sent off to bed. On Saturday nights it was hockey, and for two hours or more I could see myself playing right there in Maple Leaf Gardens, every week a hero, the big star of the game, and the crowd was roaring for Eldon Harris.

Then there was the war. Good programmes like *Half-Hour with Mr. Jones* and the reports with Matthew Halton, who made it sound like it was happening just down the street. Old Goodhead used to have large maps of Europe and the Middle East across one wall of the classroom and we'd chart the progress of the war by sticking miniature flags into the map, the Union Jack for our side and the swastika for theirs. I even put up a map in my own room, adding Russian and American flags, and I remember asking my father why we didn't have our own Canadian flag and he told me that what was good enough for the King was good enough for Canada. If war had been a subject in school I'dve been top of the class, more than a match for Goodhead. As it was he didn't like it when I had all the answers.

It was an exciting time.

When the last woman came out all the men went in, and while some of us just stood and had a pee, others crouched to have a shit. I stood, enjoying the relief, watching a grey squirrel up in a tree chattering and swishing its tail. Poor bugger, having to put up with the stench.

For me, time often seems to stand still, like a photograph, and I'm able to see things that I normally wouldn't notice. I had one of those moments when I went to join Connie and Janice to eat our sandwiches. Connie didn't hear me coming, and I saw her isolated from everything else, looking tired, not just in her face but in her whole body. But more than that, she looked old. For the first time I could see beyond the grey streaks in her hair to the dark eyes, almost hollow, and because of the way she was holding her head the skin under her chin seemed loose and like wax. Around her cheeks there were wrinkles where her hand had forced the flesh up, distorting one eye. I had brought us to this, sitting in some fucking field eating peanut butter sandwiches, both of us older than we should be, not knowing each other any more while we waited out the years.

"*You'll be skilled for nothin'. Then whata you do?*"

She turned and saw me, looking up with a tired smile and offering me the bottle of warm water, and it was gone. Warm water, for Chrissakes!

I met Connie at a Christmas party in 1948.

I say "met" her, I saw her, like in that song, across a crowded room, sitting next to some guy at a piano playing "chopsticks" with one hand and holding a beer in the other. To say it was love at first sight wouldn't be fair because she hadn't yet seen me, but speaking for myself, I was smitten, captivated, enchanted, you name it. Then she laughed with her eyes sparkling, surrounded by a sudden golden light that dazzled my eyes and made my knees wobbly. Okay, so I'm exaggerating a bit, but that was the way it seemed.

Someone put the record player on and I cut through the crowd and asked her to dance. She was wearing a white, square-necked blouse with puffed sleeves and a striped dirndl skirt (she told me it was a dirndl later. To me it was a striped skirt), bangles on her arm and her hair was wavy and pulled back, held in place by a flowered clip. When she looked up and I saw her eyes, deep blue, soft and warm, I went into partial shock and almost backed out but she agreed to dance and I was stuck.

I didn't put a foot wrong as we drifted in the crowded basement, not saying a word for at least ten minutes. Thank God someone invented the long playing record. The perfume she was wearing smelt fantastic, and we seemed to fit naturally into each other's arms, her hair soft on my cheek and her arms cool to touch. I didn't even notice her figure until the floor got more crowded and we were forced closer together and I felt her breasts pressing against my body through my shirt. Then it started to happen.

"Er . . . d'you feel like a drink? It's getting pretty hot in here."

Those were my first real words to Connie Martin, forced out in an emergency situation that had to be attended to before she thought she had some sex maniac on her hands.

"Nope. I'm quite happy dancing. I like that music."

Yeah. Well that's all very fine, but I have this problem, see. I was beginning to sweat and then the idea hit me. Grabbing my handkerchief I quickly broke away and acted out the most dramatic sneeze I'd ever seen, doubling up at the same time in an effort to shift the position of the swollen mass caught at the wrong angle in my shorts.

"Bless you."

"Thanks." I sneezed again just to make it look real and coughed a bit. "Something in my throat."

"Maybe a drink is a good idea."

"Okay. What'll you have?"

"Rye and coke."

"After beer?"

"Why not?"

"Yeah, why not?"

That was my introduction to Connie. I remembered her slightly. She was a year ahead of me, and I knew that she lived up near the highway. As the evening went on I discovered that she served behind the counter at Howard Dusty's drug store and came with a guy who'd passed out upstairs.

She remembered me from my hockey days and knew that I'd been in the army, but that was all. It was enough to start with.

Our first date was to the movies to see *The Treasure of the Sierre Madre,* and during the Christmas holidays I drove her around in the Chevy, which was no big deal in twenty below zero. But it was in the Chevy that we kissed for the first time with the windows steamed up and freezing. I took her to a New Year's party that some guy at the mill threw and it seemed that everyone got drunk except us, so most of the evening we had the dance floor to ourselves and floated around looking into each other's eyes and feeling the shocks of electricity go through our bodies. At least, they went through my body. I was on Cloud Nine. On the way home we stopped and parked in the cut-off near the highway and took turns drinking from a mickey of rye I had in the glove compartment, my arm around her and her head resting on my shoulder, kissing occasionally while we watched the frost patterns form on the glass.

I think that when God created the earth, He deliberately designed northern Ontario as a plot against young love. He figured if he provided plenty of blackflies and mosquitoes in the summer, populated it with low income earners who couldn't afford the luxury of motels, where they existed, gave the people a puritanical outlook so that no one dare try to get in to the town's hotels for fear of being caught, made the houses small and equipped them with radios and the CBC and then, in the winter, engulfed everything in below-zero temperatures, young love would be squelched very nicely. And He did a good job.

Not only does the amount of clothing needed to keep warm remove any hope for a gradual, casual approach, but it also shrinks your balls and cock to a point where you look like a midget. With the engine off and a mickey of rye, you have about fifteen minutes to try and make some progress, which in the end is worthless unless you have somewhere to go to take advantage of it. In which case you'dve gone there in the first place.

It was at the twelve-minute mark, more or less, when she said it.

"Why don't we go over to my place, and I'll make some hot rum."

"Won't your folks mind? I mean, it's New Year's and all that."

"They drove down to Cochrane to spend it with my aunt and I stayed to look after the dog and the canary."

It's amazing how the body temperature can start to rise so quickly.

The thing is that, in certain kinds of relationships, something seems to happen between you. Something you don't have to talk about because you both know it's there.

"If you park on Allen Street and walk back the neighbours won't start gossiping." She gave me a smile and closed the door quietly. I watched her blurred figure through the iced-up window, hurrying to the house. When I got back from parking the car we stood in the front hall for a while just holding each other with the occasional long, deep kiss in between and then, very calmly, she showed me into the living room, introduced me to the canary and the dog, called Frankie after Sinatra, then left me to go and make the drink. The room was very similar to our own living room with lots of family pictures all over the place, a china cabinet, Philips radio, worn furniture and some plaques of flying geese on the walls. I sat on the chesterfield and flipped through the latest edition of the Black Rapids Record, trying to appear casual, but within five minutes of her

34

getting back with drinks, we were stretched out on the chesterfield kissing passionately and for the first time without heavy coats. I was able to run my hands over her body, feeling the softness where it should be soft and the firmness where it should be firm, until without a word we both got up and went upstairs, holding hands.

Why didn't you talk to Rochford about us moving?"

"It wasn't the right time."

"It never is the right time with you. I don't see why we have to live in that place while those Jamaicans get a proper house."

I'd finally persuaded Connie to come down to the stream for a late wash to cool off, thinking I'd maybe interest her in a little romance to relieve some of the tension, but as soon as she started off on her pet theme of the Jamaicans, I knew that I'd have to make do with the cold water of the stream.

"I don't make the laws and nor does Rochford."

"Damned right . . . and you don't do anything about it either."

"I told you, it wasn't the right time, for Chrissakes . . . what with her bleeding like a stuck pig all over his truck, maybe even dying." It was just like her to wait and then spring it on me. "Anyway, this'll be the last summer."

"You said that—"

"Last year. I know. Lookit, a bit of hard work, a bit of

discomfort never hurt anyone. What d'you want me to do? Go on welfare?"

"I sometimes think it would be better, yes."

"A Harris has never been on welfare and – "

"A Harris has never taken a handout. Not even your father during the depression. I know, I know. It doesn't change the fact that the Jamaicans make twice what we do for half the work and they have a shower."

"Okay, okay. I'll talk to him."

"When?"

"Tomorrow."

"Sure."

She stepped out of the water and started to dry herself and I knew there was no point continuing so I lay back, the water up to my neck, and watched her, some kind of stranger whose ass was getting a little larger, towelling herself down. There was a time when I would have dried her and there would have been an excitement, a warm, loving feeling . . . but tonight she was just a middle-aged woman, distant and not caring if she didn't look so good.

The trouble was she was right. I didn't do anything about getting us moved because I knew I'd be wasting my time. The Jamaicans had the law on their side and I had nothing, so they got their house and we settled for the shed.

"I'll talk to him tomorrow. I mean it."

"It's just that I worry about – "

"Janice. I know. It's no place for a kid."

"Aren't you coming out?" She slipped on her blouse and jeans, turning to me as she brushed her hair.

"I guess so." For some reason I was thinking of the French Canadian woman covered in blood and living in the storage shed, wondering if it would have been a boy or a girl.

"They have privacy, too."

"Who?"

"The Jamaicans. It must be nice to be able to shower without being stared at by you."

"You used to like it once. What'd you prefer? That I stared at the Jamaican woman?"

"You do anyway. I've seen you. Like the day she got soaked when it rained."

"Maybe I've got a good reason."

Rochford was by the barn loading some cedar fence posts into his truck the next morning, and I hurried over to catch him before he drove off. Over by the house his eighteen-year-old son Grant was lining up the telescopic sight on a .22 rifle with the Shantz kid, who walked with a limp since he'd lost some toes under a cultivator when he was small. By the garage, Rochford's wife, an attractive blonde with a good figure and warm grey eyes, was loading some baskets into the trunk of their white Buick Le Sabre. I didn't know much about her as she kept to herself pretty much, but Grant Rochford was typical of farmer's sons in that area, lazy, not the least bit interested in the farm operation and even less interested in working the farm. They wanted more out of life (in a way I could understand that) and it meant working in town, at a canning factory, driving a truck; doing any job that would pay good bread so they could drive a souped-up heap like Grant Rochford's with the ass-end elevated, wide oval tires, aluminum rims, an engine that had something like three hundred and fifty to four hundred horsepower under the hood, air scoops, two spotlights on the bumper, a racing stripe painted down the side and a tape deck and CB radio. He worked for a construction company, and unlike the farm boys of years ago, wore faded jeans covered in patches, bright shirts open to the waist, a medallion round his neck and long hair that looked like it had been done in a woman's hairdressing place.

Al Rochford slammed the tailgate shut and walked round to the front of the truck.

"Mr. Rochford! I was wondering if I could have a word with you?"

"Yeah? What?" He balanced his foot on the front bumper to tie up a bootlace.

"It's about where we're living. The implement shed."

"What about it?"

"Well . . . it's that and the Jamaicans living in the house over there. We've been coming here a few years now . . . worked for your father and – "

"You don't like where you're living?"

"Yeah. I like it all right. It's just that – "

"Lookit, I got enough problems. You ain't black, you ain't imported an' you don't have the fuckin' government on your back making all these rules. If you don't like it I'll pay you off, forget the whole thing. I ain't in business to provide fuckin' palaces for you people. All right?"

"Well . . . I spose . . . "

"You spose right." In one motion he swung into his truck, slammed the door and started it, looking down at me. "D'you really think I like them coloureds cluttering up the place? Stinking it out? Shit no! But they work their asses off, I'll tell you that. Thing is, pickin' tomatoes ain't good enough for our own folks any more, so I haveta bring em in, like it or not. Listen, you want the Quebecker's place you're welcome to it. Even throw in a new mattress."

"No . . . that's okay . . . thanks. Just thought I'd ask." The truck pulled away in a cloud of dust and I started to walk back to the shed, the two kids staring at me.

Fuck! It happens every time. I go into these situations ready to do battle, stand up for myself, and when the crunch comes . . . nothing! They're the bosses. They know better. They always know better. And me? I need the job, so what the fuck can I do?

Stand up, for one thing. Lose my job, for another. Lie to my wife.

"What did he say?"

"He's gonna see what he can do. Look into it."

"You see! I told you so. All you had to do was ask. Why couldn't you have done it sooner so we didn't have to put up with this place all this time? When?"

"As soon as he can. There are government rules and things he has to worry about. He'll get back to us."

"Eldon . . . I can't wait to have a proper stove, a fridge and a soak in a bathtub."

"Yeah . . . it'll be nice." Jesus, woman, can't you *tell* I'm lying to you?

"I mean, we should have some rights in our own country and all."

"That's what he said. Something like that."

"Goddamnit, I've burnt the toast."

While she made some more I went outside with my coffee and lit a cigarette, feeling bad that I could lie so well. Janice was sitting there and I knew she'd heard the conversation by the way she looked at me over the top of a huge pair of purple sunglasses, half-smiling as she casually painted some stuff on her nails and then blew on them.

"What are you smiling at?"

"You."

"What about me?"

40

"You know. All that stuff you told mum about us moving outa here . . . outa this dump."

"So?"

"So. We won't and you know it."

"You mind your business."

"There's no way Rochford'll do anything, an' I betcha he never said he would. But it'll keep mum happy for a few days."

"You don't know what you're talking about, eaves-dropping."

She waved her hand through the air a few times and then started on the other one. How come she was so smart and could see through me while Connie couldn't? The sunglasses slipped down her nose and she pushed them back up, not looking at me.

"It'll keep mum happy. As long as she doesn't know any different. Like, if I bumped into Rochford and he told me he was still working on it . . . it'd keep her happy, wouldn't it?" Then she looked at me with a smile that was all sweetness and light. God help the guy she marries. He'll have to be twice as smart just to stay alive.

"Eh, dad?"

"Yeah. Your mother worries too much 'bout little things. It's not good for her and we haveta help her . . . well, relax, you know?" To have Janice on my side, helping keep Connie off my back, would make things easier for the rest of the season . . . and this really would be the last year.

"That's why she won't let me go to the Exhibition in Toronto. She says she'll worry too much. And I've never been, ever, and I'm sixteen! All I want to do is go for the day. Could you have a word with her?"

Bitch! I'm everyman's sucker. I fell into that one smooth as you like and she knew it. I couldn't help smiling. We understood each other very clearly even though she did give a sort of shrug, almost apologizing for the way she did it.

"Sure. I'll have a word with her. We won't be here next year and it might be a long time before you get another chance."

"Thanks, dad." She came over to me and gave me a brief kiss on the cheek, grinning from ear to ear. "I hate to see mum worry so much . . . "

"Bugger off." I gave her a pat on the bum and she hurried inside, her hair bouncing with her walk, ass wiggling and breasts pressing firmly against her T-shirt.

This really was no place for a sixteen-year-old girl.

Eight years ago things weren't going so good. I was out of work, had a bit of a problem with the booze, and Connie and me were going through what people call a rough period – like we were dead broke and living on what Connie made as a part-time waitress at Eddie Wong's. On top of that, or because of it, we were always arguing and fighting and things weren't any better in bed. What started it all was getting fired from the mill.

What happened was, I punched Caulfield Jr. at the Christmas party. We'd both had a few when I met him leaving the bar with a tray of drinks. It's still not too clear in my mind except I remember being pushed, bumping into Caulfield Jr. who dropped the tray, being pushed again and someone calling me a clumsy bastard. I swung around to hit the guy and got Caulfield instead. Right in the mouth.

It wasn't exactly a happy Christmas.

When I reported to work two days later I was fired and given two weeks money in lieu of notice. Not even the union could help me. I'd come a long way from being someone in that town, and suddenly I didn't give a shit any more. I guess you could say it was the lowest point of my life pretty well, I mean, things were rough during the depression and all that, but when the country was supposed to be going through a boom we sure as hell weren't getting any of it.

I'd tried everywhere in town to get work. I was prepared to do anything, but with the kids getting ready to finish the school year and needing summer jobs, who was going to take me on when they could get the same thing done for half the pay? The night they decided to cut me off at the tavern I decided to head for Toronto and work there for the summer, maybe in construction or something. My carpentry wasn't so bad, and with any luck I'd make a bundle and come back and start again.

I left the tavern and headed down to Eddie Wong's for coffee, hoping that Connie could take ten minutes off to have a cigarette and listen to the idea. But when I got there she gave me this look from the back of the restaurant that said she didn't want to know me, turned away and headed into the kitchen.

Angry, I stomped out. If that's the way she wants it, to hell with her. I wandered across the street to the seat the Lions Club put in for people waiting for the bus to Fort William or Cochrane and rolled a cigarette, watching the summer's night in downtown Black Rapids.

The place hadn't changed much from the time when I was a kid – a few extra stores, a supermarket where the old baseball diamond used to be, that grassless area of dust-covered clay, a mudhole in the spring, that was Yankee Stadium or Wrigley Field, depending on who you were playing for at the time.

Ever since the Caulfields started the mill way back

when, this has been a company town. They say that Caulfield Sr. had a finger in practically everything and owned most of the real estate in Black Rapids as well as half the town council. It was Caulfield who got them to put proper sidewalks down where we used to have boardwalk and bought and fixed up the Roxy movie house, then refused to show *The Outlaw*. I think we were the only town in Ontario that didn't get to see Jane Russell's boobs, although I remember Burns circulating a picture of her that he'd got from some American magazine. Everyone said Caulfield was a *good* man because he always gave a big donation to the church at Christmas and had his own family pew. I think the reason we went to the Anglican church was because Caulfield went. Every week we'd walk there, and every week as Caulfield's Packard passed us my father would nod to it, check his watch and say, "There goes Caulfield," as though we didn't know. Then he'd start to walk faster.

The hotel gets most of its business from the tavern and cocktail lounge that was put in after a vote (the mayor said it was time B.R. joined the twentieth century and it was rumoured he fixed the vote) that even Caulfield couldn't stop. It's been done up too, with a big dining room for Kiwanis dinners and weddings, and since the church hall burned down, dances and things like that.

They still keep a few rooms for salesmen who have the bad luck to stay over, and if you know the manager you can get a room for a few hours, no questions asked, but to take a girl there is as good as taking out an ad in the Record.

Used to be, if you wanted to get laid, all you had to do was go over to Ivy Morton's place. She was supposed to have moved in right after the mill opened and brought some girls with her from Timmins and Kirkland Lake (which, they say, Caulfield turned a blind eye to), but the depression, the war and finally a heart condition forced her to go out of business. There were always complaints from all the churches, but whenever we got a new police chief, Ivy made it her business to introduce herself and get the ground rules established. Somehow there was never a chief who could get enough evidence to prosecute.

Groups of teenage kids were wandering up and down the main street with nothing to do, smoking and laughing – the boys getting teased by little things with long hair, tight shorts and tops to match, advertising it like the flashing sign outside Wong's. Jesus, at their age I was too shy to say hello to Muriel Lobraico. Eddie Marshall drove past in the new police department cruiser, slowed slightly and waved, then drove on. He did all right for himself, considering. A gleaming '59 Chevy convertible, loaded down with kids, pulled away from a parking meter, made a U-turn right in front of me and roared off with a squeal of tires that echoed from building to building. Little bastards. How the hell can they afford it?

"Whatdaya say, Eldon?" Bert Powell, who owns the hardware store, was walking his dog and sucking on an unlit pipe.

"Not much, Bert."

The dog, a spaniel, must have been as old and as fat as Bert himself. It waddled instead of walking, too arthritic to cock its leg anymore. It came over to me, smeared hanging saliva all over my pants, and breathed the smell of rotting teeth into my face.

"How's Connie?" He pulled the dog away, stuffing tobacco into the pipe, looking up and down the street, not really interested. "I see she's working in Wong's sweat shop."

"Yeah. Part time. Makes a break for her. Gets her out of the house for a while. You know how it is." But then he probably knew that I was out of work and it was Connie who was keeping us out of the poorhouse. He could probably care less, too. His wife had never had to work in her life, certainly not since she married Bert and he took over the hardware store from her father.

Bert and me were at school together, in the same class, but the only thing we have in common, and causes us to stop and talk all these years later, is being caught together playing with a French safe when we were in Grade Six.

Bert used to steal them from his father's dresser drawer and we'd take them into the washroom, and while one kept watch, the other would fill them with water. At the time we didn't know what they were for – only that if his father hid them under a pile of socks and ties there was something forbidden about them.

That day we had planned to fill one and then climb onto the roof and drop it on a bunch of girls during the morning recess.

It always fascinated me, watching them grow and stretch, getting fat and round at the bottom, like a giant tit with a firm nipple, bouncing around with the weight of the water, suspended by three feet of taut rubber.

"It looks like Fielder's tits." I laughed at the thought of Miss Fielder, the math teacher, the sexiest thing in the whole of B.R., whose huge tits always jiggled up and down when she walked along the corridor. "Doesn't your dad miss them?"

"I dunno. He's not gonna ask me, is he, dummy?"

"What d'you think they're for?"

"I dunno. Maybe his piles."

"Yeah. Could be."

Bert led the way from the washroom, down the corridor, with me walking very close behind him, holding the swaying safe between us. Laughing, I whispered to Bert, "Hey! There's a sign on the notice board. 'Missing. One left tit. If found, please return to Miss Fielder.' How d'you like that, eh? Wouldn't you like to stroke her tits, Powell? Ohhh, what a thought." The safe began to sway with my laughter as I stared at the back of Bert's head, thinking he had no sense of humour – and suddenly he turned and ran back, leaving me standing there holding the water-filled safe and facing Goodhead and Miss Fielder. Holy Christ! There was a silence that never seemed to end as they stared at me, their smiles fading and their eyes wide. My legs turned to jelly, I was so stunned, and with them went my grip. The safe slipped gently and slowly to the floor, water spilling everywhere, settling between us like a deflated balloon, shrunken and wrinkled.

"Powell! You come back here!" Goodhead's voice roared down the corridor as he took Miss Fielder's arm and steered her back toward the staff-room, her face crimson. "You go back, my dear. I'll handle this." In the silence her high heels clicked loudly. I even noticed that she had an ass that wiggled. Turning, I saw Bert inch his way back, pale and shaking, while Goodhead's eyes travelled from me to him and back again. They had that look of anger that we knew only too well, but for some reason he was lost for words. Finally, his fists clenched tightly and his neck bulging and red, he broke the silence.

"Pick that up, Harris."

"Yes sir." I picked up the limp safe and held it out for him as he gave a slight shudder and stepped back, making a face.

"I don't want it. You'll flush it down the toilet when I say so. Where did you get it?"

"Er – well sir . . . " I wasn't going to be the one to drop Bert in the shit, but on the other hand, I wasn't going to be a hero and take the whole blame.

"My cousin gave it to me . . . sir." Bert's voice was weak. He was still shaking and looked like he might burst into tears.

"Yes, sir. Bert's uncle uses them for his piles."

"If I want your opinion, Harris, I'll ask for it."

"What I meant is, sir . . . "

"Harris! Shut up!" We waited for the sound of his voice to fade away, while I figured there was no way out of this one.

"You, Powell, get a mop and a paper bag." The way he looked at me I knew I was dead in his class from now on. "I'll take that thing with me. And you, Harris." He moved over and grabbed my hair, pulling me up so that I had to stand on my toes to ease the pain. "We also . . . happened to hear . . . ," with each word he gave my hair a twist, "every word . . . you said coming down the corridor. Miss Fielder . . . heard . . . every . . . word . . . you . . . said. You foul-mouthed little bastard." With that he gave an extra twist and pushed me away.

Bert came back with a mop and a candy bag, and while Goodhead held it open I dropped the safe in. The bell rang for the end of recess and Goodhead closed the bag, his eyes moving between the two of us. "You haven't heard the last of this." And he turned and walked back to the staff-room.

At the end of the corridor I could see a group of teachers watching, then hurrying back to the staff-room as Goodhead approached them. After he'd closed the door behind him we heard muffled laughter as Powell started to mop up the water. For once we had nothing to say.

Eddie Marshall drove slowly back
in the opposite direction while Bert pulled his pipe apart
and blew out the spittle onto the road. "I guess my Agnes
was always too busy with the kids to think about working,
what with that and the Mother's Union." He put the pipe
back together again and lit it. The dog slowly collapsed to
the sidewalk and started licking its paws. "D'you read
about George Langton passing on? Stroke."

I didn't and could care less. George Langton was a lawyer in town, and I hardly knew him except by name.

"He's over at Morgan's. Funeral on Friday. Great pity."
Brushing some ash from his shirt he gave a tug on the leash,
which the dog ignored. "Well, must be getting along.
Watch the news. Nice to see you, Eldon. Say hello to
Connie."

"See you, Bert." I got up and walked home, feeling re-
sentful and bitter. But I wasn't sure why.

Delores and Janice were in bed and Davie was glued to
the TV, watching Viewpoint, of all things. Some guy wearing thick glasses with a picture of Ottawa behind him was
going on about transporting whooping crane eggs from

some park in Alberta to Maryland by RCAF jet. Jesus, and here's me never been up in a plane. Davie was fourteen and had a job lined up at the supermarket for the summer, which burned me up. It wasn't that I was against kids working – what else was there to do in Black Rapids during the school break? – but it seemed so easy for them.

He didn't look up when I came into the room, which wasn't unusual. In fact it was getting like I didn't belong.

Slumping into the chesterfield I took off my shirt and boots.

"What the hell you watching that for?"

"Waitin' for the sports."

"Yeah? Well it's time you were in bed. Your mother'll be home soon."

"She said I could stay up. For fixing the front porch. Did you notice it?"

"Er . . . yeah. You did a good job. You're pretty clever with your hands." And he was, too.

He did carpentry at school and I taught him a few things and he took to it like a duck to water. Could saw in a straight line, do dovetails, mortise and tenon joints, things like that.

I should have noticed the porch. It was in poor shape and I'd been promising to do it for weeks, but he'dve done a good job.

"Anyway, up to bed."

He got up without a word, switched off the set, and gave a "could care less" shrug as he left the room, stopping at the door.

"D'you get a job today?"

Smartass. Goddamn smartass. No respect. The kids today have no respect. He knows the answer but he wants to hear me say it anyway.

50

"Er–no. No, I didn't. I'm hoping maybe tomorrow." God knows I'd tried. Even went to the church when I heard Fergus Downing had the flu to see if they needed any graves dug or grass clipped. Maybe with George Langton over at Morgan's they'd need one dug tomorrow. But then I had plans to go to Toronto.

"Yeah." He went on upstairs and closed his bedroom door.

A lifeless face covered by a mess of hair and two days' growth of beard stared back at me from the bathroom mirror. Eldon Harris, who was somebody once, even goodlooking some said, a guy to be reckoned with, who once, they said, had the world by a string.

I mean, it's all in the scrapbook in the dresser.

Proof.

I had a bath, shaved and splashed some Mennon on, then lay in bed and listened to Connie closing the place up. She came upstairs quietly, checked the kids, then disappeared into the bathroom, running water and humming to herself. I couldn't blame her for not wanting to see me in the restaurant–in fact, the way things were tonight, I was even lucky Bert Powell stopped to chat.

Connie came from the bathroom, closed the bedroom door to within two inches of being shut, a habit going back to when the kids were small, and undressed in the dark, probably figuring I was asleep, maybe even hoping, then got into her nightdress, another habit dating back to when Davie was about five or six years old. For me it was the pyjama bottoms. After all those years of wearing nothing in bed, it was a small but ever-present barrier.

She got into bed, staying on her own side, checking the luminous alarm clock that would go off at six forty-five in order to get Davie and Delores to school. Turning toward her I put my hand on her bare arm.

"Hi."

"I thought you'd be asleep." She didn't move except to run her hand through her hair.

"I wanted to talk to you."

"I couldn't stop in the restaurant. We were very busy."

"I figured."

Even though she'd put on some sort of powder, the smell of the restaurant clung to her hair, a mixture of stale smoke, grease from the deep fryer, and in there somewhere a sweet smell. Maybe from the soda fountain, who knows? Either way, what with my Mennon, it smelt like a whorehouse serving hot beef sandwiches, french fries and gravy, which was probably where the resemblance would end tonight. "Well, anyway, I wanted to talk to you about this idea I have."

"Can't it wait till morning?"

"No. It's important. It's about me working."

"Did you get a job?"

"No. That's what I mean. See, I was thinking that with the summer coming up and all maybe I should go down to Toronto and get a job there."

She sat up and faced me. "You'll do what?"

"Let me finish. There's lotsa construction goin' on down there, apartments and things, and they need men. I could work there for the summer and come back in time for the Labour Day weekend with a bundle. They pay good. Work my ass off, live cheap and save. Who knows, maybe I'll

52

come back with two or three grand. Set us up. That's what we'll need, see, to get us out of the hole once and for all." She lay down, staring at the ceiling, while all I could think of was how I'd love a drink, anything.

"What about us?" Finally, after about three or four minutes, she'd said something. "That means me workin' all the time, lookin' after the kids, makin' ends meet."

"I could send you money. But, you see, if you could make do and not touch what I make, we'd be set."

"I don't understand why you want to go and leave the kids. I don't care about me, but it's gonna be a long summer for them."

"Lookit, I wanna get some work. I'm goin' crazy around here. Christ, my own son can get a job an' they're prepared to wait until school finishes for him. D'you think I like not working?" I was getting angry but trying to fight it. I didn't want this to turn sour on me.

"The way you bin livin' in the tavern, you seem to be enjoyin' it. I work and you booze away the pay like it comes off trees. Well I don't like everyone seein' me working there when they all know you're down the road looking like some bum from the drunk tank."

My stomach was knotting. If I was going to go down to Toronto I was determined not to leave after a big fight with Connie, but it was all I could do not to rant and rave about how everyone was out to get me and make me look like the biggest asshole in town. I probably am, at that. After all, it was me that belted Caulfield Jr.

We lay there not speaking for at least ten minutes, until I couldn't stand it any longer.

"So. What d'you think?"

"If that's what you want. I can't stop you. When?"

"The weekend. The Sunday train from Cochrane."

"What about money? Fares, a place to live?"

"They've got hostels. How much we got in the bank?"

"Hundred and twenty three dollars. That's all we've got in the world."

"Well. If I take, say, fifty? Tide me over. How's that sound? You get paid Friday." I could feel her shrug.

"That'll leave seventy-three dollars."

"Plus your pay."

"Plus my pay."

"Listen, by Thanksgiving there'll be at least two thousand in there. At least. Promise. Whatdaya say?"

She sat up and looked at me for a moment, weighing it up.

"Yeah, all right. I'll have to iron some shirts and things."

It had been well over twenty years since I was last in Toronto but it was still like seeing the city for the first time. It had been a rough trip, and I'd been sitting up all night trying to sleep when the train finally swung to the right out of the valley that runs down the middle of Toronto and I started to notice the change.

Passing old factories and junkyards on one side I could see the expressways on the other, rising out of the ground on concrete supports and loaded down with traffic heading into the city even though it was only seven-thirty in the morning. Beyond them, the waterfront, with gigantic freighters tied up alongside the warehouses, and out in the lake the islands, where a squat ferry boat was moving across the calm water. I smiled to myself, remembering.

Out of the other window was the Royal York Hotel, and the Toronto Dominion building, the biggest I'd ever seen, stretching up, black and all glass it seemed, catching the sun. They'd printed a picture of it in the *Record* and Davie had done a project on it at school. Next to it was the Canadian Imperial Bank of Commerce building.

"Harris. What's the tallest building in the British Empire?"

"The Bank of Commerce building in Toronto, sir. It's four hundred and seventy-six feet high."

Dear Jesus, if Goodhead could see it now, a piddling, dirty, rundown thing.

The train eased into the station and I headed for the washroom to shave and put on one of the clean shirts Connie had packed, then went out onto Front Street which was already swarming with people going to work. Suddenly I felt very alone and had my first doubts about leaving Black Rapids. The traffic was loud and fast and the buildings seemed to be closing in. All the straw hats, mini-skirts and summer suits seemed to know where they were going and what they were going to do as they crossed with the light and headed up Bay Street. I bought a *Globe and Mail* and crossed over to Murray's for something to eat. Connie had packed me some sandwiches and ginger ale, but somehow a dried-up cheese and pickle on brown didn't seem that good an idea for breakfast.

The couple of days I'd had in Black Rapids before leaving were pretty strained, and although Connie seemed to go along with the idea, I got the impression that in her heart she figured I was quite happy to leave them to fend for themselves.

Even Janice seemed to doubt me.

"Why are you leaving us?"

"I'm not leaving anyone."

"Then why are you going?"

"To earn some money."

I'd taken her down to Wong's to have a sundae and then we walked along the Black River, skimming stones across the surface, trying to be casual as though it were just an ordinary outing. She'd cried when I told her the news and clung to me, sobbing into my shirt.

"I won't be gone long. Just a few weeks."

"Why can't you earn money here like everyone else's father?"

How do you tell an eight-year-old kid that no one wants to hire her father? I mean, Jesus, it's tough enough for my kids to look up to me as it is, even without them realizing that at the moment I'm not like other fathers, that the Caulfields carried a lot of weight in the town. Davie and Delores realized, and I suspected they would be glad to see me go so they wouldn't be embarrassed any more by the sight of me leaving the tavern, sitting on the Lions Club seat in the middle of the day when everyone else was working. I tried to change the subject.

"See that bird over there?"

"What bird?"

"Sitting on the dead branch."

"What is it?"

"A cedar waxwing."

"Oh. How come you know about birds and things?"

"When I was a kid I just started . . . I dunno, being interested. Used to keep record books and mark down every different bird I saw. I guess it stuck with me."

"Can you earn money with birds?"

"No. Unfortunately."

"Oh." She picked up a stone and threw it at the water, her face grim because it didn't skim the surface, sending up a big splash instead. "Will you bring us a present back?"

"Sure." I tousled her hair and she looked up at me with a smile, her eyes wide and trusting.

"Will you teach me to skim stones before you go?"

Connie cried too, quietly, the tears running down her cheeks as we lay together in bed on the last night.

"Hey, come on. It'll work out fine."

She nodded and wiped the tears with the back of her arm as I turned her toward me and ran my hand down her arm and over to her breast, circling the nipple through her nightdress with my finger, then moving lightly down to the inside of her thigh. We hadn't made love for two weeks or more and when we did I felt like a charity case, realizing that the less you have it, the less you need it. But now I wanted to smother her, tell her that it really would be okay, that I wanted her, loved her – and more important, I wanted her to feel it too. But she made no move when I tried to slip the nightdress off her shoulder, there was no hardness in her nipples. I was determined that I wouldn't leave on a sour note so I pretended I didn't notice and she made an effort of sorts, and we went through the painful motions, none of the juices flowing, both realizing that we should hurry before I lost my erection, both knowing, at the end, that it had been a disaster and neither of us saying a word.

Whatever we'd had, once, we'd lost completely. We'd hit rock bottom.

A bit of sweat is good for the soul, he'd said: *you get nothing out of this life except by hard work.*

How fucking true, goddamn him. Always right, well, most of the time, only now I either had to put up or shut up.

I looked at the Help Wanted columns over a breakfast of buttermilk pancakes, toast and coffee, with the second cup free, searching for anything that would pay me good money and allow me to go back at the end of the summer and put two thousand dollars in the bank. But somehow I seemed to get sidetracked, avoiding the issue by riding up and down in the subway or looking at the new city hall with its highly polished lump of metal outside that someone said was a sculpture done by a famous person. It beat me that people would pay money for it. I looked in store windows and at the fountains and flower displays on University Avenue where the traffic raced up and down like it was the Indy 500. And the cranes – sitting on top of half-finished buildings, up there against the sky, pointing to where the money was.

I had to wait over an hour to see the man in charge at the first site I went to, dazed by the speed of things, the endless stream of Ready-Mix trucks, cranes swinging the buckets high, wondering how, from a bunch of drawings, they could do it all without making a mistake. The interview lasted all of two minutes and it was the same at the next five sites I went to, no job if you didn't belong to the union and no union card if you didn't have a job. Finally I was sent up to the north end of the city where there was a non-union job under way, building houses. After an hour and a half of subway and bus rides I eventually found the beginnings of a subdivision in what seemed to be the middle of the country. Most of the workers spoke Italian. I found the foreman in the family room of a $45,900 Colonial with double garage, four bedrooms with stove and dishwasher supplied. His laugh bounced around the empty room and he squashed out a cigar butt on the rough floor.

"No unions? Who fed you that line? Listen, I got unions

coming outa my ass. I can't even piss without them sayin' so. Where you from again?"

"Black Rapids – up near Cochrane – er, close to Kirkland Lake."

"Listen, take some advice. Go back up there. No hassle, nothin' to worry about. Good fishin', eh? Nice talkin' to you, but shit, man, it'd be more than I could afford to take on a non-union guy. No kiddin'. Take care, eh?"

I wandered back to the main road, across fields and what had once been country lanes, past an old brick farmhouse that was being demolished. On part of the property was at least two acres of silver birches and oaks being cut down and the roots ripped out of the ground by large machines. They'd put up a sign saying "Forest Glade Estates. The Ultimate in Country Living."

I felt bitter and depressed, so much so I couldve cried. I mean, how often is it that a grown man feels like actually crying? I wanted to talk to Connie, explain how it was going, have someone tell me it would be better tomorrow. When I'd left Union Station hours earlier I'd felt alone and lost, but that was nothing to what I felt now.

It took me two hours to get downtown again and I managed to get a bed in a hostel on Jarvis Street where they served stew for dinner and had prayers afterwards with a hymn-sing. No booze was allowed and if anyone came in even smelling of it, they were out. The one thing I'dve loved to do was get drunk and forget it all, but the bed was more important and I slept for ten hours. The next three days weren't much better, reporting every morning to the unemployment office and getting nowhere. I delivered handbills at a dollar an hour, spent an afternoon cutting grass in Rosedale, and worked in the pit of a carwash where I was told I had the job for life if I wanted it.

The problem was, for eighty bucks a week, after paying for my bed, food and smokes, I'd be better off in Black Rapids. On the Friday night I was down to fifteen dollars with the weekend ahead and no chance of any interviews till Monday. I couldn't talk to Connie on the phone because they'd cut it off two days before I left, but then maybe that wasn't such a bad thing. For insurance I had a return ticket to Black Rapids tucked into the back of my wallet, and if the worst came to the worst, I could get out of Toronto in one piece.

There were about twenty men in for dinner – a variation of Wednesday's stew with dumplings, carrots and thick bread, followed by some sort of cake with a sauce and coffee. There was little talking, and when there was it came between slurps and the clanking of the spoons on the metal dishes as we hunched over, five to a bench, making sure that nothing went back to the kitchen. It was the beginning of the evening routine that ended in going to sleep, or at least trying, in a room with four other guys, everyone coughing, spitting and farting, stinking up the room even worse than it was already with its stale reek of dried piss and body odour. I found myself going to bed later and later so that my tiredness would get me away from the surroundings as quickly as possible.

After dinner we cleared away the tables and set the chairs up for the service. Sitting behind me while we waited was a large man with a red, pockmarked face and no teeth, who took a swig of Yardley's Black Label, breathing in deeply as he swallowed it, then holding his breath as he let it ride down to his stomach. It was part of his day's shoplifting: canned meat from Loblaws, aftershave from three drugstores and a bottle of wine he'd boosted from a drunk passed out on the grass in front of St. James' Cathedral.

Everyone stood when the minister came in and gave us

a smile and a nod. A small notice board said we'd be singing hymn three one six and the piano, well out of tune, played the opening bars. A mixture of loud, deep, harsh voices took over, filling the room as we gave ourselves to God as part of the deal, all of us out of step with the piano.

Now the day is ov-er,
Night is draw-ing nigh,
Shad-ows of the ev'ning
Steal across the sky.

I wonder what Connie's doing now. She'd never believe it, me standing up singing hymns. Maybe with me being away like this things'll get better between us. Who knows? On the other hand, how the hell d'you make it good again? Money in the bank you gotta have, but that doesn't mean everything'll work out.

Makes it easier, though.

Comfort ev'ry suff'rer,
watchin' late in pain;
Those who plan some ev-il
From their sin res-train.

Shit – what's sin? That's all they ever talked about in church when I was a kid, and they're still doing it today. You can't win.

Grant to lit-tle chil-dren
Visions bright of thee,
Guard the sailors toss-ing
On the deep blue sea.

On the radio they were talking about the highways being jammed with traffic going north to cottage country for the weekend. Highway 400 bumper-to-bumper. Boats on trailers, convertibles with the tops down – and look at us here. Probably less than a hundred bucks in the whole room and we've gotta sing for our supper.

When the morn-ing wak-ens
Then may I arise,
Pure and fresh and sin-less
In thy holy eyes.

That's one thing for sure, you wake up here pure and sinless, unless having a hard-on's sinful. Doesn't do you any good. Mind you, didn't do much good up in Black Rapids lately either. Just made me look like a beggar with my hand held out – a dead giveaway. And like most beggars, I'd wind up with nothing. But what're you gonna do with three kids rushing around the house? Use your imagination, that's what. Be daring. Maybe that's one of the problems. We don't try to make it exciting like it used to be once. It's dull. But then if one of you doesn't care, nothing'll perk it up. Nothing.

Glory to the Fath-er
Glory to the Son,
And to thee, blest spir-it,
Whilst all ages run.
A-me-nnn.

"Let us pray."

We all sat down and bowed our heads, some holding their hands over their eyes like a sunshade, others just staring at the floor.

Muriel Lobraico bare naked. Harris moves into the centre, he shoots, he scores! Muriel Lobraico bare naked's better.

"Be mindful, O Lord, of thy people bowed before thee, and of those who are absent through age, sickness or infirmity . . . "

It was twenty years since I'd seen Yonge Street, but I remembered it as depressing and tacky. Despite all the years that had passed, the new bars and better-looking stores, it hadn't improved much. In fact, now it was not only depressing and tacky, it was shitty, depressing and tacky. And when you read about it they make it sound like the next best thing to Broadway. I had deliberately avoided going out at night – it kept me away from the taverns, out of trouble and in money. But after a week of the hostel and its nightly dose of religion, I finally had to get away for a couple of hours just so I could breathe properly, and the nearest place was Yonge Street.

I wandered for a while, looking in windows and reading movie posters. *Oliver* was playing at one place and *Rosemary's Baby* was just up the street, shows I'd never heard of and couldn't afford anyway. In B.R. it seemed like *The Sound of Music* was at the Roxy for ever. Connie had taken the kids in the spring and Delores borrowed the record and a record player from a friend so we had it morning, noon and night until I could have choked Julie Andrews with her goddamned Do, Re, Mi. I tried my hand at outdrawing a model cowboy dressed all in black in an amusement arcade, then watched a movie of some broad with big tits and a fat ass doing a strip on a bed, writhing and wriggling and trying to look sexy as she squeezed her tits and ran her hand between her legs. Trouble was I could hardly see her, the picture was so bright and white, and at the crucial moment when she was going to take her panties off the film ran out, which just about summed up my week.

I picked up some paperbacks from Coles for the weekend – even in Toronto you've got to be able to escape – and then headed along Dundas toward Jarvis and the hostel.

The street seemed to be teeming with hookers but I only got propositioned once, ten bucks for half an hour or five for a quickie. Jesus, for a quarter I could go back and look at another movie. Anyway, for ten bucks I'd want something better than the dogs here, all smothered in makeup, looking bored out of their minds and probably riddled with clap. Outside the Warwick Hotel, lit up like day with all the bulbs and brightly-painted walls, the cops were lifting a drunk into a grey paddy-wagon while a small crowd stood staring. It seemed like a good time to go and have a beer.

The tavern was like any other tavern I'd ever been in, smelling of stale beer and smoke, with the usual glass case containing cheese sandwiches wrapped in wax paper, hot pepperoni, pickled eggs, meat pies and potato chips. On the walls were a couple of pictures of northern Ontario hanging over a shuffleboard and even the tables seemed to have the same formica, wet with slopped beer, while over the bar the colour TV beamed out a bright green picture with a double image and the sound turned down. I found an empty table and ordered a draught, which was slammed down in front of me, the waiter hotfooting it to be paid. Cash on the nose. No credit in the big city.

As my second draught came the other seat was taken by a heavily tanned man about my age with a greying beard, who went through three draughts in the time that it took me to drink my second, all the time staring at the TV as he shook salt into his glass and downed it in one go, wiping his beard with the back of his hand after each one. Finally he fixed his stare on me.

"Whatsa matter? Don't you talk?" And then he broke into a deep laugh, waving the waiter over. "Set em up again, Sam. And for my friend here. He might even smile." He looked at me again, a slight grin on his face. "How d'you like that, eh? Set em up again, Sam." He frowned for a moment when I looked blank, then tried again. "Set em up again, Sam . . . 'Play it again, Sam' . . . ah, forget it. His name's not Sam anyway, it's Fred."

The guy was nuts. He picked up the two books I'd bought and flipped through them, raising his eyebrows. One was a war book and the other *Sayonara*, which I suppose is a war book of sorts. I'd read it before and fallen in love with the girl and Japan.

"Heavy stuff. Jesus Christ, what's this place coming to?" Snorting with laughter, he returned the books and paid the waiter. "Never get time to read m'self. Oh, maybe the newspaper now and then to see if the world is still as shitty a place as I thought it was. I mean, Christ, all you ever read about is murders, disasters, some creep in Africa slaughtering thousands until someone knocks him off and then it starts all over again and who gives a shit? Eh? I'll tell you. No one. Just yesterday some old lady who lived alone in Cabbagetown got herself all smashed up, then strangled with her own stocking. Just three blocks from here! And who cares? The guy could be sittin' right in this room for all we know. It could even be you. Anyway, I won't read another paper till fall. Screw it, I don't need all that stuff. Drink up, me old darlin'. The next one's on you."

And his deep laugh roared around the room.

Two hours later we went back out onto Jarvis Street as though we'd known each other for years. What he didn't know was that I hadn't talked to anyone, I mean really talked, for almost a week.

"How far you gotta go?"

"Couple of blocks."

"Don't need a ride then?"

"No thanks."

He had a '62 Pontiac wagon parked on a meter, gleaming and reflecting the street lights like it had been waxed and hand polished every day. Around the rear windows were neatly placed decals from all over: Halifax, Vancouver, Jasper, Algonquin Park, Ste. Anne de Beaupré, New York City, Key West, New Orleans, Mexico City; even the bumpers weren't ignored, with a sticker from St. Joseph's Oratory, Montreal, on one side of the licence plate and Up Yours on the other.

Leaning on the hood he took out a big cigar and lit it, waving the flame over the end until he was satisfied it was properly alight, blowing a curl of smoke up into the night and staring after it as it drifted slowly around. For a moment he seemed lost in thought; then he seemed to remember that I was standing there. For the first time he didn't have to shout over the noise, and his voice was quiet.

"I was in Japan once. Yokohama–went to Tokyo too. Did a stint in the merchant marine." He shook his head as though he didn't believe it, taking another puff on the cigar.

As he spoke his eyes lit up and his voice started to sound like some actor on television. "It was paradise, absolute paradise. There was this gorgeous little thing, a dazzling beauty if I ever saw one, who turned my whole body, my whole mind, to mush. She had me in a trance, so much so, I jumped ship and went to live with her. And she, let me tell you this, thought that the rising sun rose over me too! They really know how to treat a guy over there. Really know. I tell you, it was a crazy three months. This weird food I even got to like, baths every night – we'd take it in turns to soap and wash each other down and then get into this tiny wooden tub, not together of course, it was too small, and sit there up to our necks in boiling water. And then, my friend, we'd retire to the bed on the floor and watch Bonanza on the tube with a cup of sake in our hands. And then! Pow! She'd start on me!" He shook his hand as though he'd burnt it, smiling again, his voice sounding proud. "She was incredible. Had tricks I never knew existed and have never seen since. My every wish, whim, fancy or desire . . . she satisfied with her undivided love . . . as only a Japanese woman can. Finally I had to get the next ship outa there. I mean, she drained me, every little drop, and when I got on board they put me in sick-bay for two weeks, suffering from exhaustion. It's the truth, so help me." His face broke into a broad grin and he went round to the driver's side and unlocked the door, waving at the street. "That's why I can never stand more than two days in this place. Look at it. No class. Not like Montreal. Must say, though, this is the only street I know where you can get insured, laid, fixed and saved all within a few blocks. And if that ain't enough, you can always jump into the lake at the end of the street. They even got a morgue down there waitin' for you. I gotta go. People to meet." He got into the car and flicked some cigar

68

ash onto the sidewalk. "Listen, you wanna work and earn some dough?"

"You know it."

"Prepared to bust your ass off?"

"Sure."

"Southern Ontario–pickin' tomatoes. Strawberries first till the tomatoes are ready, maybe some cukes. Free room, twenty cents a basket, for tomatoes that is, fresh air and you get fit. Bit a practice and you'll be up to twenty bucks a day, six days a week. You figure it out. The time you spent fartin' around this town you'da had a hundred and twenty, maybe thirty."

I wasn't sure if he was kidding or not. In fact I didn't know what to think about him, except maybe he was a bullshit artist. But the idea got me excited, and in the end, when it came down to it, I didn't have too much choice.

"How do I get there?"

"With me. Pick you up at seven-thirty, across the street from your place." His grin broke again as he started the car.

"Stick with me, me old darlin', and you'll be able to go back to Black whatever it is and slap two grand in front of the old lady and ask her how she likes them apples. Hey, what's your name?"

"Harris. Eldon Harris."

He held out his hand and we shook.

"Alex. See you at seven-thirty." He made a fast U-turn and headed north up to Bloor, Up Yours catching the light for a moment, then blurring as the tires squealed.

My old man was a boxer.
Worked in the mines in Glace Bay–even turned pro for a
while."

We were driving along Highway 401, past the east-
bound stream of cars pulling boats and trailer homes, most
of them with American licence plates. Ohio, Michigan,
New York.

I hadn't slept too well, worrying all night that I might
sleep in and miss him if he showed up, at the same time
wondering what it would be like working in the tomato
fields. I mean, I'd never picked a tomato in my life.

"For a while everyone in Cape Breton figured they'd got
a winner. Trouble was, fightin' around there didn't pay so
great, so he went to Montreal and picked up a couple of
fights, won em both, and got a shot at the contender for the
Canadian heavyweight title. Three grand guaranteed." He
took out a Montecristo cigar and removed it from its tube,
then lit a match, cupping his hands to protect the flame, all
the time steering with his elbows, smiling when he saw me
watching him.

"Developed a liking for these when I was in Havana

once. But that's another story." He broke into his grin as he stroked his beard. "I also smoke em for sentimental reasons. Anyway, so we all went down to Montreal – I had seven brothers and sisters – to see this fight. At the Forum yet. Well, I tell you, he lasted five rounds. Had the livin' shit beaten outa him. Never fought again. By the time he'd paid all his expenses he had forty-five bucks left. Forty-five! Went back to the mines and worked there right up until he got silicosis and hadta quit."

The traffic slowed, eventually coming to a stop. After about fifteen minutes an ambulance drove along the shoulder, lights flashing and siren blaring. Alex switched off the engine, stretched and drew on his cigar.

"I was about fifteen at the time, and it was the worst thing that ever happened to me, seeing my father mashed to a pulp like that for forty-five lousy bucks and then havin' to go back down that fuckin' mine. And I knew I'd be goin' down there right after him, either that or the steel mill in Sydney, just like my brothers. So I quit school right then and there and got the bus to Halifax with thirty dollars I'd saved from doin' odd jobs. No one was ever gonna kick my ass around like they did his. No one." The traffic started moving again and about a mile up the highway we passed a Volkswagen that had flipped in the centre median, the roof flattened until it met the dashboard. Alex looked at it and wound up his window.

"Shit."

Near Chatham we turned off the highway and onto some concession roads, passing neatly laid out farms with the houses and buildings set back well off the road, each one

71

with a large, growing vegetable garden. On some of the fences the bodies of groundhogs were draped over the wire, stiff and drying in the sun. Alex steered with one finger, his right arm stretched across the back of the seat.

"You'll like Old Man Rochford. Got six hundred acres – worth a fortune. He hired me the first time. He's gettin' on a bit, so his eldest son just about runs the place now. Al Rochford. Cocky bastard, but he doesn't give me no trouble. They've got about a hundred acres of tomatoes and fifty of cukes – the rest is all cash crop, soy beans, stuff like that. Now and again they move us around to another farm for the day, but mostly you'll be workin' here."

The car turned into a farm with the name Rochford on the mailbox, up a rutted road toward the main house, which even from the road looked like it needed a paint job. As we got closer I could see that the screened-in porch needed new mesh; sections of it were hanging and flapping in the slight breeze.

"He's got another son, Carson, who's the eldest, lives down the road a piece. Al's got himself a cute little wife, nice ass and that look in her eye that says he's not givin' her what she wants. It's a rare wife around here that's as goodlookin' as she is. Dunno how she stands him. I tell you, he can be a mean sonofabitch at times."

Old Man Rochford was sitting in an armchair on the front porch, a frail, tanned man, probably in his late sixties, wearing coveralls, heavy boots and a sweat-stained hat caked with dust. Beside him was a crewcut kid about ten years old, drinking a bottle of Coke. The old man squinted at us for a while and then a smile broke.

"Alex! Well, my land, dint expect to see you back this year. In good time too."

Alex went over and shook his hand, introducing me.

"Eldon here is gonna stay till Thanksgiving –"

"Unless the frost comes first."

"Unless the frost comes first. Between us we're gonna clean up."

"Only so many tomatoes to go around whichever way you divide em."

"We plan our share. How's Nancy?"

"Not so bad, not so bad. Arthritis bin acting up a bit. Spose we can't complain though, eh Grant?" The boy looked over to him, shrugging, and Old Man Rochford turned to me. "This here's my grandson Grant. My boy Al's child. He's gettin' to be quite the grownup, aren't you?" The kid forced a smile and turned away. "One day he's gonna be runnin' this place jist like his grand-dad. He's even gettin' to be pretty good with the gun. Put down ten groundhogs and three rabbits all by hisself jist yesterday." The old man ran his hand over the boy's hair, smiling, then turned to Alex, indicating me. "You told him how we do things?"

"Yep. Seven to seven, six days a week, twenty-five cents a basket, accommodation provided."

Rochford studied Alex with a serious expression, then let out a roar of laughter.

"Twenty-five cents my ass. You'd rob me blind minute I took me eyes off you. Holy Christ!" He banged the arm of his chair as he stood up, still laughing. "Twenty cents, take it or leave it. Come on inside." He gave the boy a friendly pat on the behind and steered him to the porch door. "You better go see if your mother needs you. All right?" The boy shrugged and left, letting the screen door slam behind him. Old Man Rochford, opening the front door of the house, frowned, muttering, "Little bastard could use a good belt now and then."

The living room was large, with heavy lace curtains over

the windows. The air was cool and had a musty smell to it. Rochford shuffled over to a small desk and started sorting out some papers, still muttering to himself. The room didn't look like it belonged to someone worth a fortune: worn furniture and a threadbare rug, an old pump organ at one end of the room with family pictures spread across the top of it and others hanging on the walls next to china plaques, embroidered quotations from the Bible, a picture of the Queen and several calendars, one dating back to 1955, all showing the January of their year. Leaning in a corner next to the door were a shotgun and a .303 Enfield.

When he'd found what he was looking for he put on a pair of reading glasses and went to the window for better light, finally holding out some forms for us to look at.

"See for yerselves. Tax returns for the last two years. See." He rapped the form with his hand, peering over his glasses at us. "Shitdamn, made less than five thousand both years. Can't buy a pot to piss in with that. So you understand, eh? Twenty cents. That's all. Anyways," he looked at Alex, the smile breaking again, "you do all right operatin' on the side, eh? Thought I dint know about them things. Eh? Eh?" He broke into his deep laugh again and slapped Alex on the shoulder.

"You're gonna have me in tears. There I was tellin' Eldon you're the richest sonofabitch around here. Six hundred acres, yet!"

"It ain't money in the bank though. How could I sell all we got? Bin in the family for a hundred and twenty-five years. Handed down from generation to generation an' my sons'll do the same. You look on the old maps of the district an' you'll see the name Rochford goin' back a long way. And them boys a mine, they got families of their own to pass everything on to. This way everyone gits to make a livin'.

74

Anyway, I got everything I need in this life. Nancy says she'd like to put a window in at the church, a sorta thank-you and memorial all wrapped in one. But what do I do? Sell off twenty-five acres, if they'd let me, so's I can buy a window? The hell with that. The good Lord'll take us, window or no window." He started to laugh again. "An' you, Alex, Nancy says you'll wind up in hell the things she's heard 'bout you."

Alex grinned as Rochford put his arm around his shoulder.

"So it's twenty cents, m'boy. Like I said, take it or leave it. Better find your friend a place to sleep. Try the big barn."

Arriving earlier than most of the pickers gave me a chance to get a bunk in one of the sheds instead of the barn, and Alex lent me a sleeping bag for the summer. Four other men shared the shed as well as the electric burner, the flies, rodents and mosquitoes. Alex lived in luxury, in a large tent he pitched well away from the main buildings and near the stream. As I watched him hammering in the pegs I sang the Ontario theme song.

A Place to Stand and a
place to sleep,
Jesus moth-er, it's enough
to make you weep . . .

We'd driven into Chatham to buy some food, and while I got some canned things and bread, Alex stocked up with cigarettes, beer, candy, canned meats, rye, rum and pop, loading the wagon down.

"What the hell you gonna do with all that?"

"Listen – sometime everyone's gonna run outa somethin' and it'll be in the evenin' and they're too pooped to go into town to get it." His beard parted with a smile. "And who do they come to? You name it, I got it. You want a bottle of beer, a shotta rye or whatever, for a little markup Alex'll supply you. Candles, rat traps, thumb tacks, fly papers, Tampax, soap. It's an investment. People don't buy, I go broke. So I take a risk – but I know people. I've studied their needs and habits. Lookit, you gotta play it smart in this life, Eldon, otherwise everyone's gonna walk all over you. You know the old sayin', God only helps those who help themselves. That's me, baby. You gotta be smart."

They came from all over.

Quebec, New Brunswick, Ontario, Nova Scotia. Families with nine kids, seven kids, a mother with four, down for the whole summer while her husband did a season's work on the waterfront in Quebec City. Six- and seven-year-olds were putting in a full day, working right beside their parents and returning in the evening to their barns, sheds, tents – even a mobile home.

For me, the first two weeks of picking was a nightmare. A blur of brown, green and red. On very hot days, the colours swam together every time I straightened up. It was only will-power that got me back down again, dragging my ass through the heat till my head pounded with pain, muscles tightened up and I had trouble standing again. My arms and back got burnt raw when I made the mistake of working all afternoon without a shirt, and the nights were agony when I crashed onto my bunk, exhausted, aching and smarting from the sunburn after washing in the stream, passing up something to eat so that I could just rest my body, oblivious of the other guys, the putrid air and the rain, which came through a leak in the roof one night and soaked my sleeping bag as well as me.

On top of everything else I was a lousy picker – slow, cumbersome and disorganized. But more than anything, I was getting lonely – lonely for Connie, Black Rapids and the comforts that go with them. I'd written home as soon as I arrived at the farm, and every day that passed without a reply just made the loneliness worse.

I began to get jealous – jealous of the younger guys who not only seemed able to afford trips into Chatham or Blenheim for a beer, but had the strength. I was jealous of families who were together, and although I didn't see much of him I was jealous of Alex, living in that luxury, confident, making money on the side, and by all reports outpicking everyone else. By the end of the two weeks I had had enough. I thumbed a ride into Chatham to check the train times and have a beer. I was a human being, goddamnit, not some fuckin' slave on a prison farm. No one had to put up with all that. Being treated like shit so some farmer can put his feet up on a porch and talk about how great it is that his family can make a living.

Jesus Christ!"

Alex's grinning face was looking down at me and I could see that he was holding a cup. Then he was a blur for a moment; when he came back into focus, he was still grinning.

I sat up slowly, my mouth dry and sore, head pounding, and he brought me an old, broken mirror from the wall. I realized I was back in the shed at the farm. I needed a shave, but otherwise I wasn't in too bad shape, except for a puffed cheek, a graze at the corner of my mouth and a lump on the back of my head. Most of the discomfort was inside, and I could feel the cuts as I watched my tongue moving around, searching for other damage.

"You should see what you did to him, me old darlin'. Here, I brought you a slug of rye, nothing but the best! Canadian Club – I save it for special occasions – medicinal and free of charge, courtesy of The Old Firm. Coffee's on." He handed me at least three ounces of rye and I took a sip, swilling it around my mouth and letting it sting in the cuts before swallowing it, then coughing as it took my breath away.

I remembered being in the tavern, wandering into the Women and Escorts section by mistake, the waiter telling me I shouldn't be in there in this loud voice, feeling the sudden anger at hearing that in a so-called free country; like no woman was safe in there; that there were laws that made it look like all men alone in taverns were molesters or rapists, second-class citizens. In this day and age, in a supposedly modern, progressive country. I remembered the people staring at me and this guy in the clean shirt with the girl telling me they should keep all us picking bums hidden back on the farm. That's when I told him to go fuck himself and he came at me.

"How'd I get back here?"

"Bunch of us came in and picked up the pieces and hustled you into my wagon two minutes before the cops arrived. I tell you, I was impressed. You looked like you knew what the hell you were doing. You almost demolished him in thirty seconds. If five guys hadn't pulled you off, Christ knows what would have happened to him. Trouble was you hit your head on a table on the way down – which was probably just as well. When he pulled himself off the floor he went for a bottle. Coulda bin messy."

We sat outside with the coffee, watching a pair of groundhogs in the next field, and I realized that I had missed the train for Toronto. Alex stared at the ground, lighting a cigarette, as I told him of my plans to go home. He offered me the pack, and I lit one, my hands shaking, as one of the groundhogs disappeared down a hole and the other sat up and looked around, then settled down to eat again.

"What sort of horseshit's that?" He was looking at me like some kind of officer, as though I had no right to do what I wanted.

"That's the way it is. The way I'm gonna do it."

"I'll look a real asshole with Rochford. I tell him how you need this break – things are tough and all that – and he takes my word for it. Next time he'll tell me to get lost. You're a real sweetheart."

"I can do what the hell I like."

"Sure. Like everyone else here. They all gotta right to quit – but they can't. They need the dough. So you've had a rough couple of weeks and got in a fight. So what? Next week'll be better, and the one after that. Anyway, you'll never get your money outa Rochford on a Sunday. It's a day of rest for them – they go to church. It's a big thing. What they don't do is work."

"So I'll go tomorrow. Lookit, some of those eight-year-olds pick more in a day than I do."

"Sure they do. They're experienced. Old hands. See, you gotta have a system and it takes time. One where you keep everythin' flowin' smoothly, like a car engine."

The groundhog was floating in the air. As we heard the shot, it flopped heavily back to the ground. Over on the slope, beside a fence, Al Rochford was sitting with the rifle on his knee, looking for another victim. Alex watched him, squinting as he drew on the last half-inch of his cigarette, then mashed the stub into the ground, grinding it in with his heel.

"I heard somewhere, once, that guys who get their jollies knockin' off animals like that are all screwed up in their heads about gettin' laid. Like they have problems bein' normal with women. No kiddin', Eldon. They're scared the woman's gonna take their nuts right off. I heard that somewhere. Course, with him it doesn't surprise me. And to think of that little wife of his goin' to waste like that." He grinned and opened the bottle of rye and poured two more shots. "Okay, so don't believe me, but let me tell you, me old darlin', I think your problem is that you need to get well and truly laid before you start knockin' off animals."

I laughed and my mouth hurt. "So what else is new? And even if you were right, I couldn't afford it."

"I'll fix you up."

"I just said, I got no money."

"Your credit's good. Anyway, you don't need money. Five bucks cash or twenty-five baskets of tomatoes. That's the basic minimum. Over and above that–for extras, overnights–you negotiate."

I didn't believe him. I mean, this was southern Ontario farming country where everyone went to church on Sunday. Jarvis Street, okay, but here?

"You give me all this crap about guys shootin' animals and bein' mixed up and now you expect me to believe there are hookers working the farms?"

"They're not hookers, for Chrissakes. They got class and they don't screw just anyone. They work in the fields like you or me, only this way they get a chance to make something extra. They need bread, you want to get laid. Supply and demand."

"And you're their pimp?"

He looked at me with a surprised, hurt expression, like I'd stabbed him in the back or something. "A pimp?" His voice was rising as he spoke. "Don't you have any class? Any couth? Just because you come from Black Rapids you don't have to show it! God Almighty!" He shook his head and sighed, like Goodhead used to when he was trying to explain something to me. "Entrepreneur! Entrepreneur! Haven't you ever heard of someone who's an entrepreneur? An impresario? Jesus, what did they teach you up there? I thought Glace Bay was bad enough." Then his beard broke open in a wide grin and he gave me a slap on the shoulder.

"I'll have to make allowances for the fact you bumped your head last night. Ah, c'mon. At least you could smile."

Al Rochford got up, looked over at us, then started to walk back to his house, the rifle slung over his arm. Neither of us said anything as we watched him go. Finally Alex stretched and stood up, looking back to me, nodding.

"Yep. I think Anne-Marie will be the best one for you. I mean, they're all good, don't get me wrong. There's none of your wham-bam-thank-you-Sam crap. There's Bev over on the Highdale farm, Cathy up on Old Man Rochford's brother's place and Anne-Marie at the Shantz place. No one here yet, but we're looking after it."

"What about their husbands?"

"Turn a blind eye. Except Anne-Marie's. He's back in Quebec working the docks."

"One thing's for sure, you don't do it for love."

"Neither does Anne-Marie, me old darlin'. Neither does Anne-Marie."

Anne-Marie and her kids lived in a converted chicken house that had been attached to a small wooden garage, making two rooms. Alex hadn't said too much about her, so I had no idea what she looked like even though I'd seen her from a distance in the fields. He did say that her last child was born caesarean and they'd tied her tubes so there was no way she could get knocked up.

She opened the garage door with a slight smile and closed it quietly behind me. I'd taken a route through the back fields so that Shantz wouldn't see me and felt quite nervous until she had bolted the door, turned and smiled again.

"'ello. I'm Anne-Marie."

"Eldon. Alex – "

"'e came to see me. Tell me about you."

Her voice was soft and her English not too good. She was slightly plump – although even that was hard to tell with the sleeveless cotton housecoat she was wearing. Her legs seemed slender enough and her feet were small in a pair of fluffy blue slippers.

"I made coff-ee." She tilted her head slightly to one side

as she said it, rather like a robin, and the little smile appeared again.

"Thanks." I liked her right there and then.

The garage was furnished with a table, cupboards and an electric burner at one end. At the other was a double mattress on the floor with two pillows and a loose sheet thrown over it. Next to the burner was a small oil lamp, giving out a soft, low light, and I could see that the door to the chicken house was bolted too, probably to keep the children out.

Some old Ontario licence plates were nailed on one of the walls. In the roof, hanging from a beam, were a couple of worn white-wall tires and a fading and rusty five-gallon container of British-American 10w30 oil.

" 'ow you take it?"

"Just sugar."

She smiled and cocked her head. "One . . . or two?"

"Two."

She brought the coffee to the table, offered me a cigarette from a blue package, moved the oil lamp over and sat down. "Alex say – this is your first time. At the farm. Picking."

Her eyes were something else. Wide and brown and soft and warm.

I guess eyes are the things which get me first with women – they tell almost everything. Sincerity, boredom, love, hatred – whether they're uneasy or relaxed, confident, angry or afraid. It's around the eyes that beauty or attractiveness is built. It all starts with the face and the rest of the body is secondary – important, but secondary. I've been known to be wrong, but what Alex said was right – she had class. She wasn't your average hooker. At least, not the way I remember them. Hell, when did a hooker ever make you coffee?

"It gets, 'ow you say? Lonely . . . by yourself?"

"Yeah . . . work all day . . . no one to talk to."

"You 'ave a wife?"

Christ, what did she want to bring Connie into it for? All I needed was to start thinking about her to ruin the whole thing. Anyway, just lately she could take it or leave it, usually leave it, and I'm not made that way. Shit, now I'm trying to justify it.

"Yeh . . . she's up north. Northern Ontario. And your husband, he works in Quebec?" We'll be discussing the weather next.

"He's a . . . ," she gave a small shrug, "what you say? A steve . . . steve . . . "

"Stevedore."

"Oui."

"Does he know about . . . "

"No. It wouldn't . . . be good for me."

"Yeah. You're right there."

"I 'ate to discuss . . . well, 'ow you pay. Money or . . . " Will that be cash or charge sir? Just like in the Simpsons mail order office in Black Rapids.

I could see that she did'nt like talking about it but at least we both knew I didn't have much money or I wouldn't be on the farm in the first place.

"Money. Alex said it would be –"

"Five dollar."

" . . . and next time, maybe . . . "

"Oui." She nodded and smiled when I passed her the bill, my last five dollars. I figured it would be a good investment against insanity. She took my hand and make like she was reading my palm, studying it seriously, then looked at me, cocking her head which let her hair fall straight, in line with her shoulders.

"You 'ave 'ad a 'ard life. I see pain . . . "

"From picking tomatoes."

The little smile again, then more study. "And you 'ave been in a beeg fight! And you win!"

I took her hand and turned it over. It was small and looked like a commercial for dishpan hands, with a white circle where I figured her wedding band normally was.

"And you've been talking too much to Alex."

She laughed and came around the table, standing very close to me while she felt the corner of my mouth.

"It 'urts?"

"No. It's okay." I ran my hand along the cool skin of her arm, and she leaned in and kissed the grazed part of my face.

"We fix it. 'ow long since you . . . " She gave a shrug and then a smile.

"Too long."

"We fix that too." She moved away and gave a small gesture toward the bed. "I go and see the child-ren are okay . . . and come back." She slid the bolt on the door leading to the chicken house and left me alone.

I undressed quickly, got on the mattress and pulled the sheet over me, shifting around to find a position that wouldn't make my cock look so obvious, standing up as it was, rigid in anticipation. Eventually I settled for my side, propped up on one elbow, so that it didn't look like a tent pole.

She came back to the garage, bolted the door quietly, turned the lamp very low and brought a small bowl of warm water and a face-cloth over to the mattress. Then she knelt beside me, and slipped the sheet back, smiling at what she saw. Very gently, she bathed my cock with light fingers, not knowing how dangerously close she was getting to triggering me off. When she was finished, she unbuttoned her

86

housecoat and let it fall to her waist. She had nothing on underneath. For a moment she looked at me, not in the least self-conscious. She was a little plump, but I'dve hated it any other way. For someone who'd had four kids she was in fantastic shape – well-proportioned breasts and a smooth curve, swinging in slightly at the waist, that travelled from under her arms to her hips. The smile came again and she raised her eyebrows with a gesture that asked for approval.

"*Formidable.*" It was a word I'd learned years ago and seemed to fit the occasion. I held out my hand and moved the sheet back to let her in.

For a few minutes she just nestled there, running her hands lightly over my chest while mine ran the length of her back and over to her stomach, feeling the scar for a moment and then moving on. She looked at me, waiting for me to say something, but I kissed her instead and her tongue slipped into my mouth, darting around, withdrawing, teasing and then re-exploring. Her hand started moving down my body, skimming the surface of my skin. Every time I thought she would take my cock in her hand, she'd trace a circle around it and move away.

Finally, she gently ran her fingers along it and held it, smiling at my reaction, pleased. Without letting go she sat up, looked down at me with that tilt to the head, and then drew back the sheet. Moving down the mattress she knelt between my legs, facing me, watching me with those incredible eyes, then took it tenderly into her mouth, holding it tighter as her tongue started to move quickly, then her lips.

When it happened I felt as though I would lift right off the mattress, and when it was finished she lay over me, holding my cock between her breasts while I drifted slowly back down to earth.

The next day I worked like a man possessed, watching the more experienced ones so that I could develop a system. Pick, toss, pick, toss, move the basket up. Come on, Eldon, move it, you're gonna make it, fellah. Pick, toss, pick, toss.

And I thought of Anne-Marie.

Later I had made love to her. It was leisurely and relaxed, so that when I moved inside her, she was wet and warm and her eyes were alive.

I wanted to feel that she needed this as much as me, that this was something more than just a business arrangement and that the others who came to see her during the week didn't count.

We lay there without saying a word. The yellow lamplight made flickering patterns in the roof. Above us I could see an old tire pump, a worn harness and a rotted wheelbarrow with a metal wheel throwing weird shadows. On the wall beside me were the marks of a hundred scraped fenders, grease stains and the remains of some spilt paint that had run down the siding in the shape of a blue South America.

I realized again, as I had years ago seeing Muriel Lobraico, that God had never invented anything quite as good as a woman – if He was the one who did it – and Anne-Marie was a pretty bloody good example of His skill.

I arranged to see her again the next Saturday so that we wouldn't have to worry about getting up early to catch the truck – although she took the kids to ten o'clock mass in Chatham every Sunday. She didn't say anything about staying all night, or at least until early morning before the kids woke up, but either way, I now had to work twice as hard. That would cost at least fifty baskets.

From then on the summer was much easier to take. I got pretty fast at picking, but not fast enough to make two grand, so I hunted around for some Sunday work, pumping gas in town, doing minor repairs to farm equipment, and the biggest of them all, rewiring Rochford's barn when the local guy's estimate was too high. I offered to do it for thirty per cent less and still cleared five hundred bucks. To celebrate I suggested to Anne-Marie that we go into Chatham for dinner and maybe a show, but she wouldn't. The only time I saw her, aside from Saturday evenings, was when Old Man Rochford threw his annual corn roast for the pickers from his and the Shantz farm. She had brought her kids but she stuck closely to the other French Canadian families – in fact, I hardly knew she was there. But Saturday nights it was like two lost people finding each other for a few hours of warmth, and it never failed. Walking over there, I would get this charge through my body, like I once had with Connie.

There was just a week left before I went back to B.R. when I walked over for the last time. I had a bath in the stream, slapped on the last of my Mennon, slipped a mickey of Black Velvet in my hip pocket and set out for the Shantz farm. Cutting through some of the fields that had already been disked for the next year, I came up to the garage from behind to avoid the Shantz house – but as I got to within fifty feet of the garage door, Shantz appeared from behind a silo with his son who had the lame foot limping beside him. Stopping, he looked in my direction, then walked over.

"What d'you want?"

"I came to see . . . Mrs. Savard . . . she wanted her electric burner fixed."

"Who?"

"She lives over in the garage with her kids."

"Oh." There was a silence while he looked me up and down and the son stared at me with his mouth open. His yellow teeth stuck out, badly in need of braces. "Where you from?"

"Rochford's."

"Yeah – well, she left. This mornin'. Figured the kids bin outa school too long."

A heavy, sinking feeling gripped my stomach. I hoped that he was wrong but at the same time I knew he had to be right. I could see the small window of the garage now, and there was no light coming out. It was just another empty farm building.

"You sure?"

"Why wouldn't I be? Drove em into town to the train station m'self so's they can connect in Torrona. Long ride all that way."

He started to walk toward the house, followed by the boy, stopped to make sure I was following, then continued. "Way back to Rochford's place is down that road there. I was gonna say, if you wanna check over that burner, you go right ahead. It was working jus' fine when I looked the place over 'fore payin' her off." He gave me a smile that said fuck you, Charlie, and went inside, but through the glass in the door I could see him watching me.

Even though we still hadn't had any frost the nights were cool. I walked quickly, almost blindly. It was like being kicked in the gut. Like part of me had been taken away. I mean, shit, I knew it was a business thing and all that and I wasn't in love with her or anything, but even so it hurt, but good. At least, I don't think I was in love with her. That sort of thing doesn't happen in the goddamned tomato fields. And getting along good doesn't mean you've got to be involved or whatever. Anyways, the fact she took off without telling me, without saying goodbye even, proves it. Like the scrapbook. Proof.

I stopped and took a swig of the rye, a long, slow one, that warmed its way down to the knot that was gripping me, tight and twisting – then another long one that made my eyes water. Stuffing the bottle back in my pocket I hurried on, wishing to hell I'd worn something warmer.

I could see her face in front of me, tilting the head and smiling . . . all she had to do was tell me . . . I'dve understood . . . I wouldn't have liked it . . . but I'dve understood . . . those eyes . . . look at em . . . you can always tell with the eyes . . . they show everything . . . be in Quebec tomorrow . . . she shouldn't be going all that way alone . . . with four kids . . . that fucking husband of hers . . . I hope he chokes on the money I sweated my ass for . . . but she knew I'd be coming over . . . she knew I'd get there and find the place empty . . . and if she'dve told me . . . it wouldve been easier . . . much easier.

I finished the mickey and threw it into a ditch. Dear Lord Jesus, I wish I'd had the chance to say something to her. I'm not sure what – but anything that would have let her know – well, just let her know. That's all.

The train for Kapuskasing stopped long enough in Black Rapids to throw out a couple of mailbags and let me off before it pulled slowly out across the trestle over the Black River. It was early on the Sunday morning before Thanksgiving, and the place was deserted, except for Ernie Davits, the station clerk, collecting the mailbags at the other end of the platform. Even Ken Howell's cab wasn't there, not that I'dve taken it. Who expects anyone to get off the early Sunday train in Black Rapids?

I'd left the farm the day before, saying goodbye to Alex who was getting ready to head south for the winter. Maybe Mexico or Florida, he'd said. He wasn't sure.

"Eldon, me old darlin', three months is all I can stand in any one place. I'll find a beach, do some fishin', work now and again and enjoy some of the finer pleasures of this life. Canadian winters are not for me. See yer next year, maybe."

"Maybe. I wouldn't count on it, though." We shook hands warmly at the station and I realized I really admired the guy. "You know somethin'? You're a great old bastard."

He looked at me for a moment, started the wagon and slipped it into gear, his smile flashing. "That's horseshit and you know it. Take care." And he was gone, the sun glinting off the ever-polished chrome like he'd planned it should be at that point in the sky at that time.

I'd sent a telegram from Toronto telling them to expect me and now, walking down the main street, I began to feel a little nervous. It was important that things got off to a good start again, very important. Otherwise I felt pretty good. I'd never been this fit in my life.

Turning onto Beech I saw Bert Powell coming toward me with his dog. He nodded, and stopped to let the dog pee on someone's grass.

"Eldon."

"Bert."

"Bit chilly."

"Yeah, but at least the sun's out."

"Nice day for the turkey dinner at the church."

"Yeah."

"Say hello to Connie."

"Will do – and to Agnes."

Shit, it was like I hadn't been away.

I went to the back door like I usually do, and my heart sank. There was a note pinned to the screen in Connie's neat handwriting. No one was looking out of the windows watching me walk up the street. They must have heard the train go over the crossing. The knot was coming back again as I went up the steps and pulled the note from its pin.

One line.

We missed you.

Connie was in the kitchen making coffee. Next to the stove was some pancake batter, and in the oven sausages, keeping warm. She was wearing a new dress and her hair seemed a little different. As I hugged her all the familiar scents came back to me and the knot in my stomach tightened. In comparison with her I looked a mess, my clothes rumpled from sleeping in the coach section. The coffee boiling over interrupted us.

"You must be hungry."

"You betcha. Where are the kids?"

"Away – well, they'll be back for dinner. Davie went camping and Delores and Janice are sleeping over at Mom's. I thought it'd be nice to spend some time alone."

"Yeah."

I didn't get to tell her about the two thousand, five hundred and twenty-one dollars and some change that I had on me until almost midday. And she didn't ask.

Of course, I kept going back. Year after year. It became a habit, an easy way to spend the summer, to pull in close to four grand over a season. Things didn't change much as the years went past. Old Man Rochford died of a heart attack and his body wasn't cold before his sons were negotiating to sell off two hundred acres.

The kids always bitched about going there but I told them it was good for them, helped to build character, and anyway, a hard day's work never hurt no one. I mean, kids have it soft these days.

Did I really believe that? In one word, no, but I didn't know what to say to them. Only later did it occur to me that being honest, levelling with them, would be the best thing. Tell em we needed the money, that times were tough. But by then Davie and Delores had stopped coming anyway and my promises that we'd never come back, that this would be the last year, sounded more and more phoney. I could hear my father's words even more clearly.

"You'll be skilled for nothin', then what'll you do?"

That's about the size of it, skilled for nothing. But this year will be the last, the last time we have to put up with all the shit, the way of life that slowly but surely takes away a man's pride. A man's gotta have his pride. The difference between this year and all the others is that this year I mean it. It really will be the last.

There is a moment at the end of every heatwave, a fleeting moment, when things start to change. The leaves of a tree stir slightly, followed by a gentle movement in the tall grass, and then it's still again. The swallows find more energy and the goldfinches suddenly start their rollercoaster flight again, looping through the air singing as they go. If you happen to be outside and lucky enough, you can smell it – the first breath of cool air creeping stealthily ahead of the main mass.

I was sitting watching the groundhogs when it happened, right on schedule like the radio predicted, that beautiful, fresh, cool air forcing out the clammy atmosphere of the previous two weeks, sweeping away the stale pollution of our room.

I called Connie and Janice outside and we stood there, grinning at each other, enjoying it in case it wasn't true, laughing, easing the tensions. Hell, Connie and me even fooled around a bit when we went to wash, splashing each other, getting dunked when we washed our hair and flicking towels at each other like we were kids at the Lions Club pool. For a moment there was even a sparkle in Connie's eyes as she brushed her hair, smiling in a teasing sort of way like she used to. But then it was gone just as quickly as it appeared. I think it's when you get back into your clothes that the moment disappears, when you become the person you were again, the person you're expected to be.

Later that evening Alex stopped by and invited me over for a beer, and I figured the cool air must have got to him. He had his tent pitched on the north side of some silver birches and two garden chairs set up so we could stretch out and watch the sun go down, the beer cooler between us serving as a table. It wasn't like him. Alex never gave anything away for no reason, but tonight there he was, running a comb through his beard, very relaxed as he held a bottle of beer up and let the cool liquid pour nonstop down his throat, waving at me to help myself.

The breeze had died down and the only sounds were from the crickets, the occasional late-home robin and the frogs that lived in the marshy area two fields over. A wren flew to a nearby fence, gave a brief burst of song and disappeared into one of the rotting posts. Alex belched, a long, deep one that seemed to silence the crickets for a moment. He settled back in his chair.

"So what's the occasion?"

"Does there have to be an occasion for a man to ask a friend over for a beer?"

"In your case, yes. Either that or you got stood up in town and now you're looking for someone to talk to."

"Eldon, me old darlin', you're a suspicious, ungrateful, offensive bastard. I didn't get stood up. In fact, quite the opposite. I decided not to see her tonight. She wept, pleaded, did everything she could to get me to change my mind, but I declined."

"Sure."

"It's the truth, so help me. I might add, for your information, that she's a sweet, delectable dish, the best thing that has ever come out of southwestern Ontario, and God knows there are enough dogs in this part of the world. To have found a gem like this," – he smiled, trying to look modest –

"proves that despite my age I still have the magic touch." He took out two more beers, removed the caps with another bottle, and passed one to me. "I met her at a private club just off the main drag. There she was, this cute little thing with a tight skirt covering a nice plump ass, good tits fair to burstin' outa her blouse, standin' by the bar lookin' all alone and miserable."

"How the hell d'you get into a place like that?"

"Desperation. It was air-conditioned. Just walked in looking lost and told the guy on the door that someone had sent me in the wrong direction to the washroom. He showed me where it was and I was in. Mind you, I was wearin' my best duds. So I went to the bar, bought a drink, floated over to her and we bumped and I tipped my drink like she'd made me spill it. Works every time. We were friends from then on. She lives in Leamington. Husband's an inspector at one of the canning factories around there. The miserable sonofabitch went off fishin' for a week and left her all alone, so what could I do? I have a weakness for sad dogs, cryin' children and lonely, deserted wives. I even turn to God at times like this. I'm praying that his boat will sink or he gets picked up by the police or lost in the bush."

"You passed this fantastic thing up for – "

"She is not a thing."

"This beautiful, delectable dish . . . just to have a beer with me? Come on!"

"No, I didn't. I'm in trainin'."

"For what?"

"To break my record. Three hundred and ten baskets. I figure I'll need twelve hours to do it, so I have to get into shape, and sex and record breakin' don't mix. Tomorrow's the day, now that we've got decent weather."

I looked at us, stretched out, feet up, and laughed. "You call this trainin'?"

98

"Nothin' better. A few beers, an early night, and tomorrow I'll be King."

"You're the King now. Who's ever beaten you?"

"No one. But that's no excuse. They all look to me to lead the way, show em it can be done. Especially the new ones. They're here because they've nowhere else to go, it's the end of the road. So they look to Alex to guide them, and when they see me out there they know I mean business. That you have to want to do it badly enough, to be the best."

Over the years we'd become pretty good friends, but the only time we ever saw each other was during the picking season and every year we'd sit and have a few beers like this, at 25¢ a bottle, discussing everything from storming the parliament buildings in Toronto to protest the conditions to why Alex thought Al Rochford's wife needed him in the worst way. And without fail, he'd tell me stories of the things he'd done, the women he'd made, and when he did I usually felt jealous. I never told him anything personal, figuring it was our business, Connie's and mine. It's something I've never been able to do, trust people completely. That and letting my feelings really come out. My father was always telling me to keep my ears open and my mouth shut and that way I'd never get into trouble. I should have listened instead of going around punching people up.

Alex sat up and swatted a mosquito, his face still serious.

"Yeah, I want to set a new record. One that'll stand for years, because I've decided that this will be my last season pickin'." He saw the surprise on my face and smiled. "Yes, me old darlin', this is it for me. I've spent too many years movin' around an' I've decided it's time to settle down in one place for a while. I'm not gettin' any younger, for Chrissakes. An' you know somethin'? I'm startin' to get lonely. It hit me last winter, layin' on this beach in Mexico

99

with a cold cerveza in my hand lookin' at the tide go out. I mean, I've bin fartin' around ever since I left Glace Bay. Sure I had good times – but who needs this pickin' crap, never bein' in one place long enough to pay a parkin' ticket? The thing is, it's taken me all this time to realize it, my life has bin one long series of doors closin' behind me; some woman somewhere makin' sure no one was lookin' as she let me out.

"I figured it was time I had a door of my own, so I'm gonna buy me a boat down there next winter, big enough for two, and settle down on it. You can get good used ones fairly cheap. It's time to put my feet up and relax. Bin my dream for years. You gotta have somethin' to aim for, I always say. So between now and the end of the season I'm gonna work my ass off. Think of it Eldon – the sun, sand and surf with someone who cares." He grinned, raising his eyebrows. "Now tomorrow night, that's something else. First things first. I'll meet her in the lobby of the William Pitt Hotel and we'll drive somewhere for dinner, and when it's dark, we'll head for Leamington and her apartment and really celebrate." He flipped open the cooler with a big flourish, suddenly laughing. "You know somethin'? It gives me a good feelin', toolin' down the road at the wheel of her husband's Trans Am, my hand on his wife's knee, thinkin' about him in some goddamned boat, probably pissed out of his mind, figurin' he's livin' it up. Ahhhh . . . " He sat back, stroking his beard, a smile on his face. "She really is somethin', Eldon. Blonde, gotta sense of humour, will try anythin' new – and starved of the kind of lovin' that Alex can give her." He laughed again, took a swig of beer, and became serious. "D'you think I'll do it? The record, I mean?"

It was the first time I'd seen him doubtful about anything. What he'd said was true, he was virtually the une-lected leader of the pickers in our area, a hero to many and admired by everyone else, including me. It was Alex who got the rate up to thirty-five cents a basket by threatening to get all Rochford's pickers to quit work if he didn't increase it. There was no way they would quit, but Rochford didn't call his bluff and agreed. That day Alex was at his bullshit-ting best.

It was thought to be his God-given right to operate on the side, and his business and prices grew every year as he cashed in on people's laziness and lack of planning. Even his stable of women had grown, and although the farmers denied knowing about it, every farm for miles around, in-cluding Rochford's, had its resident "therapist," as he called them. There's no doubt that Alex was a somebody around the tomato fields. Like he said, someone not to be messed with.

I used to be a somebody, too. Once. In Black Rapids. Some-one to be respected, a hero if you like.

I've got a scrapbook to prove it. My mother bought it when I started playing hockey, a large book with brown pages and a bright cover with a picture on it of a girl like Shirley Temple with her arm around a dog that looked like Lassie.

Inside, on the first page, right in the middle, she glued a piece from the Black Rapids *Record*:

In the Novice League Bill Irving's White Rose beat Homecare Hardware 3-1. E. Harris had two goals for Irving's and B. Kalentzis scored the other.

My name in print at the age of nine! There were more over the years. When I was twelve and playing Peewee I won a trophy at a big tournament in Timmins for being the leading scorer, and by the time I was playing Midget it was taken for granted that one day I'd play for the Black Rapids Raiders.

They were long, cold winters, playing on open air rinks, but it was worth it, especially if you were a hero after a three-goal game, the centre of attention, sitting around the stove in the coach's kitchen while you thawed out, drinking hot chocolate with marshmallows and stuffing doughnuts made that morning by his wife. There was no way I wouldn't make the NHL. I mean, everyone said it was a dead cert.

My first season with the Raiders wasn't that successful. I only scored ten goals and fifteen assists with plenty of bench warming in between. I had quit school, and like most players on the team worked at the mill, seeing that Caulfield owned the Raiders. All in all, life was pretty good.

It wasn't until the season had been over for a month that my father said anything about it at Sunday breakfast.

"You're wasting your time."

"What?"

"I said you're wasting your time playing for that team. It'll get you nowhere. Let's face it, you didn't exactly set the world alight, did you?"

"I thought I played pretty good, considering."

"What sorta trade are you learning? I had to do it the hard way. Not rely on special privileges because of Caulfield." My mother, as always, was hovering in the background, and she interrupted by taking the plates off the table, smiling at my father.

"We'll be late for church, dear, and you've got to shave. We have all summer to worry about that."

He pulled out his watch from the front of his coveralls, wound it, and got up without another word. From that day on he never spoke about it again.

That summer I worked my ass off, determined to put on weight and be completely fit for the next season. To keep my father happy I took up carpentry in my spare time, and although I say it myself, I became pretty good at it. In fact, toward the end of the summer I started to build a greenhouse for my mother as a surprise and got it finished by the Labour Day weekend. It was a pretty snazzy thing, with windows for ventilation, shelves for plants and a small table in the middle for potting, things like that. I painted it, bought some pots with chrysanthemum plants in them and on Labour Day we had the grand opening. Even my father had to admit it was good.

It was typical of my mother that she wouldn't say anything and I only realized some years after she died that I had built the thing facing north. I had to assume that my father knew even less about gardening than I did, because he didn't say anything either, and he'dve never missed a chance like that.

There are some days when you know that whatever you do things are going to work out good, greenhouses aside. I had that feeling when we played the first game of the new season. Even though I was playing on the third line I knew this was going to be my night. Call it confidence, cockiness, whatever, when I stepped out onto the ice for the first time something told me I was going to set the crowd on its ear, make them realize that even if I was the youngest player on the team, this kid was something special. We were playing Cochrane in Black Rapids, and the new arena was jammed with about two hundred people stamping their feet and chanting "Go Raiders go!" as I poke-checked one of their forwards in our end, recovered the puck and started down for their goal on a breakaway with two men back. It was a beautiful moment, out there all alone, the whole team waiting, depending on me, as the first defenceman came to me to take me to the boards. At the last moment I gave a slight shift and left him standing there with egg all over his face. Suddenly accelerating I got a couple of strides on the second defenceman, cut across the front of the goal, sent the goaltender sliding in the wrong direction and flipped the puck into the empty net. The ovation was fantastic and I played it very modest as I skated to the bench with half of the team draped over me patting my back, my head, my ass, you name it. What I wanted to tell them was I couldve scored going in backwards the way I felt, but instead I just nodded and said my thanks with my head slightly bowed and sat very casual on the bench, just aching to get back out and show them it was no fluke.

I became someone in Black Rapids that night.

They gave me the puck as a memento of my first hat-trick for the team. By Christmas of that season I was the league's leading scorer and when I walked down the main street in Black Rapids people recognized me. Even the coach said I'd be a cinch to make the NHL. It was a whole new world.

The Black Rapids *Record* ran my picture almost every week and called me the hottest prospect in Northern Ontario. They nick-named me "Ace" Harris, and occasionally they'd interview me after a game and I'd try to remember some of the things I'd heard on the Imperial Hockey broadcast.

"Yeah, they were a tough team. Probably the toughest."

"Yeah . . . Bobby was really digging in the corner and when he threw the puck out I saw this spot over the goalie's left shoulder and let it go."

"Yeah . . . I picked the top right corner."

"Yeah . . . it's not just me. We're a team. That's what counts, teamwork."

"Yeah . . . you get the breaks and give it your best shot."

Most of it was crap and I knew it, but it sounded good.

There were fringe benefits, too. Clothes from Bill Rogers' place wholesale, free Cokes at Wong's, invitations to parties. And the girls – who came to every home game and as many out-of-town games as they could get rides for.

And guess who they were after?

I started brushing my hair more often, using Brylcreem, smearing stuff over my face at night to get rid of pimples and shaving twice a week. In the mirror my nose looked too big, but aside from that I thought I wasn't bad looking.

At the mill everyone figured I was getting laid practically every night, especially when we had out-of-town games, and at the team Christmas party I had to almost fight them off. I mean, me? The year before I'd watched the older players going through the same thing, obviously enjoying it and obviously getting their share. I heard stories about how I was playing hard to get, how I was a loner and how after a ride back from Iroquois Falls after a game, a girl named Ruth had been the first to get me into bed!

I shouldve been that lucky.

The truth of the matter was that I was a virgin with a capital V. Oh, I'd read all those books and knew what it was all about all right. My problem was I didn't know how the hell to go about it. What to do first? How far I could go? And supposing I did go all the way, what if I knocked her up? I mean, could you see me going into Howard Dusty's drugstore and buying a package of safes? Hell, I wouldn't know what to ask for. The brand name? Condoms? Contraceptives? Rubbers? Or plain, ordinary safes?

Anyway, it would be just my luck to have the girl serve me. Then what?

The trouble with this Ruth girl was that the story got around. She was good looking I suppose, well-built and considered something of a prize among the players. What was I gonna do? Deny it and admit I'd turned it down? I say "turned it down," it didn't really get that far. What really happened was that when I got into the back seat of the car for the ride home, she was already there, like it was planned, and within five minutes she was snuggled up close saying it was cold and what a great game I'd played (she was right, I had. Two goals and two assists including the game winner. She knew her hockey all right), ran her hands through my hair (after I'd just brushed it so it looked great), kissed my ear and held my hand, all the time whispering into my ear how fantastic I was and all that crap.

I remember we were just passing through Nellie Lake and I was watching a dog pee against a garbage can, the only activity there was, when she took my hand and I suddenly found myself holding her left breast, inside her coat and blouse, its nipple erect and firm as she moved it against the palm of my hand. I sat there frozen, like some kid caught in the act of stealing, until she took her other hand and placed it over mine, pressing it into her breast as she let out a deep breath.

"That's beautiful," she whispered, and closed her eyes with a smile on her lips.

I had my own problems. Not only was I getting a hard-on, but in the rush to get a ride after the game I'd forgotten to take off my jock-strap and cup and was now suffering the consequences. My other problem was that this was the first breast I had ever touched and I wasn't sure what to do about it. It felt good, warm and firm, and I learned some-

106

thing about nipples I didn't know before. But what next? What if the couple in the front seat saw us?

But Ruth distracted me by inching her hand along my leg in a direct collision course with my metal cup, and I was suddenly panic-stricken. If it ever got out that the star of the team wore his athletic cup in the back seat of a car with Ruth, or any girl come to that, I'd never live it down. My erection started to dwindle, thank God. Then she changed tactics.

Opening her coat, she removed my hand from her breast and directed it toward her crotch, over her stomach and along her thighs encased in tight ski-pants. Relieved, I started to sweat. But then she placed my hand between her legs and from there pushed it under the top of her pants. I felt warm flesh. My hard-on started to come back. Jesus!

Now she'd pointed me in the right direction she obviously expected me to continue the path down to that sacred area which, up until this moment, had been nothing more than a thing of my dreams, of pictures in medical and hygiene books with the parts described like it was a geography lesson. Labia majora. Labia minora. In the meantime she was getting more reckless and attacked my belt and fly buttons with a vengeance, her breathing getting faster, me sweating more and more as she yanked the fly open, sending buttons everywhere, and rested her hand on my stomach. It's impossible to describe the physical and mental agony I was in because of that goddammed metal cup.

For a moment everything stood still. Her hand was cold and I could see her breath coming in spurts, like a dragon. I could have sworn her eyes were moist. Even in the gloom of the back seat, they flashed like a hunter's with the buck lined up in the sights. She smiled and started to move my hand down over her smooth skin, shifting position to make it easier for me to cover those final few inches, at the same time slipping her own hand under the top of my shorts. Dear God, what can I do now? Her smile was peaceful and she seemed relaxed, while I was sweating and starting to hear strange wailing noises in my head, getting louder and louder until the cruiser behind us overtook, the cop signalling us over to the side of the road. Ruth came to life, pulling my hand out of her pants and wrapping her coat around her.

"Shit!" She slumped back in the seat, angry and pouting, while I wondered how the hell I'd explain to my mother where all my fly buttons had gone.

The police let us off with a warning for speeding and the rest of the drive into B.R. was uneventful, the two of us sitting as far apart as possible. I got out at her place and we had a cigarette in her father's garage so that our voices wouldn't wake her folks, then another in the back seat of his car, where the game started again with Ruth telling me how goodlooking I was, what a fantastic player I was, how she liked the sound of my voice; all the time rubbing her leg against mine as she undid her blouse, revealing two large, beautiful breasts.

Let's be honest, I'd waited all my life for something like this to happen, and here it was. A real live girl offering it to me on a platter . . . and I was immobile, speechless. All I could do was stare in wonderment as she took my hand again and held it to them. Then she pushed me back, and, kneeling on the floor, placed one breast on my mouth, pulling my head toward her. I wondered how the other guys would handle something like this. I mean, hell, if I'm the star of the team and gonna get laid (for the first time yet) it should be somewhere better than in the back of some old car. It didn't seem very suave, very–well, starlike. I had all

108

sorts of things I wanted to tell her but there was no way I could speak, smothered as I was with this breast, until I finally managed to push her off and come up for air, gasping.

"Ruth . . . I don't think we should go any further, eh? I mean, I appreciate what you're doing and all . . . but well, I don't think I should take advantage of you. It's difficult for me to say this because you're so tempting and very beautiful. Not like all those others we have to put up with. With you, I'd want to go steady . . . but right now I don't want anything to interfere with my hockey. It wouldn't be fair to you. You do understand, eh? And anyway, this is no place for, well, you and me. One day it'll be somewhere better."

The voice sounded a little familiar, but I couldn't place it.

I gave her right breast a kiss (what the hell, having waited so long I couldn't just let it go) and she buttoned up her blouse.

"D'you mean that?"

"Mean what?"

"About . . . one day it'll be somewhere better?"

Jesus, did I say that? This time her eyes were moist with tears. Or was it the cold?

"Sure. But you do understand?"

"I think so. You're so fantastic out there. The way you skate, shoot the puck – so graceful."

She gave me a kiss on the lips, deep, tongue probing, and it was good. As we broke away her hand brushed my metal cup and I thought I saw a look of amazement in her eyes.

"Any time, Eldon . . . you change your mind . . . "

Almost doubled over with cramp I crawled out of the car and walked home, removing the cup at the first dark stretch of road and throwing it into the night.

So despite the rumours and stories, Eldon George Michael Harris was still a virgin, thanks to one metal athletic cup. Even so the stories didn't seem to hurt my image (even the one that I was well hung, wherever they got it). One thing was for sure, neither Ruth nor me would ever admit that nothing happened. So we were both safe on that score, which wasn't a bad saw-off when you consider it.

For the first time in their history the Black Rapids Raiders won the championship, beating out Kirkland Lake in the final. Now that was a night to end all nights.

We were playing in Kirkland Lake and a busload of fans had come down from B.R. (including my mother, who told me later that she had met a nice girl named Ruth who said she knew me) as well as the town council and the mayor, who drove down in Caulfield's Caddie. It was thirty-five below. All we needed was one win. One lousy win.

The team went down in its own bus and everyone was a little nervous, not only because the game was important, but because there was a rumour going around that some scouts from the Toronto Maple Leafs were going be there. Jesus, that was like getting the chance of a one way ticket to the land of milk and honey, about the only way of getting out of a life sentence to hard labour in Black Rapids or wherever.

I was nervous, too. Now the papers were calling me the leader of the team. Our big weapon. The major threat to Kirkland Lake. Hell, my picture was even in the local paper there with a big story about the fantastic season I'd had. Mind you, being that successful had its drawbacks. I was a prime target for boarding, body checking, slashing, spearing, you name it, and had fourteen stitches in various places to show for it.

Well, I'll tell you, things didn't go so good for the first period and a half. We were down two to nothing and they wouldn't give me any ice room, always having a man on me, hacking away at my ankles, holding, anything to keep me off the score sheet. Finally, in desperation, with nowhere to go, I let blast at the puck from about forty feet out and the next thing I know the red light is on! We were back in the game and everyone was saying what an incredible goal it was and how the goalie never saw it. I'm not surprised. I'm sure he wasn't expecting it any more than I was.

From then on it was plain sailing. We tied it up and then I went on to score two more to be a hero again. Christ, what a way to finish the season!

Caulfield had some champagne delivered to the dressing room and we whooped it up while the mayor came round and shook hands with each one of us. From then on things seemed to get a bit hazy after what seemed hours of picture taking, getting dressed and answering questions. My mother was waiting outside the dressing room with all the fans from B.R. and she gave me a big hug, tears running down her cheeks. There were more pictures, more congratulations and I could feel the champagne getting to me as I suddenly realized that this would be it until next year. I was gonna miss it.

To this day I don't know how I got to the party or even if I was invited. I suppose I must have been, because there were some other players from both teams there as well as the mayor, Caulfield, the coach and some of the town council.

It was held in the largest house I've ever seen or ever been in – a mansion on a big piece of property that belonged to some guy who owned a mine in Kirkland Lake. Just the cars parked in the driveway were enough to make me want to forget it and go home. Caddies, Lincolns, Packards, each of them probably worth more than all the cars in B.R. put together.

Inside seemed to be a series of huge rooms leading into other huge rooms, all with fireplaces and gigantic paintings on the walls, carpet that was like walking on sponge, furniture out of some movie and at least a hundred people wandering about from room to room, talking and eating small biscuit things with fishy-tasting stuff on them.

When we walked in (I think I was with the coach) I caught a look of surprise on Caulfield's face and got the idea that a mistake had been made and we weren't supposed to be there. Then his face disappeared in a mass of people as someone gave me a drink and left me to wander around. In the front hall stood a glass case on a black stand holding a chunk of rock with yellow streaks glinting in it. Underneath was a small metal plate that said "Lakeshore Mines – 1912," while on top of the case sat a half-full glass of champagne. As far as I was concerned, the sooner I got out the better, but the mayor grabbed me and took me around introducing me to people – who seemed like they could care less about meeting a hockey player from Black Rapids – and telling them I was sure to make the NHL. I felt completely out of place and when someone did say something to me I was reduced to answers of yes and no and modest thanks for their praise.

I was dying for a beer and a hamburger, but I settled for the fancy things a waitress brought around on a silver tray, things so small they wouldn't feed a fly. I found myself shuffling from one foot to the other and for some reason I didn't know what to do with my hands, so I found a quiet corner and sat down with a rye and ginger the coach had brought me and lit a cigarette. After all, I seemed to be the only person who was looking at the paintings and you can only stare at them for so long.

"You must be Ace Harris."

I looked round and up to find a woman with blonde hair and a lime green dress standing over me, swaying slightly as she smiled down between the two glasses of champagne she was holding.

"Yeh . . . that's me."

She moved round to the front of my chair and sat down on a footstool, still smiling as she handed me one of the glasses.

"No one seems to be looking after you."

"Oh, I'm doing all right."

I'm not very good at telling how old a woman is, but at a guess, I'd say she was about twenty-five, thereabouts. She was wearing glasses and had big rings on her fingers, red nails and a figure that didn't seem too bad.

"I thought you were wonderful tonight. I watch all the games here, you know, and I've seen you several times this season. That first goal was . . . superb!"

"Thanks." I tried to shrug it off. I had a feeling I might be blushing. "I saw this spot over the goalie's right shoulder and just let it go."

"Incredible precision . . . and you seem to skate so *effortlessly* . . . almost ballet-like."

I wasn't sure that I liked that and looked around to make sure that no one was listening, knowing that she hadn't taken her eyes off me, and when I turned back I didn't know whether to look up or down or where. If I looked down I'd be staring at her tits, and to look up, away from her, seemed to be rude. Always look at the person when they're talking to you, my mother would say. There was a silence and I felt I should say something, but my mind seemed to be frozen. Relax, kid. You're a hero, a star.

"They got nice paintings here."

"Oh yes . . . he's a great collector." Her voice was low, with a kind of huskiness to it that could have been natural or caused by a cold. I guessed the booze had got to her a little and I was feeling slightly pissed too, not enough to slur my words or anything, but enough to keep me riveted to the chair. She leaned over and reached for an ashtray; as she passed it to me I got a whiff of her perfume.

"Cheers." She raised her glass.

"Cheers."

"I've always found hockey so . . . stimulating. Exciting. Rather like bullfighting." She drew her legs up onto the footstool and looked at me through the glass, then over it. "There's a sense of theatre about it. All the ceremony, getting dressed for the game, putting on armour like the knights of old. D'you agree?"

"I've never thought about it." What the fuck was she talking about? Bullfighting and knights in armour?

"Have you ever seen a bullfight?"

"No." For sure she's loony. Where in hell would I have seen a bullfight? In Black Rapids? The closest thing would be two stags fighting it out during the rutting season. Oh, I'd seen pictures of it, but Jesus, what a dumb question. She put her hand on my knee for a brief moment and looked right into my eyes. She must have been talking to my mother.

"I've seen several, and there's the same kind of electricity in the air, the same kind of finesse, rather like when you

114

skate. It has a beauty, a feeling of poetry about it. Something . . . sensual."

Now there was a word I'd seen in the dictionary and it sure as hell had nothing to do with hockey. I gave a shrug and tried to be casual about it.

"I suppose. I mean, the bullfighting, not how I skate."

"You're too modest but it's very becoming. By the way, my name's Sandra."

"Hi. Mine's Eldon."

"I know that." She gave a laugh as she said it that I liked. It gave me a funny feeling inside. "I know all about you. But I must say I prefer Ace. If I had my way I'd call you El Perfecto." Jesus, I've got to get away from her. "Instead I'll have to settle for this chance to talk to you. I've often wondered what goes through a player's mind before the game. A special player like you. And when you've reached heights like you did tonight, what goes on in your mind after the game. Would you like me to show you the rest of the house?"

"Well . . . er . . . "

"They have a snooker room downstairs, and many more paintings."

She took my hand and led me from the room. I didn't dare look round to see who might be watching. We went from room to room, drinking a glass of champagne in one and leaving it in another, only to be offered more. She talked about the artwork but I didn't hear what she was saying, except that I liked the sound of her voice.

The snooker room was in use so we moved on to another long basement room that looked like the kind of English pub you see in the movies, with barrels on the bar and old pictures and shields on the walls. From there we went through a door and found ourselves in the furnace-cum-laundry room. Suddenly, without a word, she locked the door and started kissing me, her arms around my neck, pushing her body into mine, her tongue moving quickly around like Ruth's did. I stood there rigid, dumbfounded, my arms at my side, wondering what would happen if Caulfield or the mayor walked in. Or the owner of the house, come to that. But the door was firmly bolted, which made it worse. She stopped kissing me and moved back, her hands resting on my shoulders, and smiled at me.

"I've been wanting to do that since the first time I saw you play. You see, it is like bullfighting. It's a very sexual thing. You . . . don't mind, do you?"

"Well . . . no. I mean . . . "

"Then relax." She felt the muscles on my arm and squeezed them. "All gods . . . all prima donnas . . . have to know how to relax after their soul has been drained by their performance."

Now I knew she was nuts. All I did was play a game of hockey. Putting her arms back around my neck, she started kissing me again, this time slowly, deliberately and gently, while her hand stroked the hair on the back of my neck. In my pants I felt a growing bulge, and out of nowhere I heard my father.

"I've read all about those hockey players. The year Timmins won the cup. Everyone gettin' drunk and things."

And things.

She pressed herself against my bulge, then stepped back and smiled, her eyes alive.

"I just wanted to say thank you for all the pleasure you have given me this year." She pressed herself again. "Now I know you're mortal."

Then something snapped in my head as she started to kiss me again and I found myself kissing her back, running

116

my hands down her back and over her breasts. She paused long enough to say, "Oh God," and lead us to a pile of laundry on the floor. In seconds we were writhing over coveralls, sheets, pillowcases and shirts, my hands inside her dress trying to get past her bra, her hands rubbing my cock until she sat up and quickly unbuttoned her dress, unclipped her bra and let it fall away. I kissed her breasts as she sat there groaning and I thought of the possibility of someone being outside and hearing us. It didn't last long, though, as I found my belt undone, fly open and her hand holding my cock, stroking it gently as she looked at me, almost crying. Then there was no time to worry about other people as she pulled her dress up, slipped off her pants and, falling back onto the clothes, pulled me on top of her, guiding my cock into that warm, wet wonderment that, until this moment in my life, had been a plain and simple cunt. Maybe she was right, there was some poet in me.

With her hands pressing on my ass she forced me right into her, letting out little whimpers, My Gods and darlings as she did it, then, with a cry and a groan, arched her spine. That was it. The straw that broke the camel's back, so to speak. I exploded without any control and collapsed on her while she continued to writhe and moan. My heart was pounding in my head as I breathed in rapidly, sucking some of her hair into my mouth. Shifting position to get rid of it, I only succeeded in getting another, larger mouthful. There was nothing I could do, so I lay there, letting it tickle my nose as I breathed in, at the same time trying to get my hand around so that I could remove it from my mouth without making her feel bad. Even that didn't work.

I just lay there.

Well, Eldon baby, you finally did it. After waiting all these years, dreaming about it, imagining it, preparing for it, building up your expectations, it finally happened. And lasted for all of ten seconds. You and a girl named Sandra on a laundry pile in someone's basement. After all that, ten lousy seconds. If you'dve blinked you might have missed it.

She opened her eyes and smiled at me. "Tell me . . . what were your first thoughts the moment after you erupted and unleashed your soul into me?"

She's gotta be kidding. What were my first thoughts? What does it matter anyway? And what's all this crap about erupting and soul? I mean, if you really want to know, it happened so fast I didn't have time to think anything – except I was wondering why the hell she was moaning and groaning, carrying on like that.

"Well . . . er . . . I don't know really. I don't remember . . ."

"For a moment your mind was above it all . . . a transcendental experience, an ethereal stopping of time where all your tensions were dissipated? Right?"

"Er . . . yeah . . . somethin' like that. Like you said."

My elbows were starting to get sore, so I eased myself away and lay beside her, thankful to get the hair out of my mouth. Suddenly I felt kind of pleased about it all. Here I was beside a woman for the first time, and despite the dress rolled around her waist and being a little weird she looked pretty damned good. She didn't seem to mind my looking at her – at her white breasts (I couldn't really call them tits any more) and that little world surrounded by the neatest patch of soft hair leading to her long legs, tanned, obviously from watching too many bullfights. In fact I think she enjoyed my looking, as she blew me a kiss. "Ace Harris scores again? Eh, El Perfecto?"

Time of first goal, ten seconds. A new record.

Her eyes went from mine, down my body, and paused as she nodded, smiling. I looked down, a little embarrassed, to find that I was raring to go again, having gotten a little worried at the way it faded so quickly. She let out that nice little laugh and gently pushed me on my back and moved on top of me. Christ, the books didn't say anything about this! Very slowly she lowered herself down, guiding me into her as she closed her eyes and let out a sigh. I started counting to myself. At fifteen seconds I figured this might be different. And it was. She leaned over me and whispered, guiding her breasts to my mouth, "This is how all matadors . . . enjoy their evenings after a fight."

I guess bullfighting can't be all bad.

"Whatdaya say, Eldon?"

"Nothin' much."

The mayor peered into his glass like he'd lost something, then held onto my shoulder for support.

"Good party, eh?"

"Yeah, it is."

Sandra had gone upstairs ahead of me so we wouldn't look too obvious, but when I got up there she was nowhere to be seen, so I helped myself to some champagne and wandered around, finally bumping into the mayor and the coach, who were both pissed. Still holding onto my shoulder the mayor looked at me, his bloodshot eyes squinting as he stepped back like he was trying to bring me into focus. "I see you were talking to . . . talking to Sandra."

Oh, shit! Here we go. They know already. Does it show that much?

"Who?"

"The woman in the green dress. Sandra Caulfield. She's Caulfield's niece."

Jesus H. Christ! He's kidding me. Caulfield's niece! What crap.

119

"Lives here in Kirkland Lake. Her father's worth a fuckin' fortune, I've heard it told." He leaned a little closer, lowering his voice. "They say she's one of those brainy types. Goes to university down in Toronna there. Doin' some strange thing to get a degree so's she can have fancy letters after her name. Somethin' about sports and ath-er-letes."

"And bullfighters." My voice was a whisper.

"Yeah. Very odd. Shy girl."

"I spose."

"Gotta get you a drink, Eldon. That was quite a night you had for yourself."

"Yeah . . . it was."

"What you smilin' at?"

"Nothin'."

I had to admit, it was kind of funny, being part of someone's show and tell project.

They organized a big parade the following weekend, to celebrate the victory and show off the cup that we'd won. The team was supposed to ride in open convertibles (some borrowed and some loaned by Black Rapids Chevrolet), but when the time came to assemble at the mill it was so cold they couldn't get the tops of the cars down, so we wound up driving through town in the backs of pickup trucks, led by the highschool band and the school cheerleaders.

It's not easy to have a parade in B.R., because there's nowhere to parade. One trip down the main street and that's it. But the mayor was determined, and the route called for us to go from the mill, past the school, round by the station, along Main, up Pine past the Anglican church (so that the minister's wife could watch from her wheelchair), then along River to the Catholic church (to keep things even with the Anglicans) and then back onto Main for the second time as we headed for the arena, where the mayor was going to present each player with a memento on behalf of the town and the Most Valuable Player award to me.

It didn't work out that way. By the time we got going an hour and a half late the team was half pissed from the rum we'd been drinking to keep out the cold; the cheerleaders dropped so many batons they quit when we reached the school; there was no one waiting on Main Street, so the band quit; and as we passed the minister's house, the goalie fell off the back of his truck when it hit a pothole, saving the bottle he was holding with his glove hand, pulling it to his chest as he rolled. At that point we decided to forget the rest of the route and drive directly to the arena.

A great roar broke out from the large crowd as we walked in, all wearing our new black and red jackets with the championship crest on the front, our hair brushed, all chewing gum to get rid of the smell of the rum. People grabbed our hands as we moved through to the chairs that had been set up for us, slapped us on the back and yelled smart-ass remarks. The mayor introduced each one of us to the crowd, and when I was called up to get my tie-pin with the town crest on it, the cheering was deafening. It was a glorious moment.

I stood, looking down from the stage, at a sea of faces; while the mayor held up my hand like a fighter who'd just knocked out his opponent, the applause and cheering went on and on. Finally I was someone in Black Rapids. This was what it was all about. The mayor put his arm around my shoulder and shook my hand while Fred Smith from the *Record* took pictures, getting us to do it again because his flash didn't work, causing the crowd to cheer even louder. "Sure beats that bullfighting, eh, Eldon?" the mayor shouted into my ear with a grin on his face.

Then he stepped up to the microphone. "And now, ladies and gentlemen, I have the honour of presenting the team trophy awarded every year to the most valuable player. You all know who's gonna win it, eh?" The cheering got louder as he turned to me. "I give you Ace Harris!" It was deafening as they started to chant A-C-E . . . A-C-E . . . ACE! The mayor held up his hands, then mopped his face with a handkerchief. "This boy has performed wonders all season. I've never, in all the years I've bin associated with the Raiders, seen someone of his age with so much talent, so much ability. Someone who seems to have leadership built into him. I tell you, this boy's gonna go places! Right to the top! Up there with Charlie Conacher, Howie Morenz! The best of the NHL!" The cheering grew to a roar as he presented me with the trophy, shook my hand and we posed again for Fred Smith. "Eldon boy, when you make the NHL, don't forget us here, eh?" The mayor was shouting it, grinning from ear to ear. "We're proud of you – and you deserve it. Give em a wave."

I started back to join the team, pushing my way through the wellwishers as they slapped me on the back, shook my hand, roughed up my hair and told me how great I was. In the background I saw Ruth's face appear, mouth something at me, then disappear into the mass of people. I saw my mother briefly, crying again, and beside her my father, who was actually smiling, although he hadn't been to a game all season. I never did find out how my mother managed to get him there.

And then, suddenly, I was face to face with Muriel Lobraico. She was wearing a fur hat and coat and seemed just as surprised as I was. I hadn't seen her since I left school almost two years ago, and in that time, she had become even more beautiful than I remembered her, including that day I watched her swimming such a long time ago. Now her eyes were very alive and she was smiling – the one girl I'd been so scared to talk to, to ask for a date – and we were standing two feet apart with at least three hundred people looking on.

"Hello, Eldon."

The strange thing was that despite all the noise I could hear her.

"Oh . . . hi, Muriel. How yer doin'?"

"Fine. Congratulations."

"Thanks." I could feel myself start to blush. "Hot in here, eh?" Shit. You'd think I'd be able to do better than that. Here I am, a hero, a star, a Somebody. And that's all I can come up with? "I didn't know you liked hockey."

"Well . . . I'm not crazy about it. My dad's here. He's on the council so . . . "

"That's nice. So how's everything going? School, things like that?"

"Fine. That's a nice tie-pin they gave you."

"Yeah. Got the town crest on it and all." Trouble was, I never wore a tie. Nor did most people in B.R. except maybe the mayor, Caulfield and a few people like that. "Muriel . . . " Now's the time, kid. Ask her for a date. You'll never have a better chance, and how could she refuse you in a crowd like this after that reception?

"Yes?"

"It's er . . . it's nice seein' you again after so long."

"Nice seeing you. Take care." The crowd started to move, and then there were ten people between us. She smiled and turned away, then looked back, but it was too late. I'd blown it. I just couldn't say it. It was that simple.

They had a table set up where they served coffee and doughnuts after the presentations, and I bumped into my father there. He took out his watch, checked the time, wound it and then returned it to the breast pocket of his Sunday jacket, which he'd worn over his coveralls for the occasion.

124

"Good turnout, eh, son?" Jesus, why do fathers have to call their sons "Son"? I mean, hell, they went to a lot of trouble to give me a name. And always in front of people. The minister was nearby and my father edged us closer to him, then, as though he'd just seen him, acting all surprised, grabbed his hand and shook it, pushing me in front of him. "Father Campbell . . . it's good to see you."

"Of course . . . it's Mr. . . . . "

"Harris. Work at the mill. We come to your . . . "

"Of course, of course."

"This is Eldon, my boy."

"You must be very proud."

He took my hand and smiled at me, trying to think of something to say. My father thought the sun shone out of his ass but everyone knew he was a two-faced sonofabitch, telling us what sinners we were from the pulpit while all the time he was having it off with Hilda Ecclestone's mother. But everyone said that was all right for him because she was a widow and lonely and his wife was a spastic in a wheel-chair and he wasn't getting any, but he was devoting his life to her anyway and was a real Christian.

Bullshit. And he didn't even know who my father was for a minute. Mind you, that was typical of my father, try-ing to make nice to his betters, as he called them. Maybe that'd teach him. I don't know what, but maybe something.

Father Campbell (it was a High Anglican church, what-ever that is, so the ministers were called "Father," which was a sore point in our house because it made us sound like Catholics) let go of my hand and moved away after telling me that God controlled the puck and made it work in mys-terious ways (I wondered if He could stickhandle too), and we moved back to the coffee lineup.

"D'you like the presentations?" I felt I should make an effort, seeing he'd shown up.

"Very nice. I spose the tie-pins come out of our taxes, eh?" He laughed when he said it. His little joke. "Made your mother very proud."

"What about you?"

"Well, me too. I mean, it is only a hockey game after all. We shouldn't take it too seriously now, should we?" I shrugged it off, not wanting to get into that again.

"You want another doughnut, dad?"

"No. One's enough. Somehow it doesn't seem right, us livin' it up like this, all this food, while there's a war goin' on. People starvin' and dyin' over in Europe."

What the hell did he bring that up for? I know there's a war on for Chrissakes, but us not eating doughnuts or having a party isn't gonna change things one bit over there. I mean, I feel sorry for them and all that, but what the hell can I do about it?

He took his watch out again and started looking for my mother. I began to feel angry with him. Why the fuck d'you come? Why d'you bother? Go home, for God's sake, and have your afternoon sleep. There were a lot of things I would have liked to say to him, but all I could do was pick up a jelly doughnut and stuff it in my mouth right in front of him. The trouble was, he was already edging toward the door and he didn't even notice.

"Don't be late for supper, son. Your mother's cookin' a pot roast. Mustn't let it spoil for her, eh?"

I got home well after midnight, a little drunk and happy, not caring what he said. They were both asleep, or at least my father was, and my mother was probably pretending.

It had been a good party. The coach took a room at the hotel and we all sat around and drank beer and relived the season. For some reason there were no girls there, maybe because it was the last time we'd be together until next year, and it seemed like a family breaking up. Oh, we bragged about them, and my reputation as a stud grew. But I knew better.

I thought about Muriel and wondered what Ruth had been saying about me, listened to dirty jokes and told a few, and when it was time to go home we all slapped each other on the shoulders and said how fantastic we were. In a way it was kind of sad. No more being a hero, no more travelling, no more girls till next season. Life would go back to normal, whatever that was.

I walked home and met five people I knew. They all said, in one way or another, hiya Ace, whatdaya say Ace, you really slew em Ace. Ace. A hero. Ace Harris. I was really someone in Black Rapids. A star. Someone. The next week they published my picture on the front page of the *Record*. The mayor was holding up my arm and I was looking out over the crowd. I bought twenty copies and sat in my room and looked at the picture for hours, soaking up the glory. On the front page, yet.

Fred Smith gave me an enlargement and my mother had it framed and hung it in the living room next to a picture of their wedding.

But it's the one in the paper that counts. The one everybody looks at. It's in my scrapbook. That's proof. That I was someone in Black Rapids.

Once.

Alex had the perfect day for his record attempt. The forecast called for lots of sun with a high around seventy-five. In fact, when I went down to the stream to wash first thing, it was chilly. The guy on Janice's radio had been screaming that it was only sixty-two in the Chatham-Leamington area and wasn't that great. Yeah, it was.

It was great because Connie was happy thinking that we might get out of the implement shed; Janice was happy because she reckoned she'd get to the Ex in Toronto; Alex was happy about the record attempt and the wife of the canning factory inspector who'd be waiting for him tonight; and I was happy because—well, I don't really know. I guess because I could breathe again, Connie and Janice were off my back for a while and it was a nice morning. The only thing that spoiled it was having to beat the shit out of one of the rats caught in the traps. It's the garbage that does it. I mean, we wrap it up in plastic bags and all, but they only send the truck round twice a week.

One thing that made Alex happy was that he was going for the record on the Rochford farm, which meant no bouncing, dusty truck rides that poop you out before you start. Just a leisurely walk across a couple of fields, and there you were – facing one big mother of a field of tomatoes.

Alex was already there when we arrived, pacing up and down, anxious to get on with it, like a boxer before a big fight. The word had spread quickly, and for once the day ahead didn't seem too bad. There was even a feeling of excitement because the routine was going to be different, so much so that Alex was already taking bets, giving good odds, five baskets to one, that he'd make it. And there were suckers who took him on, some risking up to ten baskets. Ten slaved-for baskets!

"So, me old darlin'. Are you gonna make a small wager?" He smiled through his beard, his eyes sparkling as he kept moving.

"For Chrissakes keep still."

"Gotta keep the old adrenalin flowin'. Five to one. Good odds even if I say so myself."

"It's rigged."

"Sure it is. There's no way I'm gonna miss. No way. And then tonight, Eldon m'boy, we're off to celebrate. I might even take tomorrow off and give her the time of her life."

"If you break the record all you'll want to do is sleep."

"You gotta be kidding. Have you ever known me not to do what I said I was gonna do?"

"No."

"Well then?"

"I'll cheer for you."

"Cheap bugger." He started to laugh as the last truckload of pickers arrived. "I don't blame you, me old darlin', it's a fool's game. Now we can get going. Wish me luck."

"You'll do all right, don't worry." He had planned the

whole thing like a military operation, getting up early to walk the field and place bottles of water and beer in strategic positions so that nothing would hold him up, and now he suddenly climbed onto the tailgate of one of the trucks and yelled for quiet, about to address his troops. He looked like some ancient warrior, tanned, his beard glinting in the sun as he watched the strange mixture of people below him gather around the truck in their wide-brimmed hats and dirty clothes. Refugees with nowhere to go, waiting for a truck to take them to a better life. Believers standing at the feet of Christ waiting for him to do his thing with the loaves and fishes. Even the birds went silent.

"Today is the day!" He took a pause to let that sink in. They all knew what he meant.

"Way to go, Alex." A voice from the crowd, then another silence as they looked up at him, almost with awe. He made the summer tolerable for them. He gave them some kind of hope, even if they didn't take it and do anything with it. Alex showed them that it could be done. That slaving your guts out wasn't the worst thing in the world. Mind you, I couldn't think of anything that beat it.

"I just want you all to know that I'm starting on the east side and God help anyone who gets in my way. I got bottles planted here and there and if any sonofabitch touches them . . . " He let it fade off. No one would tamper with them, but he was just making sure. "All bets will be paid at the end of the day. All right?" There was a murmur from the group that they understood. "For those who don't speak the Queen's English. Vamoose . . . er . . . vamoose outa my way. I don't *parlez-vous français* too good but I'm sure you get my meaning, eh? So let's go get 'em!"

"God save the King!" The same voice from the crowd. Alex beamed down at them and gave them the thumbs-up sign.

130

"You better believe it, me old darlings."

"And you, you old darling, get your ass off that truck and get to work. You're holding everything up." Al Rochford had appeared from nowhere, standing with his foot on the rear wheel in his sport shirt, beige pants and Kodiak boots. He was one of the new breed of farmer, running a big operation that needed accountants to juggle the investment in equipment, the loans from the government, write-offs, depreciation and stuff like that. It was a far cry from the days of Old Man Rochford, who managed with an old, thumbworn accounts book, a bit of guesswork, and a lot of faith that the Lord would be good with the weather and his health. Today, time was money. Standing around was losing money. It was the same in the old days too, but somehow it didn't seem to matter so much.

Rochford's voice rose as he turned to the crowd of pickers. "Okay. Let's go. Get a move on. This ain't no summer resort. Move it!"

Alex jumped down from the truck, coming face to face with Rochford.

"Knock it off, eh? You treat em like a fuckin' chain gang." He was quite a bit bigger than Rochford and the sparkle in his eyes of a few moments ago was a glint of anger now. Rochford should know you didn't try to make a fool of Alex in front of the other pickers.

"Lookit, you want to play Mister Big you go right ahead. Set your record. But don't hold things up. I pay em to do a job, to meet a quota. They don't like it they can move somewhere else. Okay?"

"This'll be the biggest day you've had all summer and you know it. We'll probably get tomorrow's quota too! So get off my back. Fuck off to your pretty farmhouse and count your dollars! We'll all go to work when we're good and ready!" He walked away, taking out a cigarette and lighting it, and sat on the stump of a tree staring at Rochford until, finally, Rochford went to his truck, slammed the door, and drove off. Alex's face broke into a grin as he looked around. "So what are we waitin' for? Let's go get em!"

Alex hurried into the field, followed by all the pickers, who seemed to have more life than usual, some even laughing. As the morning went on his voice would bellow through the silence every time he filled a basket. Three. Ten. Fifteen. Twenty. Twenty-one. Twenty-two . . . We always knew how he was going, and when he reached fifty he'd let out a whoop, throw a tomato into the air, then stand with his arms outstretched as he tipped a bottle of water to his lips and let it pour down his throat in one go. Even his belches could be heard from a long distance. What all this did was help inspire the others, really rev them up, me included. I mean, when he's filled twenty baskets and you're still on number eleven . . . well, that's the stuff that champions are made of. So we all worked a little harder, forgot the sweat soaking our clothes, the aching muscles and the buzzing insects. It was a challenge, and in the end everyone came out ahead – even Rochford.

We moved across the field slowly in line abreast, like a battalion of soldiers searching out the enemy but never finding them. A ragged battalion that had been through hell's fire and out the other side, knowing there was no way back, wondering how they got to be there in the first place, and in the end not really giving a shit. Out in front was Alex, working furiously, the mad general knowing that to survive you had to win.

I was in the army once. I volunteered.

About a month after we won the championship it was announced in the *Record* that the league was to be suspended until after the war was over. Too many teams had been weakened by players joining the service; rather than run a diluted league, all competition would be stopped until the situation improved.

When I read it I felt like throwing up. I mean, it couldn't be true. It was a joke or something. My whole life, my future, depended on hockey. It was gonna be my ticket out of Black Rapids. It was the only thing I could do that was any good. I was getting to be pretty okay at carpentry, small stuff, nothing big, but who the hell wants to be a carpenter all his life? And I was only just beginning. If last season was anything to go by, next year would be even better. Okay, so a lot of the time I'm big-headed about it, boasting, enjoying all the attention. Being a hero, my name and picture in the paper and all that. But hell, I was good, shit-hot, and it didn't hurt to be confident.

I knew my father had seen the paper the moment we sat down for dinner. I came in late as usual and my mother met me at the door trying to tell me something, but I wasn't really listening because I was still shaken to the core. And I'd had a few belts from a mickey of rye to try and unwind, so I ran upstairs to brush my teeth to get rid of the smell of booze. When I got back to the kitchen he was sitting there, rolling a cigarette. He swept the spilt tobacco from the table into the pouch, the *Record* neatly folded beside his plate. Then he nodded to me and struck a match on the underside of the table, inhaling deeply and blowing the smoke toward the ceiling.

"D'you see the paper?"

"Yeh."

My mother served me my dinner and then took his plate away from him. "Not now, dear. Let him eat first. I'm sure he doesn't want to talk about it just yet."

"Why not? It's not the end of the world, yer know."

"Dad . . . I read it. Okay?"

"I won't say 'I told you so,' but now you're gonna have to start thinking about yer future."

"More jello, dear?" My mother was trying very hard to change the subject, but he wasn't having any.

"Fran, will you stop flappin' around like a mother hen for God's sake! It's about time he faced up to facts and took some responsibility for his life instead of fartin' around at the mill between hockey seasons! There ain't gonna be no more hockey seasons for a long time. Till the war's over, they say, and that's gonna be a long time comin' you mark my words. I always did think we took things too casual in this town. Like we weren't even part of the world." He sat there nodding at his own brilliance, then got up and went over to the window, standing with his back to us. "Well?"

"Well what?" I hadn't had time to think about the future other than it had been fucked up good and proper, and as I

134

looked at his back I saw myself, maybe thirty years from now, standing there after a lifetime at the mill. A lifetime in that same boring, shitty, old-fashioned mill.

"Haven't you given it any thought at all?"

"No."

"Well I would, if I were you. There's gonna be a scramble for jobs among those hockey players. Looking for somethin' secure all of a sudden like. You're all gonna have to give up the pipe dreams and work for a livin' like everyone else. I'll tell you now, Caulfield won't keep em all on 'cause most of em don't know their ass from a hole in the ground. Now in your case, I might be able to pull a bit of weight. Get you somethin' decent. I'm well respected around there 'cause I've kept my nose clean all these years." He turned and started stabbing at the air. "And most of the guys got no time for you hockey players gettin' special treatment all this time. There'll be a day of reckoning, you mark my words. You're lucky. You got me there and I might be able to help you. So maybe this news ain't so bad after all. Maybe it'll bring you back down to earth instead of walkin' around like King Shit figurin' you got it made."

There was a silence. A long silence. Then it came to me out of the blue, and before I knew it, I'd said it.

"I'll join the army."

He looked at me with a totally stunned expression, then walked to the table and ground out his cigarette, never taking his eyes off me.

"You'll do what?" He sat down slowly, fumbling for his tobacco and cigarette papers. "You'll do what?"

"Join the army. You know, volunteer."

"Oh for Chrissakes, let's not be stupid about it. I mean, I know there's a war on and all that and we all gotta do our bit, but that's the stupidest thing I've heard you say yet and

I've heard some dillies from you, believe me. Did you hear that, Fran?"

"He's not being serious. Are you?"

"Why not? What's wrong with it? He's always sayin' we should be doin' our bit and the sooner I go and help the sooner it'll be over and the sooner I'll get back to playin' hockey."

"Ah!" He pounced on it like a goalie smothering a loose puck. "You got ulterior motives, eh? To hell with fightin' for your King and country. You just wanna get back to playin' hockey. Sweet Jesus!"

My mother came and put her hand on my shoulder, giving it a squeeze. "It could be dangerous, Eldon. You could get killed or something."

"Him get killed? You don't think they'd trust him with a gun or anythin', do you? Christ, when I took him huntin' that time he was too chickenshit to finish off the moose. He couldn't pull the trigger, for Chrissakes, and the thing was just lyin' there. And then!" He looked at me, his mouth twitching and his eyes loathing me. "And then he couldn't even clean it. Couldn't even slit it open and pull out the guts! I've never bin so embarrassed in m' life. I had to do it for him . . . in front of my friends. Claire Audenaert was there an' he musta thought I had some kind of cissy for a kid!" He'd managed to roll another cigarette and lit it, walking over to the window. "If he went in the army he'd be in the cookhouse, God help em, or cleanin' out the cans. Anyway!" He turned back to us triumphantly, sucking in on his cigarette. "Anyway, he's too young. They don't take em his age. Squirts."

"Oh, that's good. I was worried for a moment." She took her hand from my shoulders and carried on with the dishes, while he stood looking at me like he was dealing with a five-

136

year-old, a slight, jeering smile on his face. Almost in tears and unable to stand it any longer, I exploded. It was the end of the world.

"Goddamn you! You don't realize what it means! I was gonna make the NHL! Everyone said I would. I'd be some-one! Now it'll never happen! You gotta keep playin' to be good. And I'm good! So what that I couldn't shoot a fuckin' moose or cut it open? So what? What does that prove? Eh? You think you're so goddamned big sittin' out there knockin' back a twenty-sixer of rye with all your buddies, gettin' pissed till you can't shoot straight! What's that make you? D'you ever get your picture in the *Record* for shootin' a moose? Or blastin' some bird to smithereens jus' cause it happened to be sittin' there? You shoulda bin real proud of that! You jus' don't like it because I'm good at somethin' you don't even understand! I'm the best player they ever had in Black Rapids! Even at my age. It's the one thing I was better at than anyone else! Imagine that! Better than anyone else! I coulda gone somewhere–bin a pro–an' you didn't want to know about it. The big fuckin' moose hunter–"

His hand caught me on the ear, knocking me off my chair, taking the dishes with me as I grabbed the table on the way down. For a moment we glared at each other and then I got up. "Fuck you!" I screamed, and ran to my room, crying for the first time since I was a small kid.

Two days later I caught the train to Fort William, lied about my age, and joined the army. It was May 1944.

I was seventeen, and the furthest I'd been from Black Rapids was Noranda to play hockey. Big deal.

Fort William was something else. I mean, it's a big town and anyone who lives more than ten miles from the town limits is considered to be from the sticks.

Like the guy in the recruiting office. When I told him where I was from he said oh yeah, I read about that place once on a weather map. Didn't think it was for real.

Jesus.

Anyway, I was impressed with Fort William, what I saw of it. There were at least three restaurants, a movie house that opened every night, docks with huge grain elevators standing there like some picture in a geography book and a main street that looked like the newsreels of New York. Well, almost.

Then I went into shock.

The next few months were a daze, a blur of train rides, parade grounds, rifle ranges, polishing boots, buttons, yeah, even cans (how come he was so goddamn smart?), running with full pack, yelling sergeants, yelling corporals, more train rides, throwing hand grenades, polishing boots, making beds, inspections, mock battles with tanks, crashing into bed, staggering out of bed, nursing cuts, bruises, aching muscles I didn't know I had (and I thought I was in good shape), more running, running, running and always a sergeant one step behind, yelling.

I tell you, I thought I was gonna die and I hadn't even seen the enemy. I did see Toronto from a bus, Kingston and the lake from a train, Montreal from another bus and then Halifax and the Atlantic from a boat.

D-Day had been and gone, thank Christ. I mean, when I read about it, guys gettin' killed right in the water before they even made the beach, I realized for the first time what I'd let myself in for. But then, when I was hanging over the rail of the boat somewhere in the Atlantic, throwing up for the tenth time, or was it the twentieth, it didn't seem to matter any more. Dying on a beach seemed a kinda nice idea in comparison.

I wound up in Holland, 3627836, Private Harris, 3rd Canadian Division, up to my ass in water in a flooded field with a bunch of other guys, fighting for the next flooded field so that we could take some dyke in order to move on to the next flooded field.

I spent my first night in battle on a piece of high, dry land, under a bush, scared shitless, thinking of my mother and old Goodhead at school. They say you think of your mother when you get scared, but all I could think of was her telling me, when I was a kid, not to sit on damp ground otherwise I'd get piles. I laughed, and the guy next to me told me to shut-the-fuck-up or else we'd be spotted and killed. So I shut-the-fuck-up, and like some crazy person, thought of Goodhead.

"Harris! Yes, you, Harris. Read your assignment on Holland."

"Sir. Holland is officially known as the Kingdom of the Netherlands. In 55 B.C. it was conquered by Julius Caesar. It has a lot of low-lying areas near the sea and the water is kept out by walls called dykes. It became the Kingdom of the Netherlands in 1815 and they grow tulips there."

"That's all?"

"Well . . . no . . . the capital is Antwerp and it's on the North Sea or thereabouts."

"Antwerp?" He said it in such a way I knew I had to be wrong. Now he was going to make me squirm. "It's really Antwerp, eh, Harris?" I stood, shifting from foot to foot, the whole class enjoying it, waiting for the right answer to hit me.

"Tell him, Muriel."

"Amsterdam."

Boy, he really knows how to hurt a guy. Hell, he could've picked anyone but, no, he had to choose her. Sure, I knew it was Amsterdam, but Antwerp was pretty close. It was a natural mistake.

"Thank you, Muriel. I hope you got that, Harris."

She blushed when she sat down and Goodhead stared at me for a moment, making me feel a real shit, before he told me to sit. On my desk was a small piece of paper with the word Amsterdam on it in Muriel's handwriting. She'd tried to let me know. Tried to help me and I didn't even see it. Boy, what a dummy.

"What's that you've got there, Harris?"

"Nothing, sir."

"You wouldn't be lying, would you?"

Goddamned right I was, but there was no way I'd drop Muriel in it. I had the piece of paper in my hand and slowly I closed my fist and screwed it up into a ball.

"Okay, Harris, let me see. Stand up."

"I don't have anything, sir."

"You're making it worse for yourself, Harris."

He had one foot on his chair and was leaning over his desk tossing a piece of chalk from hand to hand, enjoying the sport of baiting me. I was playing for time, easing my right sneaker off. It would be like shooting the winning goal with one second left, coming in from the wing at an acute angle with only a small hole to get the puck through. Hit the post and that was it! Goodhead would get the rebound.

"I said stand up, Harris!" he yelled, and started to move from the desk toward me, his face getting red with anger. I took a quick glance down at the sneaker, sized up the shot, and dropped the ball of paper. There was no way I could look down to check as I stood up, felt for the sneaker with my toes, and forced my foot into it. As my heel came down I felt the lump of paper jamming into my foot and Goodhead grabbed me and hauled me into the aisle.

"Open your hands!"

I waited for a moment, put on a hurt, innocent look, and opened both empty hands in front of him. For a moment he was speechless. Then he checked the floor, my desk and my pockets. Nothing. He was fuming, and he knew that I knew that I had him beat. His neck muscles bulged and he clenched his fists until the chalk broke with a loud snap. He was saved by the recess bell. Everyone got up in a rush to leave, and I stood there motionless until the room was cleared.

"I won't forget this, Harris." His voice was seething.

"Forget what, sir?" All innocent again.

"Get out, you sneaky little bastard."

Despite the fact it was hurting I was determined not to limp. Later Muriel and I both thanked each other, and I screwed it up by blushing.

We seemed to spend days shooting at people we couldn't see, moving slowly forward, checking out buildings, farm houses and barns for an enemy who was never there, even though minutes before they had been shooting back. Other days nothing would happen because of fog or we were told to stay where we were. I tried to look at it in a sensible way. I had volunteered, and here I was. Wearing a uniform, carrying a gun, fighting to help free Europe and that was that. There was no way I could quit now. To be honest, that first night I couldve easily got up and taken off. I don't know where I'dve gone, but anywhere would have been better than under that goddamned bush waiting to get shot. Three things stopped me. Not knowing where to go, the fact they're supposed to shoot cowards, and if I ever got back to Black Rapids, I'd look a real horse's ass. Oh yeah, there was a fourth thing. I'd never hear the last of it from my father. So I sat there and thought about naked women, but in the cold and the damp it didn't do a damn thing.

For the next couple of days it wasn't so bad, in fact I even felt brave with those Spitfires flying overhead.

Then I came across my first dead body.

It wasn't really my first. I saw my grandmother down at Morgan's Funeral Home looking like she was sleeping, only her face seemed waxy. Everyone said that Morgan had done a good job on her. He had too, I suppose, only I was surprised that he hadn't shaved the hairs that stuck out from the moles on her chin. I mean, she used to cut them off because I remember, when she would come to visit and give me a kiss, the stubble from the moles sticking into my face. It wouldn't have hurt Morgan to have cut them off, and she'dve liked it.

My grandmother was one thing, but the body in that field in Holland was something else. It was just before dark and we were squishing our way through the field toward a dry area where we were going to dig in for the night. Some of the guys were moving ahead checking for mines and I was in the rear carrying the Piat anti-tank gun when I stumbled on something soft and spongy and almost lost my balance as I staggered, trying to keep the Piat out of the water. The body, which must have been stuck in the mud, floated free and came to the surface right beside me, a swollen, white, revolting mess with a hole in the chest and half the face shot away, one eye staring up at me and the hair, what was left of it, sitting on top of the water, strung out like string, like the kids who used to float on their backs in the river in Black Rapids.

For a moment I was paralysed as it drifted toward me. Then, in a panic, I thrashed my way forward through the water, splashing, almost falling again as I tried to get away from it. I didn't want to stop, to look back, to do anything except get away from that God-awful thing that was once alive and walking through this same field. Only when I started to throw up did I stop running, holding my Piat close to me as I leaned over it and puked and puked and puked, my eyes and nose running as I tried to get my breath when the vomit caught in my throat.

Slowly I raised my head and looked around. There

wasn't a sound, and in that strange, eerie light, the men ahead were just weird shapes against a grey sky, all turned toward me, watching. Then, without a word, they moved on and the silence was broken by the noise of squelching boots and slurping water.

"It could be dangerous, Eldon. You could get killed or something."

"Him get killed? You don't think they'd trust him with a gun, do you?"

Fuckin' right I could get killed. So much for all he knew.

I think I was finally relieved when I saw it happen. When it did, I was so goddamned busy looking after myself and fighting it didn't seem real. We'd been sent in to clear out a small woods where there were two tanks for sure and God knows how many Germans, preventing us from reaching a canal that we'd hoped to cross before dark. They had us pinned down in a ditch while we waited for an air strike that never came because the Air Force was fogged in at their base. So the sergeant decided to give it a try anyway, sending the forward group across a 150-foot clearing between us and the woods. Battencourt, a guy from Hamilton I knew slightly, was the first one I saw get it.

He left the ditch crawling, then half running, keeping as low as he could, weaving from side to side as he went. The other guys gave him covering fire while I sat with the Piat and watched. I suppose he was three-quarters of the way across when he just kind of flew into the air and landed on his face.

He didn't move.

It was just like the mock battles back in Canada, only this time he didn't get up and say goddamn you guys. It didn't seem real.

Then their tanks started on us and I didn't give it another thought, I was so fuckin' scared. I mean, I'dve been happy to have spent the day flat out in the ditch until a shell landed 200 feet away and killed five guys in one go, sending one of them up into a tree where he hung in his stockinged feet with his guts hanging down. I was just about to throw up when the guy next to me gave me a shove and told me to move my ass, we were pulling back.

"Him get killed? They don't take em his age. Squirts."

Fuck you, Charlie.

As a squirt it didn't seem right for me to question what the sergeant was doing but it seemed crazy to me to try and cross that clearing when with a bit of luck or something we could make a big loop through a field to the south of us, cut back up onto a sideroad and come at the woods from the rear. I mean, when you're hunting moose you don't go chasing them upwind. Sure it would take longer, but what the hell, what was one more afternoon? Of course I didn't tell the sergeant this, but he overheard me spouting off my views to a buddy of mine from Regina named Gimby.

"If you're so fuckin' smart, Harris, how come you're not a sergeant? Eh?" Strange how he sounded like Goodhead, only with this guy you didn't fool around.

"Sir . . . I was thinking . . . well . . . I just thought that maybe we could . . . " I shrugged like I was in front of the class, " . . . it was a dumb idea . . . sir."

"That's why you're not a sergeant, Harris."

"Yes, sir."

A funny thing happened. An hour and a half later me and Gimby, three other guys and a radio operator were sent to make a loop through the field to the south of us, cut back onto the sideroad, take a look at the woods from the rear and report back over the radio.

"You gotta big mouth, Harris."

"Yeah, and don't I know it."

We were crawling along a ditch, line astern, and Gimby was muttering all the way, complaining about me shooting off my mouth. For being so outspoken they had shoved me to the front to lead the way, and I figured the sergeant had nothing to lose. What worried me was that our guns might open up and a stray shell would find its way towards us, our asses bobbing along as we hauled the Piat, radio set and Sten guns. It seemed peaceful enough, the battle on the other side of the woods carrying on in an almost monotonous fashion. Where we were you could hear the occasional bird. If you stuck your head up, there were some farmhouses off in the distance.

It took us just over three hours to make the trip, and when we got to the rear of the woods we saw why the Germans were stuck in there. The back half of the woods was surrounded by a bog, and there would be no way they could get their tanks out. Nor would it be the smart thing for us to try to go in that way.

Shit.

It had seemed like a good idea and it would have been, except for that bog. The radio operator tried to raise the sergeant but all we got was static. Christ, I couldve done better with two tin cans and a piece of string. No wonder it took so long to win the war, with crappy equipment like that.

We lay low and had a cigarette, wondering what to do

next. It's a funny thing, but with no one to give orders you feel kind of helpless and we sat there, still trying the radio, like a bunch of stunned kids.

"Lookit, I think we should head back. At the rate it took us to get here it'll be dark if we leave it any longer." I was surprised to hear myself say it, but the thought of sitting there all night, behind the German lines yet, didn't appeal to me and I was all for getting the hell out.

"Supposing he's sent some more guys after us, then what?" Gimby seemed quite happy to stay.

"We'll meet em on the way. But he won't. Six of us is worth risking, but not any more."

"He figures we're disposable?"

"Sure. Why not? That's what privates are for."

"Privates with big mouths."

"Okay, okay. So I shot my mouth off. I've learnt my lesson."

"We didn't have to learn it with you. Be just our luck to be picked off by some eager Kraut on the way back."

"I bet they're scared shitless. Anyway, they're too busy with the guys out front."

"Why don't they surrender?"

"How would I know?"

If someone had told me at the end of the hockey season that by October I'd be sitting in a ditch in Holland, behind the German lines, wondering why a bunch of them didn't surrender, I'da told 'em they were full of shit. But here I was, listening to the battle less than a mile away as the crow flies, feeling quite calm about it but anxious to get moving. It just didn't seem safe.

We all heard them at the same time – two big-mothering tanks moving slowly through the woods toward us with about a dozen troops walking beside them. My heart stopped and a cold chill ran through my body.

147

"Holy Christ." Gimby whispered the words hoarsely, looking at me as though it were my fault.

The tanks came closer and closer to the edge of the woods, then stopped and swung around with their ass ends facing us. The troops started to dig trenches.

"They'll never get through those roots."

"What the fuck do you care?"

I didn't, but it seemed a sensible observation.

It was strange watching a bunch of Germans up close. Apart from their uniforms they looked just like us, or some of us – unshaven, dirty and miserable. There was one sitting inside the turret of one of the tanks who seemed to be in charge, and once his privates or whatever they called them in their army had started digging, he lit a cigarette and watched them. Officers are the same in any army. Have it soft. One of the soldiers flushed a partridge and they laughed, the officer saying something before disappearing inside the tank. Then I laughed.

"I don't see anything funny." Gimby was worried and he ducked his head down in disgust.

"It's simple." I wasn't sure if I should say it or not, having already got us in this mess by being a big-mouth.

"What is?"

"We just knock em off. We've got the Piat anti-tank with us. Stens."

"You crazy or something? There's twelve of them out there, plus whoever's inside the tanks. They've got two big guns and there's only six of us with no protection. Anyway, our orders were to take a look and report back."

"Yeah, on a fuckin' radio that doesn't work. We got em cold. Their guns are facing the other way, their ass end where the engine is is wide open and the Krauts on the ground can't shoot with shovels. By the time they know what's hit them it'll be game over. It's either that or wait

148

until dark to get outa here, and then we have to find our way back."

I loaded the Piat and checked my Sten. "Whatdaya say?"

"I don't like it. We'll be in deep shit for disobeying orders. And anyway, suppose we miss? Then what? There's no place to run and hide here, kid. They'll make mincemeat of us." Gimby looked at me and I realized he was scared, really scared. In a way he was right. Suppose we missed? It would really be game over then. I felt the cold chill of my own perspiration, heard my heart pounding away, saw my hand shaking slightly. Gimby wasn't the only one.

The Germans stopped to have a cigarette. I started thinking about that guy in the tree and Battencourt lying out in the clearing and I was goddamned if I was just going to sit there and wait for it. I thought about it carefully before I spoke. "We don't have too much choice. Anyway, what the fuck d'you think we're over here for? I'm not gonna wait like a sittin' duck till dark, get lost and maybe taken prisoner." I could hear my father laughing at the news of that, hear him telling my mother that that was what you got, sending a boy on a man's job. "You know somethin', Gimby? I heard that sometimes they don't even take prisoners – just line em up and shoot em. Who can prove anything, and what will it matter?"

I would say that it was all over in less than five minutes. First we hit the guys with the shovels, spraying them with the Stens while they danced around before they hit the ground, then I lined the Piat up on the furthest tank (something told me that if we hit the closest one first, we might not see the other in the smoke and it could get away), looking down the sights at the huge mass of steel sitting there like a wide-open goal with the goalie out of position. Then the turret started to turn back toward us and I let go.

"For Chrissakes!" Gimby yelled at me as the shell went sailing right over the top of the tank into the woods. "Let me do it!" He tried to wrestle the Piat from me, his eyes wild and his voice high-pitched, but I managed to shove him away, shaking violently and sweating like Niagara Falls.

"Fuck off!" The other turret was moving now, starting to turn toward us as we reloaded. This was no time to be arguing over who should fire the bloody gun. Okay, so I missed. That was one of my problems playing hockey. When I had all the time in the world I usually blew it, but give me a fast wrist shot anytime and I could snap it into the net before the goalie had a chance to move.

Loaded. Up to the eye. Fire! He shoots, he scores!

The tank went up in a lazy cloud of black smoke and orange flame as the shell slammed into the engine compartment, reminding me of burning leaves in the fall back in B.R. For a moment it even smelt like it until the stench of burning oil started to drift our way. Then I went for the second tank while the others cut down anyone who got out alive. The quick shot does it every time.

We all lay there trembling, waiting, watching for any sign of life, listening to the ammunition exploding inside the tanks. Then, suddenly, we felt elated, the fumbling panic of a few moments ago forgotten. All I could think of was that I wanted to pee badly, my gut ached so much. I crawled onto my rubbery knees, trying to ease the stiff bones and muscles, knelt there, and with my head down, had the best pee of my life.

I mean, it would have been embarrassing for my folks to have their son killed while peeing in Holland because he didn't keep his head down.

One hundred and thirty-six!"

Alex's voice boomed across the field and he came jogging off into the shade like a quarterback who's just thrown a long touchdown pass.

"One hundred and thirty-six, Eldon me old darlin'. Not bad, but I'd hoped for a hundred and forty before the break. I figure I have to average at least twenty-eight an hour for the first eight hours, then drop to twenty-five. Guess I'll have to pick up a bit." He stripped off his shirt, did some light running on the spot, unearthed one of his bottles of water, rinsed out his mouth, then drank the rest in one go. Connie and Janice had gone back to the shed to have their lunch and I'd brought mine to eat with Alex.

"Janice's radio says it's gonna rain this afternoon."

"Ahhh . . . you can never believe them forecasters. Don't know if they're punched or bored."

"I can tell you, Janice's radio is never, but never, wrong." Even now I could see the clouds forming in the west, but if Alex said it wasn't going to rain then I guess it wasn't. Beside one of the trees Alex cleared away some dry grass, reached down into a deep hole, pulled up a bottle of beer and one of his Montecristo cigars, and stretched out on the grass with his head against a shallow bank. "Nature's own refrigerator, eh?" He laughed and slowly undid the cigar tube, sniffing the cigar as he pulled it out.

"You not gonna eat?"

"It slows you down. One beer for energy, then water for the rest of the afternoon to replace the sweat. That's all you need. Anyway, I've got a date with the canning inspector's wife tonight. I'll eat then." He roared with laughter as he took out a match. "D'you like that? I'll eat tonight." And he roared again. "It's the thought of her that inspires me." Lighting the cigar he lay there, very relaxed and obviously happy with the way the morning had gone, then held the cigar out and admired it.

"Did I ever tell you about Havana? Now that, my friend, is a story! It was before that Castro guy took over – we were there pickin' up a load of sugar and had a couple of days to bum around, so I went into town and checked into one of the big hotels. In those days I always had a big wad. Anyway, every time I had a few days on shore I'd take along my officer's uniform that I'd won in a poker game from some guy off a Swedish ship. I'd made a few alterations to make it look Canadian – gave myself the rank of Lieutenant-Commander – I mean, in those foreign countries who the hell would know the difference? Must say I looked pretty good in it. Anyway, I was playin' at the blackjack tables when I met this Cuban gift from heaven called Theresa. My God, you shoulda seen her!"

As he always did during a story like this, he kissed the air and outlined her shape with his hands. "Long black hair, a body that could only be called . . . exquisite, forced into this gold dress . . . I tell you, she was somethin' else." He stopped for a moment so I wasn't sure if that was the

152

end of the story or not, something he always did to perk up interest. Finally he shook his head at the memory, took a puff of the cigar and carried on. "Of course, she was impressed to hell with the uniform and my stories of storms at sea and fighting U-boats durin' the war."

"You never said you were in the war."

"I wasn't for Chrissakes, but she didn't know that. Now you've ruined my train of thought. Will you shut up and let me finish?" He looked up at the sky for a moment, frowning as he thought, then at me, a smile breaking. "So there I was impressing her with my stories, my charm, winning at the tables – savwer-fare they call it, those who know – and she asks me back to her place for a nightcap. Now let me tell you, me old darlin', it – was – a – *place*! Right on the ocean, full of big rooms, courtyards and terraces, tiled floors, archways leadin' everywhere. It was . . . " he took a big puff on the cigar and blew smoke up to the tree, " . . . a Garden of Eden, Babylon, ancient Rome and she was Eve, Cleopatra, Rita, all rolled into one."

"Who's Rita?"

"The cannin' inspector's wife. Anyways, it turns out that her husband, Theresa's that is, was some big-wig in the Cuban army under this guy Batista who used to run the country, and Hubby was away for a week on manoeuvres in the mountains. So, we had this wild weekend together; brandy on the patio, champagne in a sunken bathtub, breakfast watching the sun rise, and in between, screwing wherever the fancy took us. I tell you, it's not good for me to think about it with all those tomatoes to pick. You want a beer? There's another down the hole."

"No thanks."

"It's the truth, so help me. On this last night we made love on a tigerskin rug, on this huge bed with satin sheets and in the bathtub. It was somethin' fan-tas-tic! There I was afterwards, relaxin' in the tub with her, lookin' into these beautiful deep, brown eyes, her beautiful dusky figure with the most perfect tits I'd ever seen – up until then, that is – eating caviar and drinkin' more champagne . . . when her husband came home early. We heard him call from downstairs in Spanish or whatever they talk there. Well, I tell you, I almost died on the spot. Here's this guy, an army General or somethin', who'd be bound to have a forty-five on his belt, comin' up the stairs and I'm in the tub with his wife. And she's layin' there paralysed. Frozen rigid.

"Finally she managed to say 'Eeee kill you.' That's all it took. I was out of the tub, grabbed a robe, ran through the bedroom, and for some goddamned reason picked up a box of cigars that was on the table, ran out onto a terrace, down some stairs, over a wall and found myself on the beach. Jesus, did I run. The only guy on the beach, in a white robe, runnin' like hell, and it musta bin near midnight. Anyway, I found a cab, told the driver my clothes had been taken while I was swimmin' – he didn't ask why they didn't take the robe as well – and he took me back to my hotel, where I made a fast change, paid my bill and got another cab back to the ship. The pity of it all was that I left my uniform there. I mean, I'd put a lot of work into it. It was my passport." He smiled and drew on the cigar, looking at it lovingly. "That's why I smoke these."

He sat up, checking his watch. "Fifteen minutes to go." Swilling down his beer, he lay back and closed his eyes, letting out a sigh. "I often wondered what happened to them when Castro took over. They probably stuck him in front of a firing squad, and her . . . who knows? When I get my boat maybe I'll sail over there. They like Canadians down in Cuba."

"You really think you'll get it?"

" 'Needum badlium, conquestium mondo.' That's bin my motto. Latin, more or less. If you need somethin' badly you can conquer the world. I'll get the boat next winter and Rita tonight."

"Her husband's obviously too trusting."

"He sounds a real jerk. Goes bowling, curlin', fishin', beers with the boys. Can you imagine anything worse than spending a whole evenin' drinkin' beer with a bunch of guys? No, she needs attention, care, understandin' and a lot of lovin'."

"Does she know you're a picker?"

"You kiddin'? I told her I was a salesman. In my duds I could be anythin'. Depends on the circumstances. This time I'm a salesman in precious stones. Gives me a chance to hold their hands while I look at their rings and give my expert opinion on them. It breaks the ice. Hey, you like that? It breaks the ice. Anyway, women are always interested in diamonds and things and it gives me another chance to tell em how cheap their husbands or boyfriends are."

"Supposin' they know you're givin' them a line of bullshit?"

"I don't. I read up on it in the library. I even carry a small gemmologist's glass."

"A what?"

"Gemmologist. An expert on gems." He looked at his watch. "Twelve minutes."

"What was that Latin again?"

"Needum, badlium, conquestium, mondo."

"Not bad."

"Yeah, I like it." He stood up and started to do some exercises, touching his toes, stretching his arms and bending his knees, keeping the cigar in his mouth all the time. "It's important not to tighten up."

"Why don't you just keep goin' through the break?"

"Against the rules."

"Whose rules?"

"Mine. All records have to be set under constant conditions."

"If no one else is competing it doesn't matter."

"It does to me. You gotta have standards. Objectives. Somethin' to aim for, otherwise what's the point? Me, I got my boat and a new life ahead. Now, take you for instance. What do you ever aim for? I mean, what sorta challenge is it to drive a goddamned school bus or a snow plough?"

"I'm the best they ever had. On the plough, that is."

"So what? It's just like Rita's husband inspectin' all those fuckin' tomatoes day after day. He probably figures he's the best too. So what? You gotta get out there and hustle, baby. Do it yourself. Me? I'll be the best tomato picker in southern Ontario by the end of the day. Complete with proof."

"You are already."

"Yeah, but that's not enough. I gotta prove it to myself. Make sure I'm not slidin' backwards, 'cause people respect a champ and when you're number one you respect yourself. You take the easy way out."

"I do?"

"Sure. And you know it."

The sound of Al Rochford's pickup pulling into the next field, followed by another truck, interrupted us. For a few minutes we watched while they rolled boulders into some groundhog holes, attached long lengths of plastic pipe to the exhausts of the trucks, stuck the free ends well down into holes they hadn't blocked, and started the engines.

Alex spat into the grass and we turned away. "Listen, Eldon, if you wanted to you could take the world by the balls and swing it around." His face broke into a broad grin when he saw I was pissed off at being lectured. "Hey, I think I've touched a nerve. Lookit, sometimes I get a little hyper, all tense, so I run off at the mouth a bit, okay? But we all gotta have dreams and do somethin' about them." He put on his shirt, swilled out his mouth and jogged on the spot. "Tonight, me old darlin', before I go out, we'll celebrate with some Canadian Club. How's that grab you?"

"Yeah. It'd be nice."

He checked his watch again and jogged out to the field.

"Way to go, Alex."

Turning, he held his arms high and picked up his pace, stopping to face the other pickers as they ambled back to work like a slow-moving bed of wilting tulips in their strange hats.

"God save the King!" His voice roared out, followed by his deep belly laugh. "Alex'll rule the waves. You'd better believe it!" Then, stuffing the cigar into his mouth, he hurried to where he'd left off and the sound of Al Rochford's gun in the next field came as a starting pistol, as if he had it planned. A weaving ball of fur trying to escape the gases didn't make it more than twenty feet from a free hole.

I headed slowly out to my baskets, still pissed off. I didn't want to hear about his goddamned women and how easy everything was. Oh, he was right. What do I aim for anymore? Like I said, once I was doing all right. Had it made, more or less. Somewhere back there.

They made us all corporals for knocking off those tanks, and two days later we were rotated back behind the lines to some town whose name I can't remember, let alone pronounce, to catch up on our sleep and generally relax – "generally relax" meaning getting drunk and finding a piece of tail.

I got drunk.

Sure, I'dve liked to have got laid, who wouldn't, but when it came down to it I didn't know what to say. The fact she couldn't speak English and I couldn't speak Dutch didn't help, so we sat and had a drink or two and smoked my cigarettes while out of the corner of my eye I watched the other guys coming on strong with their girls.

My problem was I couldn't bring myself to do it, you know, kissing em and feeling em up, even if they did seem to enjoy it. Don't get me wrong, I've got nothing against girls. I just didn't know how she'd react. She might make a fuss so that I'd look a horse's ass in front of the others.

One by one the guys would leave with a girl on their arm and a grin on their faces. Gimby left with a big blonde named Greta, and as he passed my table he asked me why the hell I was taking so long. Well he might.

My girl wasn't bad looking, well-built you might say, but her teeth were pretty rotten, not that you'd notice unless she smiled, which she seemed to do all the time. I wondered if they were this friendly with the Germans who were here just a few weeks before, then figured they weren't. Hell, they were on our side.

Before it became too obvious that I was retarded when it came to women, I got up, paid the bill, took her by the hand and led her out, trying to look as confident and smug as I could.

"Make like you're a Piat, Harris."

"Maybe you'll get a third stripe for this one."

"Hey, someone's cradle-snatching Harris."

Hoots of laughter.

"Fuck off."

"Attaboy, Harris. See you back there. Save some for tomorrow." Bastards.

My father thought I might get involved with girls when I joined the army, so the day before I caught the train to Fort William he gave me my first and only sex talk.

He waited until my mother was out shopping, then called me into the living room. I knew something was up by the way he was shuffling from one foot to the other, winding his watch and not looking straight at me.

"What with you goin' in the army and things . . . I thought we should have a talk."

"What about?"

"Well . . . the . . . facts of life. Things like that."

Holy shit! He'd caught me right off guard. I'd heard about parents telling kids these things, but you never expect your own folks to do it.

159

There was a long silence while he put his watch away and took out his cigarette papers, stuffed them back into his pocket and took out a British Consul from a wooden box they'd been given as a wedding present. Normally he only smoked real cigarettes on Sundays and at Christmas, preferring to roll his own. As he lit it, he nodded down at my crotch.

"You know what that's for?"

"Well . . . er . . . yes. Of course."

"Good. Well make sure it stays inside your pants, buttoned up. That way you'll stay outa trouble."

"Yeah . . . sure . . . "

"Good."

Visions of Sandra Caulfield began to flash through my mind, then Ruth in the back seat of the car, then Sandra again. It was so vivid she couldve been in the room with us.

"Well . . . I gotta get some sleep. On the late shift." And with that he left the room and me standing there.

Walking her home through the narrow streets of the town, parts of which were completely wiped out, I thought of that afternoon in the living room. It had taken all of twenty-three words and a minute of his time, and here I was, ready to test his advice. I looked at the destruction and tried to imagine what it would be like with half of Black Rapids a mess of rubble and ruin. I couldn't.

We held hands for part of the way and then put our arms around each other.

"It's a nice night."

"*Ya.*"

"Terrible thing. All this mess."

"*Ya.*" She smiled and held me tighter. God, she must think I'm saying romantic things to her.

"You're very pretty."

"*Ya.*"

"You know somethin'? I've never walked arm in arm with a girl before."

"*Ya.*"

I just hoped I'd be able to find my way back to the tent-camp they'd set up on the outskirts of the town.

"My . . . house!" She pointed to a small, cottage-like place across the street, which didn't seem to have been touched by the war, and we stopped alongside an old stone wall. I figured there was no point in fooling around any longer so I took her in my arms and kissed her. To be honest, it wasn't very exciting. Not only did her breath smell but she giggled. I tried undoing her top coat and slipped my hands inside and touched her breasts through several layers of sweaters, leaning in to kiss her when she started to protest. But she fixed that pretty good by moving and neatly ducking down and away from me, buttoning up her coat at the same time. Shit, and he told *me* to keep it buttoned up!

"*Nein,* Eldon." She pointed to the house. "Papa." Then she giggled again. Wouldn't you know it? Of all the girls in that room I got stuck with one who giggled, had a father at home and didn't think it was patriotic to give herself to a Canadian soldier fresh out of battle. So I smiled back at her, led her across the street to her house, said good nacht, and started the long walk back to camp, cursing and fuming.

To make sure that the other guys didn't realize that I'd struck out I killed time by walking around the streets. The air was damp and chilly and I could see my breath. I thought about the girl, then about Ruth. Mine for the taking, and like a stunned bastard I turned her down. Maybe I got a problem. But then there was Sandra. No problem there, except she was the one who wanted it. Jesus, a few evenings with her would cure me. I mean, there must be something wrong with a guy who makes it with one girl, turns another one down and then can't get to first base with the third one. The language. That would be it. But then the other guys made out okay. They seem to know what to do. I get all tongue-tied. Scared. And I still blush, for Chrissakes. Of course, the other guys all come from big cities. There's more opportunity there. I mean, even Miss Fielder didn't have dates in Black Rapids so that shows what kind of place it is. I remember overhearing my mother talking to Bert Powell's mother about it. Saying what a nice girl she was and how lonely she seemed since she came up from Toronto and maybe they should try and get her to come to the church. I couldn't believe it. Miss Fielder? Hell, any time I wanted to get horny I thought of her. How I was injured, not seriously, playing hockey, and she came to visit me and felt so sorry for me she took off her clothes and got into bed with me and held my head on her tits and then . . .

It was getting cold, so I walked faster and lit up a cigarette. Miss Fielder would have cured me too. Maybe there isn't a cure. It's some rare disease and I'll be like it all my life. Hell, a guy who's a corporal, shot up two tanks, star of the Raiders, should be able to handle a girl. Supposing everyone found out? God, I'd want to die.

You might die.

Yeh, that's the point. It couldve been the other way around and the Germans couldve caught us. Jesus, what a thought. It mustve bin awful for them, fried up like that in that tank. And those other guys. One minute they were diggin' and the next they were dead. But they mustve felt those bullets ripping through them first.

162

You've gotta go back, kid, do it all again, five days from now, and there's no point in being scared because there's no one you can talk to – not even that Dutch girl who giggled. Supposing she tells her friends and her friends tell the guys that I've got a disease? I must look it up in a book. See if there's a name for it.

Two o'clock. That's enough time. Mess up my hair, loosen my tie. Christ, it's cold. Anyone who walks the streets just to fool the guys must have rocks in his head. But then I've got a disease, and they don't know that. Wouldn't understand. Maybe I should volunteer to go back to the front early.

Are you crazy or something?

Well, what would you do? I mean, I've got another five days and walking the streets in the middle of the night sure as hell is no way to spend it.

Maybe you'll meet a saint and she'll understand and cure you.

There is no cure.

Tough.

Yeah.

"Hey, Harris. How'd you make out?" Gimby was already back and in his cot when I crept in.

"Fine. How about you?"

"Bloody fantastic. We screwed so hard I almost wore it out."

"She was goodlookin'."

"And built, man. Built! We found this place, a barn or something, and wow! She had the biggest boobs I've seen in years. How about yours?"

"How about what?"

"Was she any good? I thought for a minute you weren't gonna get anywhere."

"She was great. I mean, fantastic. I thought she'd never want to stop. Finally I had to drag her home. There's only so much a guy can take."

"Yeah. Musta bin saving it up just for us."

"Yeah."

"Yours looked like she was built too."

"She was. Like melons. We did it under the stars."

"Musta bin cold."

"Are you kiddin'? We worked up such a sweat, I'm telling you. We just lay there and caught our breath and cooled off before she wanted it again." Just imagining it gave me a hard-on.

"I told mine all about our battle with the tanks, only it was me who blew them up."

"Didn't think she could speak English."

"She couldn't. But you gotta say something, eh?"

"Yeah."

"Better get some sleep so we've got our strength for tomorrow night."

"Yeah." I lay there staring up into the black feeling pretty depressed. It was going to be a long five days.

"Hey, Harris. How come you could see the stars in that mist?"

"Eh?"

"How come you could see the stars?"

"Who the hell was lookin' at stars, Gimby? All I could see were these gorgeous tits and her white skin gleaming in the dark as she put her arms around me and pulled me to her." Not bad! Almost like a poet. If I ever live up to my imagination I'll have it made.

"Holy Jesus," Gimby groaned, and gave a big sigh.

164

"Will you guys quit playin' with yourselves and get the fuck to sleep." The voice came out of the darkness from one of the other cots and I was glad he'd put a stop to the conversation. I mean, I was starting to get carried away.

I spent the next four days in bed with a streaming cold, which suited me just fine. It gave me time to try and think up a cure and I didn't have to face the problem again, at least until the next time, if there was a next time.

"That'll teach you to get all romantic about it, Harris. Maybe next time you'll find somewhere dry." That was Gimby's parting line as he went back into town. He thought it was pretty funny.

The war dragged on. Although the Allies were making great progress on other fronts and all the talk was about the end coming very soon, it still seemed a long way off, like when I was a kid in school, waiting for the summer vacation.

We spent the winter of '44 along the Maas river, then moved to the Nijmegen peninsula where we made routine patrols and the occasional raid on the German lines. Seeing someone get killed or stumbling across a body didn't have the same effect on me any more. They were just faceless people in a uniform and you knew there would be more where they came from, so you watched them die and thanked Christ that it wasn't you and hurried on in case some Kraut already had you lined up in his sights.

There were always rumours floating around about some big offensive, but it never seemed to happen and the days got shorter and gloomier. So I spent my time in slit trenches, writing letters home, thinking about hockey and getting sick of Spam and all that canned food that came with our Compo rations. I was getting to the point now where I could grow a fair stubble of beard during the time we were at the front, shave in freezing water, shit leaning up against a tree, sleep standing up and handle the Sten, Thompson and Bren guns like it was second nature.

But my disease wasn't getting any better. On the other hand, my imagination was getting to be fantastic.

Even the fact that Antwerp was now free and full of hookers didn't help, at least from my point of view. Here was a city that had a permanent military establishment to begin with, loaded down with officers and non-coms, plus all the troops of various nationalities and ranks who came there on leave, and because it was a port city you couldn't move for naval types and merchant seamen. The hookers were outnumbered by about ten to one, and they're pretty smart. They go where the money is. First the Yanks, then the Brits, with officers first in line. When they've finished with the army officers they turn to the navy and air force officers, then to navy ratings because they look good in their uniforms and they've got more money to spend. Somewhere along the line you get to 3627836 Corporal Harris, 3rd Canadian Division, wearing a crummy uniform that makes him look like a janitor, trying to compete with a PFC who fought under Patton (they all fought under Patton the way they talked) who's handing out cigarettes, gum and nylons like they're going out of style and looking as though he's just stepped out of a movie in his snazzy uniform.

Even Gimby gave up in disgust, declaring that even if he found a hooker, there was no way he'd spend the kind of dough they were asking for a quickie knee-trembler against a wall in some back alley.

166

So we went sight-seeing, got drunk, and when we went back to our lines we lied like hell.

Later on I got a copy of *Forever Amber* that was making the rounds and figured that was better than nothing.

I got a great charge out of crossing the Rhine.

We weren't the first to do it by a long chalk, but when we did, sitting on a scout car, Thompsons at the ready, it felt good. It was a milestone. Suddenly it all began to seem like there was some point, even if the people we saw in the towns and villages looked just like the people in Holland, harmless and a bit stunned.

I could see old Goodhead moving the Union Jack on the map in the classroom and giving the kids a lecture on the importance of it all, not knowing that his least favourite pupil had crossed into German territory as he fought battle after battle to help defeat the Hun.

Holy Christ, I'd love to walk into his class in uniform with my two stripes and tell em a few stories.

We were in the thick of things and heading toward a town called Emmerich when I figured my time had come. We had been moving forward pretty fast with little opposition and took over a farmhouse for the night to wait for the final thrust into Emmerich.

It was like heaven. After ten days of continual fighting and hardly any sleep, here we were with mattresses, those crazy covers the Germans use on top of the beds, and plenty of decent food left behind by the fleeing farmer and his family. There were ten of us and we were pretty well equipped, with a jeep, a truck, Brens, Thompsons, and Piats. Sentries posted, we settled in for the night, guarding various windows with the Brens just in case. The only thing wrong with the place was a huge pile of stinking manure out in the yard.

When they launched their counter-attack at five minutes after midnight, all hell broke loose. Their heavy artillery seemed to be concentrating on our main line to the west of us, and when we checked in with forward headquarters we were told to stay put for a while, our tanks would be moving up within the hour, so we sat there in the dark watching the sky light up from explosions that seemed to be getting closer and closer, convinced that we should get the hell out while we still had the chance. Gimby and me were detailed to put the truck and jeep in the barn so we stumbled through the dark feeling very exposed, and in our hurry to get back inside to the safety of the thick walls, managed to knock over a water trough and put the truck into the mud. We tried to pull it out with the jeep but it didn't budge except to sink in up to its axles. Why the sergeant had waited until it was dark to get this done God only knows, but there was no point in worrying ab t it now, so we put the jeep away and hurried back to the house.

The tanks never came. When we made radio contact again we learned that the Germans had made a sweep around us and we were cut off. That was just bloody marvellous. Ten of us, and by the sound of their artillery they had the whole of the German army just down the road. And we'd had the chance to pull out. What's more, those Krauts we'd so efficiently chased out earlier were probably just itching to show us how smart they were.

The first shell hit the pig barn at 0215 hours, and from then on we didn't have to worry about being in the dark any more. Not only could we see for miles by the flames, but we knew that the Germans now had one hell of a view of our farmhouse. Then nothing happened for another hour so we sat there twiddling our thumbs listening to Redford, a private from Kamloops, telling us about hunting bear up in the Rockies, until the next shell came at 0324 hours and scored a direct hit on the truck wallowing in the mud. It went up like a box of fireworks, ammunition and all, giving us our first injuries from flying glass.

"You guys were really smart, eh? God help us if you ever had anything important to do." The sergeant was pretty pissed off.

"Maybe we should send for a tow truck." The voice came from the dark.

"Gimby and Harris – now we got another smart-ass. That truck was our way outa here. Now we got one jeep for ten guys. I'll tell you now, if anyone walks we know who it's gonna be. Eh Harris? Gimby?"

Gimby was beside me with one of the Brens laughing when we heard the burst of machine gun fire and then he was sprawled on the floor with a huge, gaping hole in the back of his head.

"Over by the gate!" The sergeant screamed it out. "Redford, take a look at Gimby. Harris! You paralysed or something? By the gate, for Chrissakes!"

I was paralysed. Frozen rigid. But part of me was working like a machine and I opened up with the Bren, spraying the area near the gate. I couldn't see anything out there, just shadows from the flames, and what I could see was a blur through the tears flooding my eyes. The machine slapped on another magazine and the robot finger squeezed the trigger. There's no point in anyone looking at Gimby. You can't be deader than he is. Another eighteen inches to the right and it would have been me sprawled out there, spewing blood onto the stone floor with my brains splattered on the back wall.

"Harris, cover the east window in the kitchen."

I stumbled out of the room dragging the Bren with me, stopping to kneel beside Gimby for a moment, tears pouring down my cheeks, then clattered into the kitchen and set up in my new position. Bastards. Fucking bastards.

"Still not getting through." The radio operator was set up on the kitchen table eating bread and cheese with a German beer beside him, carrying on as though nothing was happening.

"Gimby's dead."

"Shit." He went back to turning the knobs and took a bite from his sandwich.

My eyes began to focus and I felt a headache starting to grip the sides of my head and neck as I stared out into the weird light, seeing all kinds of strange shapes and movements as the flames rose up and died down.

I don't know if there was a lull in the shooting or what, but I heard them before I could make them out with my eyes.

Running down on one side of the house, about fifty feet away, was a stone wall about three feet high, and it was over this that I saw the second one roll and slip to the ground, then a third. But it was the first one who had caught my attention. Maybe he shifted a stone or his gun hit the wall as he went over; whatever it was, it was a foreign sound and I heard it. Then everything happened in a rush.

I crammed myself tight to the wall to get a better angle through the window and fired into the dark area where I'd seen the figures, then there was an explosion in the next room and screams pierced the air as a figure ran back to the wall outside. My Bren stopped firing and the robot changed magazines in about five seconds flat and I caught him as he was about to climb over, leaving him like a rag doll draped over the top of the wall. Smoke and dust started to drift into the kitchen as I ran through to the other room, bumping into Redford stumbling around in a daze, coughing and bleeding.

"Grenade." He rasped it out like he was being choked.

"Give me a hand." We groped our way through the thick air, glowing red from the flames outside, kicking aside the furniture and rubble as we looked for the others.

The sergeant and two others had been killed outright and the rest lay either wounded or unconscious or both, moaning and gasping for air. With the radio operator, we dragged them into the kitchen and under the table. While the others worked on them I gathered up all the guns and ammunition I could from the bodies before I laid them out in a corner. Then I ran upstairs into the main bedroom to take a look from there, away from the smoke, dust, blood and death.

The room had a smell of lavender and mothballs about it. It reminded me of my grandmother's room, except that it was covered with shattered glass. I could make out a large bed, a dresser with photographs on it (my grandmother's had a picture of me when I was a baby on a sheepskin rug, naked yet), a wash-stand in the corner, and when I kicked it, a chamber pot. The drapes moved gently from the wind outside, occasionally flapping in and out of the hole that had once been the window while I stared out into the dark, waiting for my eyes to get accustomed to the light, listening.

Nothing.

Then the flame of the machinegun as it raked the downstairs walls, broken by the sound of smashing china, falling pictures and splintering wood. I half-crawled, half-stumbled back down the stairs, yelling to Redford to get the Piats. Only then did it occur to me that I was the highest-ranking person left, so if anyone was going to give orders it had to be me.

We found one Piat twisted and bent next to a window. The grenade must have landed right beside it. I took the other upstairs while Redford rounded up some shells, and we sat and waited for the next burst. We had very little ammunition left, so there was no point in firing wildly into the dark. On the other hand, if we didn't fire something they'd think we were all dead and move in on the house.

Redford went back down and fired off a few rounds from a Thompson in short bursts and it had the right effect as they returned the fire immediately, raking the side of the house again, giving me that tell-tale flame to aim at.

I let the first shell go and in the eerie light of the explosion I could see the shapes and forms of army vehicles back behind where the flame had come from. Literally shooting blind I let the second shell, then another, go to where I thought the trucks were standing, until with the fifth shell a truck bloomed out into a beautiful ball of fire. Against the flames I could see people running as the other trucks started up to move away.

"I made contact. The tanks are forcing them back. They hope to be here by seven o'clock."

"Yeh, but we might not be."

The situation wasn't very good. One of the wounded had died, which left us with a casualty list of five dead, two wounded and three lucky ones able to fight and hang on. Our ammunition was almost out and the tanks weren't due for hours, even if they made it on schedule. We moved the wounded down to the cellar and took turns watching from the upstairs window while the remaining two had something to eat and drink. Never in my life has a cigarette tasted so good.

Then they opened up with the heavy stuff.

There was no point in trying to fight that, so we all moved to the cellar and waited as the shells came ripping through the house, which started to crumble over our heads. Surprisingly, I felt very calm. It was quite easy to accept the fact that despite all my good luck, it was just a matter of time now. Redford had found a bottle of German cognac and we had a few swigs, passing the bottle around while we leaned against the cold walls and let it burn our throats, raw and dry from the dust and smoke.

We talked about home, why we had volunteered, how it had turned out to be the biggest mistake of our lives.

We didn't talk about Gimby or the others, piled under the kitchen table. Or the fact that we all knew we'd had it.

Instead we told dirty jokes and passed the bottle like the last day of the season in that hotel room back in B.R. We talked about girls, lied about girls, even laughed. But there was a break in the voice. It didn't sound real. It wasn't. I just wished I hadn't been so chicken with that girl back in Holland. And with Ruth. Muriel, come to that. I wished I'd listened to my old man.

I wished Gimby hadn't been a friend.

And then there was silence. A deafening silence. And we sat there and looked at each other and didn't say a word. For a long time.

I was the first to move. I got up slowly from the floor,

straining my ears, tip-toed to the stairs and up, tried the door to the kitchen, opening it to reveal a blinding shaft of daylight from a gigantic hole in what was once a thick stone wall built God knows how many years ago. The room was full of debris, fallen beams from the ceiling, plaster and huge chunks of splintered stone. A small bed had fallen through from upstairs and lay propped up with one leg in the sink, the mattress and pillows spread around the room. The table was supporting a massive beam, probably oak, and underneath were the bodies, untouched except for a fine coating of white dust that made them look like warriors from an Indian war, slightly ugly, some of their limbs sticking out at weird angles, especially the sergeant, who had one arm and one leg stretched stiffly in the air, like a photograph of someone landing after they'd done the pole vault.

Through the hole in the wall I could see the sun coming up over a small hill in the distance, breaking through a fine mist while a couple of cows grazed on the slope. Somewhere, way off, I could hear the birds, even a cuckoo echoing in the silence. Gimby had told me about the cuckoos. Said they lay their eggs in other birds' nests. We don't get them in Canada, at least not that kind. But we do have cowbirds, who do the same thing. The sound of the cuckoo seemed haunting this morning and rather peaceful at the same time.

Through the one remaining window I could see the charred remains of our truck, twisted and black and looking very fragile. Behind it, the smouldering frame of the pig barn, its white-hot sections glowing, was sending out a fine smoke which seemed to mix right in with the mist as the sun glinted off floating particles. Redford had come up behind me but I told him to wait, then I carefully climbed over the rubble to get out of the cellar, turning to go into the other

174

room. The wall with the window where Gimby had died was no longer there; in its place was a full view of the main farmyard. In the middle of the yard lay a dead German and beside the wall were three more, the one who had thrown the grenade still draped over the top of the wall, his arms and legs sticking out at strange angles.

I saw them when I looked back at the gate. They were about a half a mile down the road, driving directly for the farm, two German scout cars and a half-track with five men on board and five more on foot, guns at the ready. They seemed relaxed, laughing and not too concerned. Checking my watch, I figured it was at least an hour since the heavy firing stopped and three hours since a shot was fired from inside the house. They must be pretty confident that no one survived the last onslaught. It was now six forty-five so the tanks should be here any time.

But they aren't here now, so forget em. They can't help you, kid. Three choices. Surrender. Get rescued. Die.

I hurried to the cellar and briefed the others, sounding them out. If we could only hang on. But there were the wounded to consider, our low ammunition supplies, the little protection. On the other hand maybe they wouldn't want to take prisoners and then, bang, bang, game over. We also didn't have time to fart around like it was a class discussion.

You're in charge here, kid. Captain of the team, in the last period, three men in the penalty box and needing a goal to win.

This is no time to be playing kids' games. Get with it. Do something.

"Okay. I'll take the Piat. Redford, you bring the Bren. There's a nice bunch of rubble upstairs and we've got a clear view right out into the yard. They're gonna come through the gate sure as God made apples. We get only one chance of surprise."

"What about me?" The radio operator was pacing nervously.

"Feed us with ammunition, bring up some Thompsons and Mills bombs."

"Supposing they're coming from the back too?"

Shit, I hadn't thought of that. But what the hell, my father was always saying something about the devil you can see is better than the one you can't.

"We'll have to worry about that when it happens. Let's get going."

"Maybe we should surrender." The radio-operator was giving me problems with his nerves. When he was behind his machine twiddling knobs, nothing worried him. Now he had time to think about it he was getting scared.

"They've got flamethrowers on that half-track. They're here to clean up." I didn't know if they were or not, but even though his face went white, he didn't say another word and we moved upstairs.

Crawling through all the crap and corruption on the floor, we settled into our positions as the lead men reached the gate and ducked down behind the wall, the scout car moving up and stopping on a slope, protected by the wall, while the half-track stayed back.

And we waited.

It was obvious that if there was any chance of getting out of this in one piece, we'd have to wait until they were as close as possible and not take any chances with wild shooting.

In my head I went over a checklist. Piat. The last eight shells. Thompson. Six magazines. The radio-operator standing by with more. Eight 36 gauge Mills bombs. What are they waiting for?

Mustn't move. Not a muscle. My throat was thick and

dry and my mouth tasted foul. God, I'd love a beer. That cuckoo again. Nice sound.

The scout car started to move and the lead men appeared and came into the yard, waving in the half-track. Stopping again, the officer called out in broken English that anyone inside had three minutes in which to surrender, then lit a cigarette and snapped orders at the men on the half-track, who started to get the flamethrower ready. Shit, they did have them. I couldn't believe that they could be so casual about it, so careless, taking it for granted there was no one left alive, taking no precautions against a possible sniper in the rubble or over in the big barn. Oblivious to the fact that some of them were gonna die, that they were going through their last motions on this earth.

How many times had I been in that situation and not known it, only to have something change it and let me off the hook? Redford looked over at me and forced a smile. My stomach gurgled. My heart was pounding, and only then I realized that my headache had gone.

The officer was close enough that I could see he needed a shave as he stood there, looking pretty good in his snazzy uniform, even if it was muddy. Gotta admit they look pretty smart.

Then Redford's foot dislodged a piece of rubble, a piece of the stone wall, and it tottered dangerously, swaying like a trapeze artist, then rolled down the full length of an angled beam and hit the floor with a thump in a cloud of dust.

The Germans stood there for a brief moment, looking, not sure, maybe half a second, but enough time for me to squeeze the trigger and get in a shot at the scout car. Fifteen feet from me Redford opened up with the Bren – and then came the return fire, smashing into the rubble in front of us and into the wall, what remained of it, behind us. Reloading as quickly as I could, I fumbled and cursed while the scout car spewed smoke and the half-track moved crazily, trying to get out of the yard, followed by some of the German soldiers running for the cover of the wall, the overturned trough and the big pile of manure, two of them dragging the wounded officer with them.

The second shell disabled the half-track as it went through the gate, and through the smoke I could see four figures lying on the ground where Redford's Bren had dropped them. A third shell put the half-track out of commission and I flattened myself out as they returned the fire from at least three different angles. A framed, faded photograph, the glass smashed, stared me in the face. A young man stood next to a young woman sitting in a chair, both looking very serious, his hair plastered down on top of his head and hers up high with a bun on top. She was quite pretty, wearing a long dress with a high collar, her hands folded neatly on her lap. Probably the farmer and his wife. And here they were, in the ruins of their house, staring back out of the photograph at some kid from Black Rapids, Ontario, Canada, who was fighting for his life.

The firing stopped and I raised my head slowly, looking across the yard. There's no way either of us would attempt to cross that open space, so in a way it was a stand-off, except that I figured we had the advantage and it was important to make the most of it.

"Hey, Redford, chuck a grenade into that pile of shit!" As soon as he let go I threw one too, then, as fast as I could reload, slammed three more shells from the Piat into the brick wall where I thought the others were. Firepower.

178

Make em think we're really heavily armed and well entrenched. Might as well go out in style.

They fired back, but this time it was only sporadic.

Another pause. The smoke and dust was choking again.

Wham! The trough splintered as the Piat hit home and two guys went running into the mud behind the wreck of our truck. Redford raked it over with the Bren and then let a burst carve up the wall.

One more shell left for the Piat. Better hang onto it.

The radio operator crawled up, deathly pale, with the last of the magazines.

"I think we've had it, Harris." His voice was a rasping whisper and his eyes were blinking rapidly. "Sonofabitch, eh?"

"How are the guys downstairs?"

"Praying hard."

"Tell em to save some of that bottle."

"There's no more left, you know."

"Of the bottle?"

"Magazines. Grenades we got lots of."

"Yeah. Keep your head down."

Just to let em know we were still in business I sprayed the wall again with the Thompson while Redford went for the wrecked truck.

Then it happened.

One by one they came out from behind the wall with their hands up, through the gate, into the yard. Over by the wreck two more dragged themselves out of the mud and staggered to join the others.

I couldn't believe it. Six of em.

"Christ." I looked across at Redford and he was grinning from ear to ear, then back to the Germans. The officer wasn't with them.

"I don't believe it. I mean, Jesus Christ . . . " Clipping a new magazine to the Thompson I looked at the radio operator, who was staring at them with a blank expression on his face.

"Grab a Thompson and watch that wall. Redford, cover me!"

I stood up slowly, my knees shaking, and stumbled through the rubble into the yard, the Thompson trained on the line of Germans. Motioning for them to lie down on the ground I checked them for weapons, then looked around. Behind the slightly flattened manure pile was one dead and one wounded, and out behind the wall was the body of the officer, badly mangled and burnt. Jesus, what a way to go.

We took the jeep out of the big barn and locked the prisoners in, leaning a long plank of wood against the door, and then, for the first time since their first attack at midnight, I tried to relax. My legs felt like rubber and my body seemed drained, every muscle aching. My hands shook as I lit a cigarette and sat down in the warm sunlight and took a swig from the bottle of cognac, rinsing it around my mouth and letting it burn its way down to my stomach.

"We did all right, eh?" Redford was sitting with his back against part of the trough, his Bren trained on the barn.

"Yeah, I suppose we did."

Then I thought of Gimby and my guts twisted like someone had kicked me, forcing me to turn away from Redford in case he saw the tears in my eyes. In the distance I heard the cuckoo again.

"D'you hear that?"

"That bird, you mean?"

"Yeah. It's a cuckoo. Lays its eggs in other birds' nests."

"Is that right?"

"Yeah."

180

They gave me a medal. The Distinguished Conduct Medal. Redford and the radio operator got Military Medals.

They said we were brave and all that stuff and there was going to be a big presentation with Field Marshal Montgomery giving out medals to a whole bunch of guys, but on the day he didn't show up and someone else, with crowns and red things all over his uniform, took his place. I think he was a General. The funny thing was that I could have cared less. It didn't seem to matter. It was self-preservation.

Someone told me after the ceremony that if I'dve been an officer I'dve got the Distinguished Service Order. That really pissed me off. Not that I didn't get the medal, but that if I was supposed to have been so brave, what the hell difference did it make if I was a corporal or an officer? I mean, brave's brave and rank has nothing to do with it at all.

But it does.

After the war was over I stayed on with the occupation army until 1946, figuring that I might as well enjoy some time as a soldier without having to worry about making it through to the next day or spending my time in slit trenches eating Compo rations.

And there was a lot to see, as well. It was like Goodhead's geography lesson come to life. I was able to take my leaves in places like Paris, Rotterdam, Amsterdam and London. I even went to the south of France and got some time in on the beach, renting a room in a pension with a huge, soft bed, but although the sun was nice and the girls goodlooking, I didn't really enjoy it. I got very lonely and homesick as I struggled with the language, and I spent days when I didn't talk to anyone. I was a sergeant by then (when they promoted me they talked about signing on as a regular and gave me the extra stripe as bait) and had money in my pocket, looked good in my uniform, or as good as a guy can in the things they gave us to wear, so in a way I had it made.

Things changed quite a bit when I bought myself some civvy clothes, and I came to realize that out of uniform, a captain's on an even footing with a sergeant when it comes to girls. I was even taken for an American, which didn't hurt, and slowly but surely my disease was cured by a variety of girls who thought I was goodlooking, rich and a possible ticket to the USA. But even those experiences wound up being pretty dull because of the language problem. Oh, I learned a thing or two and became a lot more confident, but it wasn't what I'd hoped for. So I wasn't surprised, when I eventually got to London, to find that I preferred it there. Even though things were in a mess and times were tough, I could sit in a pub and talk to people, know what the hell I was ordering in a restaurant (in France, *la grande omelette jambon* was my steady diet, being the only words I could remember), read the street signs, know where I was going on a bus or train – well, more or less – and understand the newspapers and movies.

On my final leave there I met a girl named Joyce. She was a barmaid at a pub I went to for a late beer, and it was there that I realized for the first time that the eyes are so important. I was in my civvy clothes because Canadians weren't too popular over there at that time, some guy having killed a girl in Surrey, and everyone figured we were animals, crude and uncouth, whatever that is. But then they thought that about most people who were foreigners. I was sitting in a corner drinking a pint of black-and-tan when she caught me looking at her and there was a moment where we locked on, so to speak, just looking at each other. She had a nice figure, what I could see of it, but this time I wasn't looking at tits or anything like that, it was her face and eyes that got to me.

I had another beer, making sure she served me, and eventually asked her for a date. I remember she blushed a little, but she said yes and after the pub was closed we wound up having some stuff they called coffee at a Lyons Corner House, which was like a large version of Wong's only much dirtier and with worse food.

She lived with her sister and brother-in-law in a basement flat in a place called Clapham Common and we caught the last bus out there, riding upstairs at the front, and then spent what seemed like hours walking the Common and talking. I mean talking. I think I got carried away, it was so long since there'd been anyone to share things with. The only lie I told was to bump my age up to twenty, the same as hers, but from then on I didn't need to lie. I saw her to her flat, made no attempt to kiss her or anything, then caught a cab back to my room.

183

She had time off during the day, when the pub was closed, and walked me around London showing me the sights, the bombed-out places, the famous places, and we walked through the parks holding hands, fed the ducks in St. James' Park, laughing and talking, talking, talking.

I kissed her for the first time standing in the rain on the Common, the water streaming down our faces, and it was slow and gentle, long and very special, like we both knew it was going to happen eventually. On her day off we went to Epsom Downs for a picnic, and later back to her flat, where she had arranged for her sister and brother-in-law to be out until at least midnight. It was a cramped place, damp and cold, with a gas fire in the living room (she called it the sitting room) and little electric heaters in the other two rooms which were only switched on when the rooms were being used. We bought half a bottle of gin from an off-licence and sat in front of the gas fire while I told her more about Canada, wrapped in sweaters borrowed from her sister's room.

Yeah, we made love. And it was fantastic. I mean, totally different from the other times. More personal. I knew this girl.

I didn't want to go to bed with her like the others, cash in advance, knowing that twenty minutes later I'd be back in some bar or out in the street while she was getting ready for the next one. This meant something. It meant . . . hell, I don't know what it meant, except that it was more human, yeah, human. It was something we both wanted to do.

She had a beautiful body, at least I think so, small and white like the sun had never seen it, with perfect breasts and long legs. She was very gentle with her hands and wasn't the least bit shy about herself. When I finally moved into her she held me very tightly to her as we waited, not wanting to miss that first real moment, before she kissed me and we started to move slowly together.

184

Later, as we snuggled under the blankets and thick eiderdown comforter, I kidded her about her cold nose and cold bum. The radio was playing music from *Oklahoma* as we finished the gin.

It was a great feeling, lying there without a care in the world, to have finally arrived with a woman that made me feel so good. I guess the difference was that I cared.

When I woke up it was dark and she was sitting on the edge of the bed in a robe with her hand on my cheek. It seemed like the most natural moment in the world while we looked at each other, grinning.

"Are you hungry, luv?"

"Yeah. Very."

"I cooked up some things."

"What time will the others be home?"

"We've got lots of time yet. Lots of time."

She gave me her brother-in-law's dressing-gown and we sat down in the tiny kitchen to a dinner of eggs, sausages, chips and thick, strong tea with bread, margarine and marmalade on the side.

There's something about a short relationship. Like you want to be awake for every minute so that nothing will be wasted. I didn't know it at the time, but that's how it was between me and Joyce. We knew it was coming to an end and it was important to make the most of it.

So she quit her job and we took a train to Brighton on the south coast, checked into a boarding house as Mr. and Mrs. Harris, and spent a week in the wind and rain. On the one hot day we sat on the beach watching the ships off in the distance and doing English things like having afternoon tea and walking the prom. When we weren't doing that we were making love in a creaky old bed, making sure that every hour stretched into two. It was the first time in my life

I'd ever spent the whole night with a woman, shared a bed with a woman, and it was beautiful. I mean, just waking up and finding her there was something else; her hair spread all over the pillow, those fantastic eyes opening just before she said good morning, snuggling into me as my hands ran gently over her body until she pulled me to her or rolled over onto me. And we'd lie there, in no hurry, enjoying every sensation.

The bathroom was down the hall, and a couple of times we snuck in when no one was looking and had a bath together (another first for me) in the huge tub, soaping each other down, drying each other and, one morning, making love on our robes spread out on the draughty floor. When we came out an old lady stared at us all the way back down the hall, complaining that she'd been waiting fifteen minutes and that she'd report us to the manager.

The whole war had been worth it for that one week away with Joyce; for the things I learned. No one had ever told me that women enjoyed making love too, how it felt when you knew it had been good for her, when you saw that look in her eyes that told you that she was happy, that it made you feel good too. It spoiled me for the rest of my life, because anything from then on would have to measure up to it. Of course, I got to realize that women were different from each other and some even didn't like it at all. But at that time, with Joyce, it was all magic. Even simple things like walking down the street, sharing some chips in newspaper. Gone were the days of ass-grabbing, back seat necking and quick lays in the laundry pile. They wouldn't recognize me in Black Rapids.

The day before I was due to go to Liverpool to get the boat back to Canada, she told me that she was married.

We were standing in Waterloo Station drinking more

crappy coffee and eating stale buns waiting for the next train to Clapham Junction–the L on platform two at sixteen minutes past the hour. She cried as she told me, holding onto my arm, and all I could think of was that she looked even more beautiful when she cried, so I kissed her and wiped her eyes with my handkerchief–and then we had to run to catch the train, just getting through the gate before they closed it. The carriage was full and we had to stand, swaying with the motion of the train, while people glanced over the top of their evening newspapers at us and then looked away as we hung onto each other and Joyce cried.

We got off at the next station and sat on the platform, not noticing the dirt and grime, the trains rushing through sucking Joyce's hair over her eyes.

"I wanted you to know. I hadn't planned to tell you but it didn't seem right in the end. It was like I'd been unfaithful to you . . . and I didn't want you to, well I didn't know what you might be thinkin' about . . . the future." She pushed her hair back and wiped her eyes. For the first time she looked afraid. "You know? Like you said, you might come back over one day. See, when you first asked me out I didn't know it was gonna end up the way it did, with me comin' away with you to Brighton."

"For a dirty weekend. Isn't that what people do in Brighton?" I tried to make her feel better by not being too serious about it, and she managed to smile through the tears. "Where is he?"

"In Malaya."

"That's a tough place to fight."

"Yeh."

"How long have you bin married?"

"Two years. We met at the Palais and it all seemed very

romantic at the time, what with him in uniform and goin' off to war like. Really we've only bin married a week. That's all the time we had together before he left. My father told me I was stupid and too young and kicked me out of the house. So I went to live with my sister." I tried to light a couple of cigarettes, finally succeeding on the fifth match, and handed one to her. "We didn't have a honeymoon or anythin' – just a week at his mum's house in Wandsworth. You're the first man I've bin out with since then. Honest." She looked away, running her hand through her hair, then looked at the train ticket she'd screwed up in her hand. "You're not mad or anythin'?"

"Are you kiddin'?"

We kissed again, caught the next train back to Waterloo, and checked in to the Strand Palace hotel for my last night in England. For some reason I wanted to protect her, keep her away from ugly things, make her happy. I guess I was in love. So I blew the wad and we had dinner in a fancy restaurant, a bottle of champagne in the room and we made love, only this time it was a different kind of lovemaking, quieter, longer, more careful, and we held onto each other and talked all night about the craziest things, trying to keep the clock from moving too quickly, until finally daylight crept through the window, a grey, ugly daylight.

I didn't know it at the time, but that was the day my father died. I got the message when we were about eight hours out of Liverpool and I didn't feel a thing, except for a trace of anger. It was just like him, when I'd finally done something worthwhile, not to be around to hear about it. My mind was confused for most of the trip, scrambled up by thoughts of Joyce, my father, going home, leaving Joyce, her outline standing against the window in the hotel room, the daylight bright behind her head, then catching the streaming tears as she turned slightly when I opened the door to leave; the aching emptiness in my guts that I couldn't explain.

They let me off the boat in Quebec City, and before I caught the train for that long ride home I phoned my mother. It was a long, awkward conversation, full of weepy silences, and I realized I didn't know what to say when someone had died. I was used to ignoring it, taking it for granted, or if it was a friend like Gimby, not talking about it at all to anyone. I told her I'd call again from Toronto and got on the train feeling totally lost and very lonely, like I felt in France.

There was a wait between trains in Montreal and I perked up a bit by enjoying my first hamburgers and milk shakes in two years, seeing the clean city with all its buildings intact. But it didn't last very long and I drank myself to sleep on the overnight to Toronto with the duty-free rye I'd picked up on the boat.

When I saw the tacky, grey, ugly, shitty city they called Toronto, I knew what my problem was. I didn't want to go home. It was like I had been let out of Black Rapids on a pass and when I got back the gates would clang shut behind me, the key would be turned and I'd be locked in there forever. I'd never get out.

But my father had set the bait by dying. My mother was alone and waiting for her only son. There was no way I could turn around and run away. No way.

If Toronto is this bad – hell, you can't even get a drink – then think how bad Black Rapids will be. The pits. And I thought it was the big time. Once.

"It was a heart attack. He was sitting at the kitchen table, winding his watch, and he just slumped forward." My mother wiped away some tears and put the kettle on for coffee, keeping her back to me so that I wouldn't see she was crying.

I knew how she felt about being seen crying. I'd spent a couple of days in Toronto at the Ford hotel, avoiding the final step of catching the train north to Black Rapids, spending my time walking the streets, riding the ferry boats, trying to find something good about the city that would make me want to come back and try my luck. In the end I decided that anything would be better than Black Rapids, even Toronto. At least it had big stores, more than one movie house and . . . well, big stores and more than one movie house. The Ex was something, I suppose, but hell, after the places I'd been to it wasn't much. The girls were better dressed than in London but they seemed to giggle a lot, like that girl in Holland, and were, to me, well, immature. Anyway, I wasn't interested in girls. Joyce was still very much a part of me and those kind of emotions were something new. Something I had to learn to handle.

I was the only person to get off the train, and my mother was there to meet me. Crying, she threw her arms around me and went to say something but the words wouldn't come out, so I led her to the cab and we rode home, the only time in my life I've taken a cab in B.R.

It was like stepping back in time when I went through the front door, greeted by familiar smells and sights that first pleased me, then depressed me as I felt the world closing in and the emotions of a teenager rushing back. The confidence I had developed in two years seemed to be deserting me.

It wouldn't have surprised me to have seen my father sitting at the kitchen table, ready to ask how the hell I managed to survive and who made the mistake of giving me a medal.

"It was sudden then, eh? He didn't feel a thing?"

"No. The doctor said it was instantaneous."

Like Gimby.

"He'd had one attack before. Just after you left."

"I remember. You said in your letter."

"He had to retire because of it."

"Yeah."

"They gave him a gold watch."

"His old one musta bin worn out."

"No. He still used it. Kept the new one beside the bed. I still wind it every day. It gains a little bit."

"It must have bin a shock for you."

"It was. D'you still like lots of sugar and cream?"

"I don't know. I haven't had a decent cup of coffee since I left."

For some reason she took me on a tour of the house. In the living room my photograph was still hanging beside their wedding picture. God, I looked young.

Nothing had changed. The furniture was still in the same place and my bedroom was just as I'd left it, full of hockey trophies, pictures of the Maple Leafs, souvenir pucks. My first hat-trick, winning the league, winning the cup, all mounted and engraved.

"That was nice they gave you a medal. There was an article in the *Record* about it. I cut it out and put it in your scrap book. Your father was very proud."

"That's nice."

"I thought you might like to have his watch. He'dve liked you to have it."

"Which one?"

"His old one."

"Sure. That'd be great."

I didn't have the heart to tell her I was wearing a brand new Rolex I'd bought from an American in Amsterdam. It was probably hot, but it kept good time.

She cooked me a T-bone with french fries and made an apple pie for the occasion. We ate without talking and I realized, watching her, that she had aged tremendously. Her hair was now almost completely grey, her face heavily lined and tired-looking, and her hands red and wrinkled, the knuckles swollen, locking her wedding band on forever.

For this you spend a lifetime in Black Rapids.

"So tell me what's bin goin' on since I left."

We were sitting in the living room, trying to make conversation as the evening dragged on and we waited for the late CBC news. I had finally brought a bottle of rye down from my room and poured a stiff shot with water.

"You haven't started drinking, have you?"

"Just the odd one, now and again."

"But you can't drink till you're twenty-one. It's against the law."

"Yeah, well, in Europe you can. I guess I just picked up the habit."

"You will be careful, won't you? Liquor does awful things to people. I don't think your father would have liked it."

"No . . . I suppose he wouldn't."

"He was a very upright man."

"Yeah. So bring me up to date, mum. What's bin happening?" I tried to say it lightly, like I was really interested, taking a sip of my drink and making a silent toast to my father. I'm sorry you died, but here's to you anyway. Now why would I do that, for Chrissakes? Just because he's dead I feel I've got to say something or think nice thoughts?

"Well dear, nothing too much when I come to think of it. Things don't change around here. Oh, one thing that would interest you. Poor Mr. Goodhead died."

Jesus!

"A nasty business. In a car accident last winter. It was a little embarrassing. He had Miss Fielder in the car with him."

Jesus Christ!

"There was a lot of talk about it. He was supposed to have been away moose hunting but it turns out he'd . . . well, been away with Miss Fielder. To Toronto."

Now that was a set of points to have on your wall. Goodhead and Miss Fielder, for Chrissakes! I couldn't believe it.

"What happened to her?"

"Concussion and shock. She went straight from the hospital back to Toronto."

I started to laugh. "Old Goodhead screwin' around with Miss Fielder – "

"Eldon!"

"Well, I mean, him of all people."

"Him of all people. He had a wife and three children. You can imagine how they felt. It was tragic. A real scandal. And there we were, all feeling sorry for her because she didn't have any social life. It was terrible."

"How long had that been going on?"

"Dear, I wouldn't know. It was none of my business. I just felt so sorry for his wife with everyone knowing. About two years, they say."

I poured myself another drink and lit a cigarette, smiling to myself.

"It's not funny!"

It wasn't, but Goodhead had played an important part in my life and at last I knew he was human.

"It turned out that she really wasn't liked around town from the minute she arrived, and now we know why."

"But I thought you said – "

"There she was, breaking up a home and teaching children while she had the morals of a tramp. Imagine if she'dve joined the church!"

"It wasn't Goodhead's fault, eh?"

"In a weak moment I suppose . . . "

194

I'd always thought of them both being quite old, but thinking about it again, I figured she must have been about thirty when it happened, which would put her in her twenties when she first came to the school.

"He seemed to be such a nice man, too, and his wife is so sweet. I don't understand why he would do such a thing."

I guess she wouldn't.

"They had a lot of trouble replacing them. It took almost six months."

Which figures. The only teachers we get in northern Ontario are the ones who can't hack it down south, who aren't good enough to teach in Toronto or places like that, so their only choice is to come up north and teach in the small towns or don't teach at all. So we get the dregs, and then they wonder why the kids aren't too bright. But Jesus, Goodhead and Miss Fielder. I think I was a little bit jealous. After all, she came to see me when I was injured playing hockey and . . .

"D'you remember that nice girl Muriel Lobraico? She's gone down to Toronto to university."

My stomach did a violent churn. It was beginning to feel like my past was coming back to haunt me.

"She's the first to go to university from here since Eddie Romandel went in 1934. Her parents were very proud."

Two people in twelve years. Eddie Romandel never came back, not even to visit. He went on to be a lawyer or something.

"D'you remember her, Eldon?"

"Sure. She always was a brain."

"Very pretty too."

"Yeah."

Before we turned in for the night I caught up with all the goings-on. Caulfield had retired and was living in Palm

Beach (it took him a long time, but he got out) and his son had taken over the mill; the minister's wife had died and he had married Hilda Ecclestone's mother; Bert Powell was going around with Harper's daughter from the hardware store and his father had died of cancer of the bowel; that nice girl Ruth who used to go to the hockey games was engaged to marry someone from the mill; Eddie Marshall had joined the police department and Eddie Wong's son had taken over the restaurant.

I went to bed feeling very down, what with everyone either dying or leaving or having a business to take over, so I had a few extra belts of the rye and lay on the bed staring at my father's watch on the dresser; at the pictures and trophies from my hockey days, the map of Europe with the pins in the same position as I left them. All I felt was a numbness, like I was a stranger in someone else's room and the kid who won all these things, lived in the room, had been a hero, had left town and would never come back, like Eddie Romandel.

The final nails had been driven in when my mother told me that my father had left a three-thousand-dollar insurance policy and by the time the funeral had been paid for (he was buried in an oak casket, for Chrissakes, and Morgan gave her time to pay), as well as the new fridge and radio and the doctor's bills, she'd have five hundred and ten dollars in the bank.

"Don't let that worry you, dear, I'll manage somehow. It's earning a little interest."

Staring at the cracks in the ceiling I thought of Toronto, London and Joyce, evenings on the Common, how beautiful she looked when she was above me, the shape of her arms and the way her breasts brushed my chest, and tried to blot out what I knew now were the facts of life. Goddamn him for dying!

196

Standing beside his grave the next day, heads bowed, looking at the dried-up flowers in their cracked pot, she told me that they had kept my job open for me at the mill. "When Caulfield Jr. gave your dad his watch he told him that if there was anything he could do for him not to hesitate to ask. So your dad said he hoped that there would be a job for you when you got out of the army. And Caulfield said that as long as his family was running the mill, there'd always be a place for a Harris. Wasn't that nice? And so thoughtful of your dad to ask, to be concerned about you."

When I thought I'd been holding my head bowed for the right amount of time I took her arm and led her away, wondering why I still hadn't felt a thing, unable to connect that mound of earth and burnt grass with my father six feet below us. "We should get some fresh flowers."

"That would be nice, dear. I haven't felt up to it. To walk all this way. And it upsets me. But with you here, it'll be different."

I looked up some old friends from my hockey days and had a few beers with them at the tavern, but somehow it wasn't the same, and after half an hour I realized there was nothing to talk about. It was like they hadn't grown up. Even talking about old times seemed unimportant. It didn't matter any more. In just two years, everything had changed.

I took my discharge at Fort William a week later and started work at the mill when I got back, feeling angry, bitter and completely frustrated. The only highlight of the whole homecoming was a special ceremony at the town hall where the mayor made a big thing about me winning the Distinguished Conduct Medal, delivered a speech in front of the whole town council and presented me with another tie-pin with the town crest on it. My picture was in the paper again and for a while it was like old times, except now I realized it didn't mean a goddamned thing. The war was so remote for these people, something that had happened thousands of miles away on a strange continent and they heard about it on their radios. Even during the ceremony the councillors looked bored to tears, and when it was over they went right on discussing a new by-law about septic tank regulations.

"What are you going to do now, dear?"

My mother and I were standing on the town hall steps looking out onto the almost deserted main street as the last of the daylight faded away, me in some clothes that I'd bought in France and my mother in a dark dress and a hat with a veil that came over her eyes out of respect for my father. My time in the war was now officially over, and it struck me as being funny. Here I was, after all that fighting, fear, blood and death, standing on the town hall steps with my tie-pin in my hand, my mother holding onto my arm, and both of us with nowhere to go.

"Why don't I take you to Wong's for a sundae?"

"Oh . . . I don't think I should. It wouldn't look right. So soon after . . . the funeral. People might think I was being a little frivolous. Why don't we go home and I'll make us a pot of coffee?"

"Yeah. Sure."

My love life was no great hell either. I was still mooning over Joyce, and none of the girls I met came close to her.

After a while I deliberately set out to get laid, and that's not easy in B.R., as a way of trying to blot her out. I mean, I didn't want her to become another Muriel, giving me mental blocks so that I'd wind up never being able to ask girls out. Well, it didn't work out so hot. Oh, I got laid all right. Once in a motel on the highway just out of Black Rapids and once in the girl's living room while her mother was upstairs in bed with flu and her father was on the night shift at the mill, but both times they just lay there, making no attempt to get involved or trying to make it something special. And they didn't feel right. Either their arms were too fat or their legs were too heavy and when I held them they didn't fit in the way they should; even their perfume was wrong. And after it was over there was nothing to talk about, so we drank cheap rye and smoked, stinking up the room, and when, in the motel, we tried again (I mean, I'd paid for the room anyway), there was no way I could get it up, so we finally dressed and sat staring at the walls. The old disease was coming back. Then I thought of Ruth. She'd solve things.

I met her on the main street by accident, and at first I didn't recognize her. Those beautiful breasts were now gigantic mountains wedged into a whole range of fat and blubber. At least a hundred and sixty pounds. Maybe more.

"Hey – Ace Harris!" Her voice bounced off the buildings and people turned to look as she ran toward me in her tight shorts, fat legs flopping from side to side, breasts moving like Atlantic swells under her tight blouse, and sneakers.

"Hiya Ruth. Howareya?"

"Hey . . . do you ever look good." Her voice tended to whine a bit. "Bigger, stronger, tanned. Wow! The army musta bin good for you."

"You're lookin' pretty good yourself. I hear you're engaged."

"Yeh, how about that, eh?" She flashed a diamond engagement ring which peered up between two rolls of flesh on her stubby hands. "Harry Inglis. You must know him. Works at the mill."

I'd seen him, a puny guy with greased-down hair, supposed to be a good pool player.

"Yeah, I know him." Jesus, what a couple. They'll look like Laurel and Hardy. Reminded me of the joke in school about the fat woman who married the skinny guy and after they'd made love she said thanks for the tip.

"Aren't you gonna buy me a coffee or somethin'?"

"Sure, why not. For old times' sake."

She took my arm and gave it a squeeze, flashing her teeth at me.

"I haven't forgotten your promise, Eldon Harris. I'm gonna make sure you keep it." And she laughed out loud as we went into Wong's.

Not again. Yours for the asking and you're gonna turn it down, kid. You really must be stupid.

Yeh, but look at her. I mean, who'd want to . . . wallow in that?

Lotsa guys. It's just what you need to forget Joyce.

Sure. No way, kid. Not this time either.

"You really broke my heart that night, you know that, Eldon?"

"Come on . . . you didn't give it another thought."

"I did so." She was silent for a moment, probably remembering that night. It seemed like ten years ago. "Okay then. You hurt my pride."

"We were just kids."

"Not me. I knew what I wanted."

"That was no place to – "

"You know . . . everyone thought I did."

"I know. I heard."

"It was a good feeling, even if it didn't happen. Just knowing that everyone thought we'd – "

"Yeah."

She laughed. Her face was still very pretty. "You gonna play this season?"

"I don't know."

"Don't know? You gotta."

"It doesn't seem so important now. Making the NHL. Maybe I've bin away too long, lost my touch."

"No way. Hey, I read about you again in the paper. You looked pretty sharp in that uniform. You've really seen things, eh? I mean, really seen life?"

"Yeah, I spose."

"It musta bin awful. I cried when you left, d'you know that?"

"No."

"Well I did. Even if you did . . . well, behave that way, I still cried. I mean, you were what the Raiders were all about. You gave em class. And I was in love with you, of course."

"You were?"

"Sure. We all were. But me more than the rest. I'd never met a guy quite like you. I mean, you never ass-grabbed or tit-squeezed. I couldn't believe it when you . . . well, turned me down. I knew you could have anyone you wanted and probably did, but that I couldn't believe. It made me feel . . . really cheap, you know? Cheap." She stared into her coffee and we sat there in silence for a while. "He's a nice guy. Real nice. We're gonna be really happy, I know it. He's like you, very gentle."

She nervously lit up a Sweet Cap and blew the smoke toward a flypaper on the ceiling."We're saving for a house and things but until we get it we'll live with my folks. He's got a good job at the mill. We're gonna be very happy. I mean, there's not much else to do in this town except get married, is there?"

"I suppose not."

"And the mill's a good place to work. Harry says there's a good future there."

Yeh. Spend a lifetime there and wind up with one gold watch, a three-thousand-dollar insurance, and when all the bills are paid, five hundred and ten dollars in the bank. That's the future at the mill.

She smiled again and finished her coffee, smearing lipstick around the edge, stubbed out her cigarette so that it still managed to burn in the ashtray, drifting over to me, then checked her face in a compact mirror.

"I must be going. I'm cookin' dinner tonight." She laughed nervously, "Imagine me a cook? Bin nice meetin' you, Ace."

"Yeah. Like old times."

"I won't . . . I won't hold you to your promise." She blushed a little and looked down.

"No . . . it wouldn't be right. What with you getting married and all."

"Yeah."

"And it wouldn't be fair on Larry."

"Harry. You're right. He's such a sweetheart. I just know we're gonna be really – "

"Happy."

"Yeah. Not live like my parents. I wanna learn from their mistakes."

Amen.

"I was sorry to read about your dad in the paper."

"It was in the paper?"

"Yeh. Said somethin' about the father of Ace Harris and how he worked at the mill and all."

"Oh."

She eased herself out of the booth and suddenly leaned in and kissed me on the cheek.

"It was too bad about that night."

"Yeah. It was."

It was, too.

It came midway through the afternoon. A fine, light drizzle, falling gently. In the west the clouds were heavier and within the hour the light drizzle would be a steady downpour, lessening Alex's chances of breaking the record as the rain threw a blanket of gloom and discomfort over everything.

I had taken a break to have a cigarette, standing under a tree watching the bobbing hats move up the rows like an oriental picture come to life.

"Two hundred and eleven!" Alex stood up and held his arms high like a drowned Christ on the cross, his clothes soaked, his hair and beard dripping, looking over to me then back up at the sky. "I must go down to the sea again, to the lonely sea and the sky!" He sounded like one of those English actors you see in historic films, his voice loud and deep. "And all I need, Eldon me old darlin', is a tall ship and a star to steer her by. We're not doin' badly considerin'. Just ninety-nine more to go. Ninety-nine of these mothers." Across the field rows of hats looked up, then went back down as the lines started to move again. Hell, I wasn't doing so bad, with a hundred and seventy-six baskets. If I really set my mind to it I could probably pick as good as Alex. He swung into motion, talking as he moved up the row. "If this fuckin' rain holds off I've got it made. It's a plot, Eldon. A plot. The Rochfords go to church, you know. Probably prayed like hell for this just to screw me. That's Christianity for you. Love thy neighbour." His face broke into a grin, "Love thy neighbour's wife is more like it, more important, eh?" Laughing, he tossed a tomato at me. "With this rain and a dip in the stream I'll be like a newborn babe for her. A newborn babe. I tell you, you'd love this little Rita, just love her." His pace picked up even more and he was working furiously as he moved away, chuckling to himself.

Janice left the line and came over, her hair wet and stringy, her T-shirt clinging to her and her bum moving with its perpetual wiggle.

"Hi, dad."

"How's it goin', love?"

"A hundred and three."

"Pretty good." It was a funny thing, but women always seemed to be able to pick faster than men for some reason. They say the size of their hands has something to do with it, but I don't know.

"I'm soaked."

"Why don't you quit for the day. Slip back to the shed."

Her face brightened as she squeezed water from her hair.

"Yeah? That's great. I can put my hair up. Have you talked to mum yet about the Ex?" They've also got memories like elephants.

"No. But I will. Promise." Always promises.

"The summer's almost over and then it'll be too late. Maybe we could go together. Mum's always sayin' you should march in the veterans' parade or go to that reunion."

"No. That's not for me. It's all past and forgotten. Anyway, why would anyone want to see a bunch of old men showin' off their medals, eh? It's kinda sad, seein' their pictures in the paper. It's like that's all they got left in life, nothin' but memories of somethin' that happened years ago. We've got Remembrance Day for that." But then, what have I got left? No memories. Just a blur.

"Yeah. We get the day off from school." Every so often I'd get a letter in the mail saying that the regiment I belonged to was holding a reunion at the Royal York in Toronto and they would be pleased to see me there. It was usually held around Veteran's Day at the CNE, about once every five years, and I think I was invited because I got the medal. On the envelope they always used DCM after my name, which gave the mailman a charge. But I knew those sort of occasions were usually for officers and they wouldn't have time for a snow plough operator, part-time bus driver and tomato picker. I mean, remembering Gimby is one thing, but I think there's something wrong with a guy who wants to relive the whole fuckin' war every five years and show off to the others about how well he's done since.

The rain got a little heavier and we moved closer to the tree, watching the others working as though it were a sunny day.

"Why doesn't mum come out of the rain?"

"I dunno. Hey, Connie!" I shouted across to her and watched her slowly ease up from the stooping position and stand with her hands on her hips like some Italian woman I saw in a movie on the late show, working in the rice fields or something. Even from that distance I could see that she was pissed off.

"So why don't you go back. I'll go and help mum."

206

"Okay. I'm getting cold anyway."

"Funny thing. I had a dream about you last night. You were quite young and all these kids were in the house for your birthday party – and everyone brought you the same present. A flower pot."

"That's crazy."

"No kiddin'. And you were cryin' and I was tryin' to tell you that it was okay, we'd buy you something else to make up for it, but you didn't believe me."

"What happened?"

"I woke up."

"So you never did buy me the things to make up for it?"

"I guess not. Maybe we get part II tonight."

She laughed in an easy way that reminded me of Connie when we first met. "Well, you talk to mum about the Ex and then we'll be even." Shaking her head like a horse so that her hair went back over her head, she left for the shed. After a few feet she stopped and turned back, still laughing. "And you get to keep all the flower pots."

I've always kidded myself that Janice and me were pretty close, but really I think I've lost her, the way I'd lost Delores and Davie before her. Like my old man lost me. They become fixtures around the house and suddenly they're grown up and you wonder what happened. And I've really tried to understand Janice, the things she does, her interests. Hell, I even found out who Alice Cooper was and went to see Woodstock so's I'd know what it was all about, what was turning them on, so I'd be able to talk to her about it.

But they don't want you to be a part of it. It embarrasses them, I guess. In fact I think I was the oldest person in the whole of Black Rapids to see it. It wasn't that bad. A bit long, I'd say, and seeing some of those people walking around naked surprised me a little. Hell, it's nothing new and I'm sure the kids in B.R. still go for skinny dips in the river like we used to. Like Muriel did. But in front of thousands of people like that? Dear Jesus. Supposing you got an erection or something? The truth is that even after I'd seen the movie I still didn't understand what turned the kids on or made them like that kind of music, although I did like the kind of free way everyone was behaving. Not worrying what people thought.

I tried to show an interest in the things she was doing at school, but it's hard when they themselves don't have any interest in school. Janice, anyway. I wanted her to read more. In my day that was the only way out of Black Rapids, through books and the radio, and my mother made sure I read as much as possible, made it interesting so that I'd want more. Now they've got TV and movies for their view of the outside world, so everything comes to B.R. instead. Well, some things anyway.

The trouble is, there's no way of turning the clock back and trying again, having a second chance at giving your kids a better life.

"You gonna let Alex pick em all?" Connie was standing beside me, soaked and unhappy, scraping mud from her hands. "If you're gonna stand around all day we might as well have not come." Alex was out there all by himself now, a lone figure at the top of the field, still moving quickly and soaked to the skin. Occasionally his laugh would drift across to us as we stood in a broken line around the edge of the field.

"Two hundred and twenty!"

"How many did you do?"

"A hundred and seventy-six." I could see that she was surprised.

"What are you tryin' to do? Beat that madman?"

"Not really. But it's a challenge."

"Maybe you could challenge Rochford to give us a better place."

"I'm doin' my best, for Chrissakes!"

"That's what you always say."

It's crazy how the weather affects people. Connie was edgy during the heatwave and now it's cool and raining she's edgy again.

"You got a cigarette?"

I passed her one and lit a match, cupping my hands. She took them and held them while she lit up.

"You're cold."

"Yeh. A hot bath would be nice."

I lit one for myself as drips of water rolled down my neck.

"Yeah, it would. Be very nice." In the west it was brightening a little. Maybe Alex would get the break he was looking for. "I was thinkin', you know, that we should let Janice go to Toronto to the Ex – "

"I wondered how long it would take her to try and use you as a last resort. I don't like the idea of her going in alone. It's too far for one day anyway – and she'll be better off out here. I've read what goes on in the big cities."

"She's sixteen! Old enough to look after herself."

"I don't think so."

"Were you old enough to look after yourself at sixteen?"

"Of course I was, but that was different. Times are different . . . things have changed."

She was right about that.

When I first met Connie things had been going pretty good, all in all. I'd been promoted twice at the mill, the first time to drive the forklift and then to the stores, and I was managing to support both my mother and myself as well as buy an old Chevy. I gave up any idea of playing hockey again when the Raiders failed to come back after the war, and although I had offers to play in Kirkland Lake, there was no way I could leave my mother. Oh, we discussed it and she said she'd be quite happy to move there and all, but when it came down to it and a decision had to be made, she suddenly felt it would be disloyal to my father to leave him up in the cemetery uncared for, after all he'd done for us. Like what? After all these years he was still calling the shots, finally getting his way about me playing hockey.

But I couldn't leave her. She had spent all her years being so dependent on him, and now I had taken his place as someone to lean on. I vowed then and there that it would be different for my wife. Much different. Also, if I was going to be stuck in Black Rapids I might as well enjoy it. I was young enough. There'd be plenty of time to leave later.

Meeting Connie made it much easier to take. For the first time since leaving Joyce in London I'd met someone who was not only beautiful but was also someone I wanted to be with, wanted to talk to, share things with, ideas, ambitions, whatever. And, as with Joyce, I didn't rush in like a bull in a china shop to see how quickly I could get laid. This was something special and I knew it would happen eventually – but not as quickly as it did when she invited me back to her place on New Year's Eve. To be honest, I was a bit thrown by it. In my mind I was prepared to wait a while longer, in a way enjoying feeling sorry for myself, the ignored hero returned from the war, his true love left across the ocean, waiting for time to heal the wound. It was like being in a movie. Bullshit, but it made me feel better. I hadn't expected to be knocked head-over-heels by Connie.

That first time we undressed each other gradually between kisses, surrounded by stuffed animals, pictures of Winnie the Pooh, Frank Sinatra, Dana Andrews and Gregory Peck, and, staring at us from her dresser, a photograph of her mother and father which made me a little nervous. But not for long. When she finally stood there in front of me naked, all I could do was sit on the edge of the bed and look at her in awe, holding her to me so that I could bury my head in her breasts before we moved into bed and pulled the covers over us. For a while we just explored each other, her hands moving lightly over my skin, down my arms, my back, along my thighs, occasionally brushing my rigid cock, teasing, stroking, until finally, she took it in her hands and gently ran her fingers from the base to the top in delicate movements before she turned onto her back. My hand circled her breasts and skimmed down her body to her thighs, her legs parting so that I could come to rest on that soft mound. Time seemed to be standing still. We kissed more and whispered each other's names as she drew up her legs and pulled me to her. It was as fantastic as I imagined it would be, and afterwards we lay in each other's arms, occasionally exchanging a light kiss, just looking at each other as if for the first time.

"Happy New Year," she whispered, and gave a squeeze while I ran my hands through her soft hair, feeling a kind of contentment I'd never known before. This time I wasn't leaving in a week. This time she wasn't already married. This time I think I was in love, for real.

A little later we made love again, and I thanked God that I knew what I was doing, that Joyce had made me realize how women feel, and when that final moment came for Connie, she moaned and gasped, building up until she cried out, thrusting me deep inside her with rapid movements, tightening her muscles until I felt myself willingly and happily turn everything over to forces beyond my control.

I guess we lay there for about an hour, slowly coming back down to earth. Then we went back downstairs, neither of us saying a word.

I left about five o'clock in the morning, slipping out as quietly as possible after Connie had cooked some bacon and eggs and coffee and we'd toasted in the New Year again with some of her father's rye – only to find that my car, sitting out there in twenty-five below, wouldn't start. No way.

It was a long walk home to the other side of town, and within minutes I was shaking from the cold. It would be just my luck to be found the next morning frozen solid, never to see Connie again. But at least they'd wonder why I had a smile on my face.

It was love all right. Mind you, it took me a long time to come out and say it. I mean, it's not an expression you just toss casually around, but I literally worshipped the ground she walked on.

I guess we'd been going around for about six months or so when I finally came out with it. I didn't have to get my courage up or anything like that, because I hadn't planned to say it in the first place. It just happened, as natural and open as anything. We'd driven up to Kapuskasing for the Dominion Day weekend and stayed at the big hotel there as Mr. and Mrs. Harris. She told her folks she was going to see some friend there while I went fishing with a guy I knew from the army. It was the first time we'd done anything like that or even had much time alone together, so at first it seemed a little strange. I'd bought some champagne from the liquor store (the army taught me something) and when we got there we put it in the sink with some ice and sat and had a couple of rye and gingers with club sandwiches sent up by room service. In the afternoon we made love, and later we had dinner downstairs, walked around the town, then came back and had a bath together (she pretended she was a U-boat captain and I was the periscope) drinking the champagne like in some Hollywood movie.

I guess it was about ten o'clock or thereabouts. Anyway, we were lying on top of the bed and I was looking at her, thinking she had the most beautiful body I'd ever seen, and feeling, well, very happy. In fact I felt so happy that I had a lump in my throat. I was choking up with this strange emotion and wanted to tell her, to shout out so that she realized how I felt. But instead I leaned over and kissed her gently and then, without having ever thought about it before, moved down and just as gently buried my face in that soft, warm mound and kissed her again and again, then with my tongue, opening it, searching, until I found that tiny button and kissed her more deeply until her back moved off the bed and I heard her gasp.

I held my head there for a moment and then looked up as she opened her eyes.

"Jesus Christ, I love you, Connie. You know that, don't you?"

She took my hand and squeezed it, pulling me easily to her and holding me very tight.

We were married a year later.

It was a small wedding with the service at St. Mark's and the reception afterwards in the church hall. I didn't particularly want anything flashy but Connie's parents insisted. I must admit Connie looked out of this world as she walked down the aisle in her long, flowing white dress while her mother cried and my mother cried. If anyone'dve walked in off the street they'dve thought it was a funeral, the way the tears were being thrown around. Connie and

214

me invited a few of our friends, but mostly the guests were relatives, and when the reception got under way and I'd had the first dance with Connie, it really became a party for aunts and uncles who hadn't seen each other in years and Connie and me were almost forgotten. By the end of the evening her relatives were lined up down one side of the hall and mine down the other.

To be honest, it was a drag, and I was thankful when we finally left to drive to Toronto for our honeymoon, stopping overnight in New Liskeard, both of us absolutely pooped, so much so that the bottle of champagne we'd bought for our own wedding celebration remained unopened and we fell asleep in each other's arms.

Wedding receptions should be banned. I bet they've screwed up more marriages than anything else. Well, got them off to a bad start anyway. Jesus, all the books, magazines and movies tell you how great and fantastic the wedding night is, how it's the crowning moment of the courtship, the moment of discovery when you give yourselves to each other in mind, body and soul, and what happens? You're too goddamned tired to know what time of day it is, because you had to stay at the reception so's you wouldn't upset your folks. Especially her folks, who picked up the tab and kept reminding me of it. You have too much to drink because everyone's either toasting you or forcing a glass into your hand, and then you have to drive or go by train to reach the spot where all your dreams are going to be realized in a wonderland of love, fantasy and romance in exotic surroundings; where you float toward each other, she in a flowing negligée, arms outstretched, music playing, champagne sparkling.

And what happens?

You fall asleep.

So much for dreams.

One thing's for sure, that wonderland isn't in New Liskeard. And it sure as hell isn't in North Bay either. We spent our second night at the Empire Hotel there, in a small, gloomy room that had about as much romance as the church hall in B.R.

It's funny though, how things change, how that room changed when we finally opened the champagne. Connie wore a filmy nightgown, I wore a new bathrobe from Bill Rogers' Clothes (he gave me it wholesale as a wedding present), and with just one bedside lamp going, we poured the champagne into some bathroom glasses and toasted each other.

"Mrs. Harris . . . I love you."

"Mr. Harris . . . I love you too."

"Forever?"

"Forever."

"And ever."

"It's gonna be great."

"I know."

We had two weeks in Toronto, staying at the King Eddie, with side trips to Niagara Falls and Buffalo, went to the Ex and took ferry rides to the islands. We even made love on one of the island beaches at night and almost missed the last boat back to the city. We went to movies and the museum, ate in good restaurants – really lived it up.

Enjoyed being Mr. and Mrs. Harris.

I don't know exactly when the magic started to fade, but fade it did. Three years, five? I don't know. But suddenly, one day, it was gone.

Maybe it was after my mother died and Davie was about a year old and we'd moved into my old house, which my mother had left to us, from the flat we'd been renting over King's variety store. I was pulling in a hundred and a quarter a week as storekeeper at the mill as well as doing the odd bit of carpentry on the side, so we weren't doing too bad. I mean, it wasn't steak and wine every night, but we were able to go to the odd movie and buy the occasional bottle or case of beer. I'd traded the old Chevy for a later used model, fixed up my old room as a kind of nursery for Davie, and Connie was able to buy some new clothes now and again. It was your typical Black Rapids married scene, only we were luckier than most in that we had a house with just a small amount owing on it.

But it wasn't what I wanted. It wasn't enough. I wanted to do better – to enjoy something of the world outside Black Rapids, the world I'd been let out to see for a couple of years with the army.

It was a long weekend. Davie had been bathed and put to bed and I was in the backyard cooking some hamburgers on the barbecue, drinking a beer and fighting off the mosquitoes when Connie came out of the house with the buns to be toasted and a couple of fresh beers.

"How they doing?"

"Fine. Couple minutes more on this side."

"I think Davie's cutting another tooth."

"Good for him."

It was then that I noticed her eyes seemed dull, the sparkle had gone out of them.

"Maybe we should go to the movie tonight." I mean, why not?

"What's playing?"

"*Streetcar Named Desire.*"

"What's it about?"

"Dunno. Marlon Brando's in it."

"I think I'd rather stay home. We'd never get a sitter anyway, on a holiday."

"We could try."

"I don't feel up to it. Davie had me up all last night with his teeth."

"I got up too. Walked him around for over an hour."

"I know you did. All I'm saying is, I don't feel like going to the show. You're gonna burn those if you don't watch out."

I flipped the hamburgers as flames leapt up from the dripping fat, squirted water on them from a ketchup bottle and took a drink of beer.

"I thought it would make a break for you, that's all."

"It would be a break just to have one night of peace."

Okay, okay, you've made your point. So we don't go to the show. "You know something? I think we should move down to Toronto."

"What?" She looked at me as though I'd said the craziest thing imaginable, like I'd suggested we go and live in Mongolia or someplace.

"We should go and live in Toronto."

"What on earth for?"

"Well, for one thing, there's more opportunity there. Lookit, I've got no future here, at the mill, or anywhere in this town come to that, but in Toronto there's all sorts of work going. Bill Reeve had a copy of the Toronto *Telegram* last week and I looked at the Help Wanted column. Hundreds of jobs. Even drivin' a truck I could make twice as much as I make at the mill. Not only that, this is no place to bring Davie up in–"

"It was good enough for us."

"Yeah. Sure. My dad worked at the mill so I worked at the mill."

"If he gets an education – "

"In Black Rapids? Come on."

"My dad got an education and he's worked for the town all his life. A good job. Responsible. You don't have to work at the mill."

"I went to school too, you know."

"You dropped out."

"Yeah, well . . . I don't think it's any place to bring him up. He needs more than the choice of working for the town or at the mill. *I* need some choice. I want you to have more than just sittin' in this crummy house day after day, year after year, with nothin' to do except . . . except . . . except rot away!"

"Oh, you don't like the way I am now?"

"For Chrissakes. It's . . . it's somethin' I've always wanted to do, ever since I got out of the army. Now my mother's gone we don't have to worry about supporting her, her being alone. I always figured that . . . when she died, we'd have the chance to move out, try our luck down there. Go where there are things happening, where they got modern houses, things for kids to do."

"What about my folks?"

"What about them?"

"It's all very well for you to want to take off because your mother's dead. But my folks are still alive. I just can't walk out, take Davie away from them, leave them here all by themselves. It wouldn't be fair. They've been very good to us. They're the only real family I've got."

"What about me and Davie, for Godsakes?"

"That's different. I'm talking about . . . about my mum and dad. My parents. I couldn't leave them here alone any more than you could your mother. Anyway, I like it in Black Rapids. You've burnt the hamburgers."

"Shit!"

So we didn't move to Toronto. We stayed and kept her folks happy. And Delores came along to make them even happier, while the distance between Connie and me seemed to be growing.

Life at the mill went on grinding away, the same thing day after day after day.

Janice was born, and her folks were elated.

Like a breath of fresh air television came to Black Rapids, and we bought a set on time. As I signed the papers it was like signing my own death warrant, and when I handed them back to Herbie Mills at Black Rapids Electric I saw him smile. His jacket became a black robe as his voice boomed out.

"*I hereby sentence you, Eldon Robert Harris, to spend the rest of your natural life here in Black Rapids, never to leave or cross the town line again, or to even think of leaving, let alone dream of it. For the rest of your natural life. And when you depart this world your body will be taken to the cemetery and buried next to your mother and father and the sentence will be continued by your children for the rest of their natural lives.*"

"Thanks, Eldon. Dumont's a good make. The Cadillac of televisions they call it. We'll be out Monday to put up the antenna for you."

"Thanks, Herb. It's amazin' what they can do now, eh? I mean, it's a bloody miracle sending pictures through the air like that. I used to think radio was incredible."

"That's progress, Eldon. If you wait long enough it'll always reach Black Rapids."

220

"Yeah."

"You can drop your payment off on the first of every month."

Once a month I would be reminded.

That was just one bill. There were clothes for the kids to buy, toys, drugs, food, gas, car repairs, roof repairs, a new septic tank.

"For the rest of your natural life."

So we watched television and shared bottles of beer and peanuts.

Our lovemaking lost all its excitement. The electricity was gone. It was routine, like reading the *Record* or making sure we didn't miss Cross Country Hit Parade, having dinner with her folks every other Sunday. No more baths together. No more worshipping. Now it took effort. Effort to keep an erection. Effort to get her up for it. Nothing spontaneous any more, like it used to be. Now it was like the train schedule and just as frequent. Sometimes I'd look at her face in the middle of it and see boredom, impatience. Oh, occasionally, if we'd had a few drinks, it would be a little like old times, but it was fleeting. Then it would be back to duty. Handouts.

We weren't the only ones, judging by the way some of the guys at the mill talked, but then as I looked around at us at the lunch bench, in our coveralls, some unshaven, teeth missing, I realized we were no Paul Newmans. But then the wives weren't exactly Marilyn Monroes, either.

It's that circle again. You can't get away from it.

221

So the years passed and the kids grew and I did more reading from the library, John O'Hara, Steinbeck, sport books – and I started drinking more.

Applications for jobs at the mill kept getting turned down. Jobs that would improve my earnings, give me something better to do, more challenging. I thought of going into business for myself doing carpentry work, but the bank wouldn't give me a loan to buy the tools, so I drank some more.

Then came the chance for the job as mill foreman and everyone said I was a shoo-in to get it, but when I went to see Caulfield for my interview he told me he didn't think I had the right attitude. I seemed to have a chip on my shoulder, he said, but maybe next time.

They gave it to Harry Inglis. Ruth had been right. He'd given her that future she'd always wanted, so I was sure she was still very happy too.

It was two weeks later that I hit Caulfield at the Christmas party. Oh, it seemed like an accident at the time, but I've often wondered. How much was anger and frustration at being turned down for the job I'm still not sure.

So my life sentence included being unemployed in Black Rapids, extra punishment for having a bad attitude, a chip on my shoulder. It also included bad scenes with Connie, her folks, and the people we owed money to. And the word spread, oh boy, did it get around fast – and with it went any hope of a decent job. Eldon Harris was trouble with a capital T, a man with a Bad Attitude. After two months of no work I finally had a break, bumping into the ex-mayor, booster of the Raiders, now retired and living out his life sentence in B.R.

He asked me home for a beer, coveralls and all, and we talked about the old days, hockey, the army and finally, my medal.

"Eldon, you did your bit for this town, put your life on the line, and who, tell me who, gives a shit today?"

"No one."

"Except me. They don't hand out those things for peeing in the snow, goddamnit. I tell you, my boy, you brought a lot of honour to this town, you gave em a lot of thrills, and I for one don't like to see a guy shat upon when he's down. I might be retired and out of the picture, but I still carry some weight. You'll have a job by Monday."

I felt excited for the first time in years, without even knowing what the job was. It wasn't at the mill and that was all I cared about. It would be different. Something different.

"I, personally, will arrange it. You're prepared to do anything?"

"You bet."

"Like drive the school bus and the snow plough in the winter?"

"You're damned right."

"You'll hear from me by the end of the week. It ain't much, Eldon, but it sure beats tie-pins, eh?"

Which was how I became a school bus driver.

The mayor said it wasn't much, but it was. It was work. It was money. And I was determined to be the best damned school bus driver they'd ever had. To make it more interesting I ran the route several times, timing myself at certain points so that I knew when I had to make up time or slow down, so that when I said I'd be there at 7:35, I'd be there at 7:35 on the dot, not before or after. The time came when people set their watches by me, and it felt good.

And then there was the snow plough. I'd say I'm about

the best snow plough operator the town's ever had. Even the mayor said that, the year we had twenty inches in one go and drifting, and I had Main Street and the road to the highway open in time for the weekend shopping. There's something exciting about being out there alone in that cab, the blue light flashing off the silent houses, trees drooping under the weight of the snow, knowing you're probably the only one out in the whole town and everyone's depending on you to keep things moving. It's a kinda faith they have.

When I go out, Connie prepares me a flask of coffee with just enough rye in it to perk it up, some soup and a package of sandwiches. Invariably, like new babies and bad news, my work comes at night. Connie says I spend too much time making sure the ploughing is neat, but to me that's important. I get a great feeling when I look behind me and see a smooth, perfectly straight cut or a driveway that, by clever manoeuvring, I've managed not to block with a three-foot wall of packed ice and snow. People appreciate things like that even if they don't realize that it takes skill to operate one of those machines.

Up where the road into Black Rapids joins the highway there's a cut-off where people can pull over in the summer and have a picnic. This is where I usually stop to have something to eat before heading back on the other side. There's something very special about that moment, with the engine off, listening to the silence. It's like I'm the only person in the world, up there in my cab surveying my kingdom, a kingdom of rugged, white wilderness, the headlights glinting off the snow-draped pines.

Or at dawn, after the storm has moved well away and left a clear blue sky, and the sun breaks over the ridge of the highway, sparkling through the trees, throwing long shadows from the frozen grass over snow that seems to glisten

224

and glitter like the diamonds in the window of Black Rapids Credit Jewellers.

And I'm the only one that sees it, sees things like five timber wolves crossing the road into the bush as casual as you like. Or the snowy owl that landed on the telegraph pole twenty feet from me . . . and I imagine what it would have been like when this area was really wild.

For those few minutes while I'm eating, I know.

Connie wasn't that impressed with my new jobs at first, her father even less so. Suddenly, working for the town wasn't as great as it used to be. Now, the important jobs were right inside the town hall. But it seemed to make things easier between us, and when Connie started working at Wong's there was a marked improvement. Not only did it mean more money but it gave her a chance to get out of the house, to meet people. We even smiled at the breakfast table and read the Cards of Thanks printed on the back page of the *Record.*

"There's quite a few this week. 'I wish to thank the following people for their help given to my son on March 5th: the telephone operator who put my urgent call through so quickly: the Black Rapids Police Department who helped with the oxygen: Mr. Howard Dusty for opening up his drugstore so late at night so that I could receive some medication: the ambulance attendants who drove my son to the hospital: Dr. Empringham who did his job exceptionally well: and all the people both at the hospital and in Black Rapids for their support at this worrisome time.' "

"Who's that from?"

"Mrs. R. Preddy."

"Don't know her."

"She's from Cochrane. Wonder what happened?"

"I've no idea."

"There's another. 'Louise McBride wishes to thank Oscar Hardy for the fine job he did in fixing her hi-fi.' Wonder what else he fixed?"

"Oscar Hardy? She's too old for him."

We took an interest in what each other was doing, swapping stories about our day – hers the gossip she picked up at Wong's and mine stories of kids on the bus; who was smoking and who wasn't, which teacher was trying to make which. Nothing earth-shattering, but it was different. Different, like it would have been in Toronto.

Connie even had an argument with her father when he made some smart-ass remark about her marrying a bus driver and she actually defended me. I think we were closer that night than we had been for years.

Then came the school summer break and I was out of a job until September, which caused things to change between us again – for the worse. What I didn't understand was why her enjoyment of our lovemaking always varied according to how things were going at the time. When I asked her one night, after a futile attempt to get her interested, she wouldn't say much. I mean, either you enjoy it or you don't; either you love someone or you don't, even though times might be tough. In fact, it's more important then. But no, she goes up and down like a goddamned barometer. She moved over to her side of the bed and smoothed down her nightdress. "Sometimes, Eldon, I think you daydream too much. You're not realistic. You get these romantic ideas and expect too much."

"What's that supposed to mean?"

"I'm not sure."

"It's just bullshit. Why can't you say what you mean?"

226

"I guess your idea of what women should be like and the way they really are are two different things."

She was right there. All my life I'd hoped things would happen one way and it would always be another. Except with Joyce. But we only knew each other for little over a week. "Things were all right once. They were exciting. Meant something. Not just a goddamned ritual."

"You can never keep that up. It changes. Everyone knows that."

"How come I haven't changed? How come I'm different?"

"Oh, Eldon . . . why do you keep on about it?"

Her stock answer to get out of the discussion. So I gave up asking. To hell with it.

On top of that the situation wasn't helped because she was the only one making money and I couldn't get a job that summer and the kids were asking out loud why their father couldn't when others could. They don't know what it's like. But they'll find out, in time, when they realize that Black Rapids is the asshole of the world.

So finally, twenty years too late, I went to Toronto to look for work and met Alex and found out how to pick tomatoes. It wasn't a bad season.

Connie came with me the next year and the year after that, like people going away to the same place every summer for a vacation, only we worked. We had to. To survive.

We went back to our old ways – bickering, arguing, growing apart. The magic of that first homecoming was just that. Magic. An illusion that was there one minute and gone the next. She was so right when she told me I expected too much. I did. But I couldn't see that it was any reason to give up hoping. Life's too short for that. There's always a solution.

But she stayed with me. Supported me. "I married you for better or for worse, didn't I?" she'd say. "So now it's worse. I made an oath." And she said it again before our trip down this year with Janice. I think it's her pride more than anything.

Her parents are in their eighties now (another part of His plot). They've been telling her for years she's wasting her time with me, but I think she wants to prove a point. Like Alex. It's important. Like it was important to me once.

I don't know why we're standing here like idiots. It's only a five-minute walk and we can't get any wetter." Connie pulled her blouse tighter as the rain continued in a steady downpour. Out to the west of us, I could see the sun shining and large patches of blue sky.

"Two hundred and forty!" Alex was still working, still determined as he came toward us, his clothes clinging to his body like lead weights. Why didn't he take a break, get out of the rain? It would be over in a few minutes and he was in good shape to set a new record.

"You've got to admit he's got guts."

"More like rocks in his head. He's insane. Talking to himself, laughing out there like some nutcase." Connie's hair was hanging dead straight and her face was sour as we watched Alex getting closer, out there all alone, water running down his face and neck, a drowned rat in a tomato field.

"This is gonna be his last year pickin'."

"You and him both."

"And he plans to buy a sailboat down south and live on it. Cruise around the Caribbean."

"Sure. If he's so rich why's he pickin' tomatoes? You can stay and watch if you like, but I'm goin' back. Who cares if he breaks a record or not? Who in hell cares?"

"Alex. It's important to him. Everyone needs a challenge."

"You keep saying that, only I don't see you doin' anything about it except tellin' me how important it is for Alex." Connie didn't like him, never had. I think he was too open for her, too confident. I took out another cigarette, using up three matches before I found a dry one. "We talked about it years ago, when I wanted to move to Toronto. We had a chance to do something, then."

"You've been lookin' for excuses all your life instead of accepting the way things are."

"That's the trouble with people in that town. They accept. They figure the train goin' down south or the bus to Thunder Bay is only for people passin' through. They figure they have no right to be on it, no right to be dissatisfied. Well, I don't buy that. I'll never just accept things the way they are. There's always a chance to change."

"You've left it a bit late, I'd say."

Alex passed us about fifty feet away and looked over, grinning. "Think of tonight, me old darlin'. That's what makes it all worth it." He shook his head to get rid of the water, and moved on. The rain hadn't slowed him up one bit.

"What did he mean by that?"

"I've no idea." Connie wouldn't appreciate a girl named Rita waiting in town while her husband was away fishing. I hadn't seen her in this kind of a mood for a long time, but on the other hand, I suppose I couldn't blame her. Everything was going to be so much better for my wife. She wasn't going to have the dreary, dull, hopeless existence that my mother and father lived through. Not my wife. Putting my arm around her shoulder, I tried to think of something to say that would make her feel better. But then it seemed crazy to try and say anything with us standing there drenched, our baskets of tomatoes out in the field while we waited for the rain to stop so we could go back to our implement shed and spend another night with the flies and the rats while the Jamaicans soaked in their bathtub. So I shrugged it off, and for a moment, when she looked at me, I thought that perhaps she was reading my mind and really did understand. But just as quickly she turned away and told me she was going back to the shed. As she moved off I gave her bum a pat, but I don't think she noticed.

Over in the corner of the field Alex stood up and turned toward us, letting out a roar – a roar that turned into a long bellow that seemed to fade off into the distance. Then he stumbled slightly, grasping at the air as though he needed something to hold onto, staggered, stumbled a few steps more, his arms reaching high, waving at the air, and started to fall slowly backwards, almost in slow motion, his arms floating gently down to his sides, bouncing off his hips and into the air again just before his body hit the ground, his shoulders crashing into a basket of tomatoes.

Around the edge of the field the figures of the pickers emerged from where they were sheltering, dark, silent, strange shapes against the trees and the black sky in the east, all looking over to where Alex lay.

Suddenly I was running the hundred yards or so across the field to him, slipping and sliding a couple of times in the mud that clung to my boots and made them heavier and heavier, the trees ahead of me blurring. When I finally reached him and knelt down to ease him off the basket I knew he was dead. I'd seen them before. Many times. You don't need to feel for a pulse or check their eyes for vital signs. You just know.

And Alex was no different from the others. For a moment I was stunned as I tried to get my breath back, my heart pounding and the muscles in my calf and thigh tightening up. Dying had never really meant anything to me. Not since that day in Holland when Battencourt bought it and that other guy was blown up into a tree without his shoes. Even when my mother died, after hanging on for a year from a stroke, I felt nothing. My whole system was numb. No emotion could get out. But Alex was something else. I mean, guys don't just die like that for no reason. At his age.

Frantically I leaned over him, forced his mouth open and started artificial respiration. Looking up I saw Connie hurrying across the field toward us, out there by herself while the others stood and stared.

"Call an ambulance!" I snapped it out like an order and she stopped for a moment, then turned and started running to the Rochford house.

Everything went fuzzy as I worked on him. Things around me came into focus for a brief moment and then blanked out again, slowly, like a slide projector when the picture stays sharp for a while and then goes hazy. I heard voices. Strange and low. Muttering.

The rain. It was stopping.

Water running down Alex's face.

A small brown toad jumped from one patch of earth to another.

People. Standing around me, watching.

Keep working. Keep working.

232

It's been known to happen. Hearts starting up again.

You're kidding yourself. There's no way, and you know it. You've seen it before.

Dear Jesus, keep going, keep going.

A goldfinch came through loud and clear, somewhere off in the distance. Pretty birds.

People again. Closing in on me. Staring down from under their wide-brimmed hats like they were watching a road accident.

No rain at all now. Wouldn't you know it?

"Okay, clear a path."

Two guys in white with a stretcher. Rochford's there too. How long? Ten minutes? Half an hour? An hour?

"We'll take over from here."

I sat back onto the wet soil, drained, brilliant colours dancing in front of my eyes, then starting to fade as everything came back into focus. Connie was beside me, her face pale and serious, her hand warm on my arm. The attendants put Alex onto the stretcher with a pillow under his shoulders so that his head fell back, then opened his mouth and slid a pale green plastic thing down into his throat, making me want to gag for him. One of them placed an oxygen mask over his face and signalled to the Jamaican, who was closest, to help with the stretcher. They picked Alex up and started the walk back to the ambulance, one of the attendants carrying the oxygen equipment.

"Can I ride with him?"

"If you want to. Sure."

"Eldon!" Connie came after me.

"I'm gonna ride with Alex."

"I heard. Is he dead?"

"I . . . think so."

Of course he's dead. Why kid around pretending? Because there's always got to be hope. He's got a boat to buy. Rita to meet tonight. That's bullshit and you know it.

"I found these on the ground. They were underneath him." She handed me a small wallet and a crushed Montecristo cigar tube. "Musta fallen out of his pocket."

"Yeah."

"You tried, Eldon. You really tried." She took my arm and for a moment there we were very close.

"I gotta go. Catch them up."

"All right! Let's move it. We gotta lot of work to do yet. What's everyone standing around for? They're pickin' up this load at six o'clock." Rochford was strutting around, a little confused. "I want this field finished by tonight!" No one moved. Just stood and stared at Alex's departing body moving slowly across the muddy field, then at Rochford as he paced. At that moment the sun broke out from behind a cloud, the first warmth I'd felt all afternoon.

"Where you goin', Harris?"

"Into town with Alex."

"You're not goin' no place. There's work to do, for Chrissakes. Anyway, there's nothin' you can do for him now."

For a moment I thought I was going to hit him, really belt him, but even as I felt the anger race through my body, something told me it would be the wrong thing to do. Not this time, Eldon, don't hit anybody this time. "Listen, I'm goin' and that's all there is to it!" Maybe it was the way I said it or the way I looked, I don't know, but he just shrugged and turned to the others.

"Let's go. We haven't got all day! Move!" But no one did.

"Lookit, this is costin' you money, costin' me money. Move your asses!"

They continued to stare, not one of them budging. The stretcher was getting closer to the ambulance and I had to go, but at the same time I felt a need to say something. "Maybe if you talked to them like they were human beings for a change instead – "

"And who the hell d'you think you're talkin' to? I pay good money an' if they're not gonna work they can all get the hell out and I'll bring new people in! Don't start givin' me trouble. I'm gonna say it for the last time! Get back to work!"

The silence seemed to go on for ever as still nobody moved, all their eyes now on me, waiting. Even Rochford was watching me. Then I found myself walking toward the pickers, my back to Rochford. "Listen, I'm gonna ride into town with Alex, to the hospital. Let's er . . . let's finish the field for the man. Everyone's a bit upset and er . . . well, we didn't come here to be treated like shit, talked to like we were the lowest goddamned thing that ever walked this earth by someone who thinks he's better than us. But we can sort that out tomorrow, eh? It's money outa our pockets if we don't, and that's crazy. Whatdaya say? If the rain holds off it'll only take another hour. But you do it on your own terms, not because we've bin threatened, because we're scared of losing our jobs. We'll do it because we want it done and we want that bread in our pockets more than anything else. We need that bread in our pockets and he knows that. So we'll pick em for no other reason. All right?"

Someone chattered away in French, translating, while I watched them, waiting, praying that they'd not make an asshole out of me. For a moment there was a lot of shuffling about and nothing happened. Rochford lit up a cigar, a grin on his face as he looked over to me. Then the French Canadian, the one whose wife had the miscarriage, moved forward, looked at Rochford with real hatred in his eyes, then turned to me. *"Ben, pour vous on va y aller."* I had no idea what he was saying, but immediately he walked out into the field to the waiting baskets and the others started to follow, Connie included, as Janice came up to me, her hair in rollers.

"I saw the ambulance arrive so I came back."

"That's good. Go and give mum a hand."

"Is he – ?"

"Yes."

"But they're giving him oxygen."

"I know. Go and give your mother a hand, there's a good kid." Without even looking at Rochford I ran to the ambulance and climbed into the back, sitting next to the attendant who was feeding the oxygen to Alex. Outside the pickers started to line up in their rows while Rochford slammed the door of his truck, gunning the engine and spinning the rear wheels so that they sank down into a deep ridge. Stupid bugger.

Looking through the rear window of the ambulance was like watching a television set as a series of images moved past: our shed in the distance, the barn, the big house, Al Rochford's wife watching us with a dazed look, crying for some reason, her hands wiping away some tears, then turning and hurrying inside, the mailbox, our trail of dust on the county road and then more dust as we passed Grant Rochford's Duster going the other way at 60 mph, the roar of his engine fading until we were back with the steady noise of the oxygen machine pumping false hope into Alex. It was another game of pretend, the attendant looking as though he really cared, Alex lying there with the mask over his face, the mud from his boots messing up the white sheet and a wet patch forming below where his head hung back.

236

"Terrible job you've got." The attendant looked at me for a moment, then returned to Alex. "How the hell d'you stand it, on your feet all day, working through that heatwave?"

"It's tough."

"Yeah, it must be. Like I say, during that heatwave I coulda understood this, but today?" He gave a shrug and we fell back into silence, listening to the oxygen pump.

They didn't put the siren on until we hit the outskirts of Chatham. Now we seemed to be going much faster, Martians whoop whooping our way through the streets.

The King is dead!

God save the King.

"By the end of the day I'll be the best tomato picker in southern Ontario. Complete with proof."

"You are already."

"Yeah, but that's not enough. I gotta prove it to myself. Make sure I'm not sliding backwards, 'cause people respect a champ and when you're number one you respect yourself."

The only good thing was that he didn't know he hadn't broken the record. I mean, he was probably dead before he hit the ground. Just like that. One second going strong – the next it's all over. That quick.

I pulled out a cigarette and damp matches, fighting back tears. I mean, he'd spoken to me only minutes before it happened.

"Can't smoke in here. Oxygen."

"Oh . . . right."

How long? One minute? Thirty seconds?

"Think of me tonight, me old darlin'. That's what makes it all worthwhile."

Maybe less than that. Fifteen seconds.

"What they paying this year to pick a basket of those things?"

"Eh? Oh . . . thirty-five cents."

"Holy Christ! And I thought we got paid bad."

It's gonna work out. They're gonna pull him through. I can feel it.

There's no way. Absolutely no way. When the heart isn't beating the brain gets starved of oxygen. When the heart isn't beating you're dead.

"It's a plot, Eldon. A plot. The Rochfords go to church, you know. Probably prayed like hell for this just to screw me."

"And there was I thinking we had a shitty job. I mean, it gets messy at times with road accidents and things but you get used to it."

Dead's dead.

"That's Christianity for you. Love thy neighbour. Love thy neighbour's wife. That's more important, eh?"

She cried. She was really crying, Alex. And you didn't even know it.

"Christ, you'd have to pick ten baskets just to make three fifty. They should do something about that."

I can see you're really worried. As long as they get their tomatoes on their plates in Toronto or wherever for three fifty for a six-quart basket and no more, that's all that matters. That's six quarts, buddy. The baskets we pick are thirty-five pounds!

"I've bin fartin' around ever since I left Glace Bay. Sure, I had good times – but who needs this pickin' crap?"

Not me. Not any more. This is my last year, too. Sure.

238

"It's time I put my feet up and relaxed. Bin my dream for years. You gotta have somethin' to aim for, I always say."

Yeah, but not this. Not with your feet up in the back end of an ambulance.

"It's not very much, thirty-five cents. Thirty-five dollars for a hundred baskets. Shit!"

Why don't you shut up and look after the oxygen, for Chrissakes! So you're a brain. You can add.

"How d'you stand it?"

"I dunno."

Your feet up for good, Alex. Boots and all.

The tall, grey water tower that said CHATHAM in big letters flashed past as we swung onto a one-way street, causing Alex's head to roll slightly. There was no point in rushing now, we all knew that, but then maybe there was an outside chance. It's been known to happen. They pulled a kid out of the Black River once and everyone said he was dead, but Eddie Marshall worked on him while someone else drove the cruiser to the hospital and the kid survived. They gave Eddie a tie-pin for that and named him Policeman of the Year.

Outside I saw St. Joseph's hospital looming up, the blue-railed ramp curving past as we pulled round beside the main building and down a slope to the emergency entrance. It looked pretty modern, so maybe they had the equipment. Maybe they could do something. And being a religious hospital wouldn't hurt. I mean, at a time like this you need everything you can get.

It all happened very quickly; the ambulance coming to a stop, doors open, stretcher out, wheels dropped, rolling through the doors, the oxygen still pumping, past brightly coloured walls, nurses, into the resuscitation room where doctors and machines were waiting.

"Are you with the patient?" A nurse wearing a blue uniform was trying to steer me away from the room.

"Yes."

"We have a waiting room just round the corner. Would you mind going there?"

"I might be able to help."

"He's being well looked after. We'll let you know how he's doing."

Don't give me that bullshit! I know already. I know, I know.

You're wasting your time, and you know it too.

They'd tried to make the waiting area more cheerful by placing orange, blue and green chairs around the walls, putting in the fanciest coffee machine I'd ever seen and hanging a painting of a woods in the fall with a stream running through it – but anyone who had ever sat there trying to read the year-old *Time* magazines knew where they were and why they were there. Nothing could disguise it. I stood shivering from the wet clothes I was wearing, struggling with the wet matches, finally managing to get a cigarette lit, feeling that I was in a strange, unreal world, watched by an old man with a red face sitting in a corner tapping his shoe on the floor. I seemed to be standing back watching myself, the sounds of the air-conditioning, the tapping shoe and the occasional call for a doctor over the PA system echoing around my head. To try and keep warm I paced up and down, walking to the large white clock hanging from the ceiling and back to the coffee machine, noticing that the old man's shoe had stopped tapping and my squeaking boots had taken over.

"You should get out of those clothes, chum. And get something hot to drink." The ambulance attendant wheeled his empty stretcher to the main door, then took some change from his pocket and went to the coffee machine to get me a hot chicken soup. "Here, this'll help."

"Thanks. I don't have any small change at the moment but –"

"On the house. They're still working on him. Be a while yet." He went back inside and I sat down. I was shivering violently and the soup felt good as it burnt its way down. It was then that I remembered Alex's wallet in my hip pocket.

For the first time I was able to find out where he lived. It was there on his driver's licence. Harpin, Alexander David. 342 Elgin Street, Pembroke, Ontario. There were several photographs: Alex on a beach with some woman, a woman by herself hamming it up, two young kids, a boy and a girl, his car ownership, two safes, about fifty dollars in bills, and in a small compartment, a tiny piece of green stone carved into the shape of an oriental person with a big grin. It was incredible how much detail they could get onto such a small piece of stone.

I removed fifteen dollars, the photographs and safes, and started to pace again. Hell, it was like stealing from your best friend, but I needed the money to get back to the farm, buy something to eat and maybe phone Pembroke. If he had a wife she should know, have his things, if she wanted them. The pictures and the safes I'd throw in the garbage someplace. No point in upsetting her any more than need be. If she exists.

After about half an hour a doctor who looked like he'd stepped out of Ben Casey, with his gown open to his navel and a stethoscope stuffed into his pocket, waved me over. From the look on his face I knew what was coming. I mean, I'd known all along.

"We did all we could. I'm sorry. Even if you'dve got him here sooner I don't think we could have saved him."

"Can't you try some more?"

"We've done everything."

"There has to be something!" I yelled at him, suddenly angry, and found myself pushing past him toward the resuscitation room. With all this modern medicine, all those machines they've got, there had to be something else they could do! Eddie Marshall saved that kid all by himself! They grabbed me before I got to the door, but not before I saw Alex lying on the table, his shirt off, mouth open, the sheets muddy from his boots. At the end of the bed was a machine like the one they'd used on me back in B.R. when I had a checkup, the kind that measures how your heart's beating, and the floor was deep in the paper that it had spewed out while they worked on him. It was there for all to see, that straight black line that ran across the floor all the way back up to the machine where it stopped when they switched it off. The line had to be jagged. Straight was the end. I knew that much.

"You've got to be able to do something, for Chrissakes!"

A nurse pulled some drapes around Alex, or maybe they closed the door, I don't know, and two doctors turned me away and took me to a room where they gave me some more soup and a dry cigarette.

Just before I left, after I'd given them all the information I could, I saw them wheel Alex out and disappear round a corner. He was all covered up, but I could see the mud stains so I knew it was him. I suppose that's the way it ends for most of us, disappearing round some corner to become a number on someone's file system.

I walked back into town along King Street, past the big houses with gigantic trees standing in their front gardens, old houses with big, flashy cars parked in the front driveways; past the new Civic Centre and then onto the main drag, where I caught my reflection in a drugstore window; this thing standing there, shaking with the cold like some rubby who's going through the DT's. I couldn't believe what I saw. It was like looking at the ghost of someone I knew vaguely a long time ago, years ago, someone who seemed familiar, except that this person had wet, matted hair, soaked, mud-covered clothes, and looked as though he'd just come back from the trenches. But worst of all, this person looked old. Very old. Someone who'd given up on life, one of the bums from Toronto who had nowhere to go and spent his time stretched out in Allen Gardens, prowling up and down Parliament Street or down on Sherbourne by the Sally Ann, waiting for handouts.

In a coffee shop people looked at me like I had the plague, and the waitress seemed anxious to get rid of me. It was while I was sitting there that I remembered Rita. Sometime soon she would be looking for Alex in the lobby of the William Pitt hotel. That decided me.

I found Honest John's Department store, a long, rambling place that sold everything from toothpaste to boots, and bought a T-shirt, windbreaker, socks, a pair of pants and sneakers. At the drugstore I got a hairbrush and some soap, then headed for the railroad station washroom to clean up and change, spending just under thirty dollars for the lot, including cigarettes. I felt guilty about going back into Alex's wallet, but there was no way I could meet Rita dressed the way I was. I figured he'd want me to do it anyway.

It was like a horror movie in reverse. The wild thing that looked back at me from the mirror changed right in front of my eyes, the down-and-out bum I'd seen in the store window, gradually changing into the guy I used to know, heavily tanned, hair long and turning a little grey, still making me look like Beethoven, like Alex said. But I still looked old. Not as bad as before, but old.

It was now five-fifteen, and I figured that Alex's date was probably for about eight-thirty, so I killed time by looking for the hotel, which was on 6th Street right opposite the old Number One Firehall. Then I went into the hotel restaurant, where I passed another hour over a hot roast beef sandwich, two pieces of apple pie and four cups of coffee. It was like coming out of the desert and finding civilization, except the local paper made me realize that Chatham was like any other town. Well, excepting Black Rapids maybe. There was Connie worried about Janice going to Toronto while right here in Chatham they were considering a curfew for teenagers because of gangs roaming the streets wrecking stuff at night. A couple had been charged with killing their kid, and some others were up on possession of marijuana charges. So much for the quiet country life.

From the restaurant I crossed the lobby to the Piccadilly Room, where I stumbled over a couple of chairs in the darkness while I tried to find a corner seat away from the blaring TV set. I've never understood why bar owners figure it's better to have people drink in almost total blackness, unless it's to hide the crappy surroundings. I ordered a Canadian Club and water and settled back with a cigarette to wait out the time. It was then, I think, that it really hit me.

I came out of the daze, back to reality, understanding clearly for the first time that Alex was dead, and I felt a strange, surging feeling grip my throat, tears forming, my eyes filling with water, the same kind of feeling I had when Gimby got it, but then I didn't have time to think about it. Anyway, it wasn't real, that night wasn't real, not while it

244

was happening. Only afterwards, like now. It was the kind of feeling I'd expected when my father died and then my mother, but on those occasions nothing had happened. Absolutely nothing, and I've felt guilty about it ever since. How come a friend can affect me this way but my own flesh and blood didn't? Why, goddamnit, at my age, do I still have to feel guilty, haunted from the grave about something I have no control over? Still be made to feel a shit by him? I know my own emotions, when it feels right to let them go, like I did with Joyce and with Connie once, although over the years even she has managed to force me to hold back a lot of the time. It's a very trusting thing you do when you let your emotions hang out, because after that you've got nothing to fall back on, you've played your ace. So you trust the person with them and hope they won't squash them and leave you helpless, because if they do, you make good and goddamn sure you don't put yourself in that position again. You've got to know when the time is right, and that seems to happen naturally, like now, only I'm glad that the bar is dark and no one can see me, because even in Chatham, in Kent county, just like in B.R., you can get stomped on.

I guess I had three or four drinks, and though it seemed like a dumb thing to do I toasted Alex, like we would have back at his tent when he'd broken the record. Then around eight o'clock I wandered out into the lobby and sat on one of the chesterfields grouped right in the middle round a table on which sat a vase of white plastic chrysanthemums. From there I could see the front door out to Firehall Number One, the entrance to the Piccadilly Room and the front desk. If she came in the back way, through the restaurant, I had that covered too.

I could imagine the style of years ago, seeing a horse-drawn cutter pull up outside and the woman I was waiting for, my lover, enter the hotel wearing a beautiful fur coat and hat right out of Dr. Zhivago, Lara, the snow still clinging to the fur and her eyebrows as she gave me that special look, that warm, special look, that said we'd be in each other's arms in just a few minutes. In Chatham? Instead a salesman, pushing a rack of clothes, crossed to the front desk to check in, booking a sample room and buying a copy of *Playboy* and *Oui* from the rack of skin magazines behind the desk. He was going to be in town for one day and was moving on to St. Thomas and Woodstock before heading for home in Toronto for the weekend.

There was no sign of Rita yet. In fact the only women who came in were with men, and they headed right for the Piccadilly Room, so I went over in my head how I'd break it to her as gently as possible. Don't worry, Alex, I won't let on about you being a picker or anything like that. Then I started to worry. Maybe it wasn't a good thing to tell her he was dead. She shouldn't have to worry about something like that. On the other hand, if I told her he'd been called away on business very sudden and had asked me to deliver a message that he'd be in touch when he got back, it might sound better. Shit, no. That'd build up her hopes.

Perhaps I shouldn't do anything, just forget it. She'd wait around for a while and then head home, writing it off as one of those things.

But that wouldn't be fair either. Alex wasn't like that. There would only be one thing that would stop him from keeping a date like this one. And it did.

If you always tell the truth, son, you'll never get into trouble. Lies lead to other lies and then where are you?

Sure. But you wouldn't understand a situation like this. It's delicate. There are people's feelings to consider, and you wouldn't know anything about that. I want to let her down gentle and still let Alex keep his pride.

Pride's no use to him now.

As long as I have anything to do with it, we'll salvage something.

By nine-fifteen she still wasn't there, in fact not one good-looking woman had been through the lobby in over an hour, so I went outside onto the street looking for a Trans-Am that might be parked on a meter or cruising up and down, but the only action was two firereels pulling out, their sirens echoing in stereo down the street, then fading off in the distance. Somewhere, someone's life was starting to change slightly, and they would try and fix it before it got too bad but it would never be quite the same again. I decided to give it another fifteen minutes and wandered back into the hotel, where the lobby was deserted except for the occasional couple going to the Piccadilly Room. Where the hell was she? Maybe there wasn't a Rita and it was one big line of bullshit.

No way. He wasn't like that and you know it.

His driving licence says he lived in Pembroke, for Chrissakes. He never once mentioned that. And men are known to brag. The less you're getting the more you brag. I know that. I've done it.

Not everyone's like you.

And don't I know it. Maybe everything he said, bragged about, was bullshit.

You're getting as bad as the rest. You did all right by him.

Yeah. I guess I'm getting edgy. Not myself. Why the hell don't they answer that goddamn phone?

You're getting just like your father.

Jesus, no.

He didn't want you to be any different from him. Maybe he was jealous of you and you're jealous of Alex.

Why should I be jealous? Oh, maybe I was once, now and then. But Alex is dead and I'm alive.

Sure.

"Front desk. *Hello* . . . front desk!" The clerk switched off the buzzing, muttered something about people being impatient, and disappeared into an office while I went out onto 6th Street to look for a pay phone, somewhere private to phone Pembroke. I'm sorry, Rita, but I got things to do. Anyway, maybe it's better this way. You'll never know, but at least you won't forget him in a hurry.

Twenty minutes later I was back in the lobby using their pay phones after a six-block search for one outside. Maybe a teenage gang stole them all, who knows? One thing's for sure, the telephone company was pretty cheap in the way they spread them around. Hell, we've got more back in Black Rapids. After half an hour of fooling around with Information and God knows how many operators I finally got Mrs. Alex Harpin on the line and explained who I was.

"You say you're a friend of Alex?"

"Yes."

"Oh." There was a long silence and I wanted to remind her that I was calling long distance and didn't have that much small change. "I haven't seen him for about five years. He hasn't bin back since then. He could be dead for all I know."

It was my turn to be silent. Behind me, a group from the Piccadilly Room crossed the lobby, laughing and shouting. "Well . . . that's why I'm callin' . . . he, well he died this afternoon. Heart attack, they think. It was very sudden."

His hands grasping at the air, then slowly starting to fall back as his arms floated gently to his side.

"Oh." Another long silence.

His body hitting the ground, shoulders smashing into the basket.

"I see."

"I figured I should let you know."

"Thank you."

"There are some of his things here . . . over at the farm. His car, a tent and things. I thought you might want to have his body shipped up to Pembroke. You know, being his wife and all."

"No . . . thank you. We weren't married in the proper sense if you know what I mean . . . just lived common-law for a few years. I got used to using his name. It . . . it made it seem better."

"Yeah. I see."

"And now I have another . . . I'm friends with someone else. We're very happy. I'd rather not have Alex back . . . to mess things up. It's an expense we don't need."

"Yeah, I see."

"He made his decision and that's . . . that."

"What about his car and things? I could sell them and mail you the money."

"No thank you. I don't want anything from him. Do what you like with them. I suppose I shouldve changed my surname."

"I spose. Anyway, I jus' thought you might want to know."

"Thank you . . . for calling."

"That's okay . . . that's okay."

I got a cab back to the farm and had the driver drop me about half a mile from the house. I wanted time to think, time to go and check over Alex's things, tidy up a bit for him, pack things up. But mostly to think. It was dark and the sky had cleared with a fairly bright moon so it was good for walking. Anyway, I didn't want Rochford to see me arrive in a cab wearing new clothes.

Sometimes it's better not to know about people. I mean, I didn't want to know about his "wife" up in Pembroke any more than I wanted to hear her write him off so quickly, like he'd never really existed. He was King of the Tomato Pickers as far as I was concerned, and that was enough.

I didn't mean to pry, Alex me old darling, but it seemed like the right thing to do. But when you're dead you're helpless to do anything, to control things so that what's your business remains your business. Hell, we've all got our "other side" except that at times you seemed to know more about mine than I did. I guess we all have the chance to do whatever we want with our lives, and you chose your way. At least you did it and enjoyed it. Most people don't.

Feeling very weary, I made my way across a field and along the stream to Alex's place. It was like the whole world had come down on my shoulders. I mean, there's no way I can take his car and his other things. It was bad enough spending his money on these clothes. The fact is, I don't like things for nothing. Like welfare. I guess I do have some of my father in me after all.

Maybe I'll sell everything and send a money order to Pembroke anyway. I'm sure she could use it.

About a hundred yards from Alex's tent I sensed there was something wrong. I don't know what it was, just instinct or whatever it is that suddenly alerts you. Maybe it goes back to being in the army, because I suddenly reverted to Corpo-ral Harris again, stopping and listening, then cutting around to the north slope that protected Alex's place, com-ing back down on it from above, being careful that my body didn't stand out against the sky.

Then I knew I was right.

The tent was gone. His car seemed to be leaning at a weird angle, and beyond it I could make out the shape of another car and hear voices.

Moving quickly and silently I got to within fifteen feet of the voices and saw the whole scene, lit by Alex's Coleman lamp. The second car was Grant Rochford's jazzed-up Plymouth Duster. I moved to the right so that the rest of the view wasn't blocked by Alex's wagon and saw the figures of Rochford and someone else, probably the Shantz kid by his limp, heading for one of Alex's garden chairs with one of Alex's beers. The reason the wagon was at such a weird angle was because it was up on blocks and the wheels were gone.

"Reach for an Old V, man."

"Right on." Someone laughed and tossed a beer bottle away. The voices came through loud and clear. I sat down, stunned. The Coleman was between us, so if they looked in my direction they wouldn't see a thing beyond the lamp.

Inside I felt ready to move in and tear them apart one by one, but instead I sat there, letting my anger burn itself off so that when I did move I'd act in a reasonably calm and rational manner. As my eyes adjusted to the light I could see other beer bottles and cartons scattered all over the place, the brown patch of grass where Alex's tent had been, more cartons that he kept his supplies in, twisted and torn open.

The bastards! The fuckin' bastards!

I guess I covered the fifteen feet between us in about two seconds flat, going for Grant Rochford first, figuring that if I could show the Shantz kid that King Shit could be brought down a peg or two, he might be reluctant to come and help.

They both seemed to turn slowly when they heard me, but because of the light they didn't see me until I was right on top of them, grabbing the Rochford kid's chair and tipping it quickly, catching him off balance so that he went sprawling to the ground on his face, spilling beer down his shirt and jeans before he got a mouthful of dirt and slid about six feet. Just as I thought, the Shantz kid got up and stood staring, his mouth open, while Rochford got quickly to his feet and came at me with the beer bottle. It didn't take much to step aside and plow my fist into his gut as he went by. He let out air like a deflated tire that smelled of stale beer and vomit, and collapsed onto the ground on his knees, trying to get his breath back.

"Okay, where's all the stuff?"

Shantz looked at me, then to Rochford and back again. "We dint take nothin' . . . not a fuckin' thing."

"Just beer, eh?" I picked up a half-full bottle of Canadian Club, just in case. "And booze? Where's the tent, the bed, his clothes . . . everything?" Moving toward the Shantz kid I swung the bottle from side to side, then grabbed him by his pretty shirt, my voice seething with the anger and disgust I was feeling. "Where the fuck is it all?"

"We dint take nothin'. Honest. It was the pickers. Honest

to God. They came up here after supper, about twenty of them, and stripped the place clean. We came to chase em off but it was almost too late. They'd taken practically everything."

I didn't believe him. I mean, I know these people. They aren't made that way. They've got respect for the dead. I shoved him away and went over to the Duster. On the back seat was a .22 rifle and a shotgun and nothing else. There was an unopened case of beer in the trunk, but not the brand that Alex drank. Slamming the lid down, I removed the guns, took the clip off the .22, cleared out the breech and unloaded the shotgun.

"You're lyin' through your goddamned teeth and you know it!" I could hear my voice getting louder, meaner, but I knew I had to control myself. No more hitting, no more. "So where'd they all come from, how'd they get the stuff out? Eh?"

Grant Rochford was getting up slowly, still hurting. "They drove, man. Right through our gate. Guys just like you. Pickers!" He spat the word out. "Shit like you, sucks who ain't worth nothin' . . . 'cept to crawl on their fuckin' knees pickin' our tomatoes! An' what we do is none of your goddamned business, man. This is our land. We own it an' you work for us! The only difference between them others an' you is that you waited till it was dark to try and clean up, but they got you beat, man . . . beat but good, cause there's nothin' left! Nothin'! Fuckin' vultures. They couldn't even wait for the body to cool off 'fore they were up here." He was gaining confidence with every word and Shantz could sense it as he strutted around like he'd stepped out of the TV screen and was acting a part, brushing off his jeans and going to the cooler to get another beer, opening it, swilling his mouth around and then spitting it out.

I felt I was losing my advantage. And when you came down to it, what could I do anyway? What the hell would I achieve if I beat the shit out of them? All they had done, it seemed, was steal a few of Alex's beers. Hadn't I already used some of his money? That was no different really.

What was really eating away at me was not only what had been done to Alex's things, but that I was helpless in trying to deal with two cocky nineteen-year-old punks except by using violence, and I knew that in the long run even though it would make me feel good to put them down, I'd probably wind up with assault charges against me – if it got out of hand, maybe something worse. I also knew that was the way my father would have handled it, and his track record wasn't anything to write home about. Kids were different these days, had to be treated differently, like Janice, and I wasn't doing so great with her.

"Let's split." Rochford threw the beer bottle on the ground and moved toward the Duster, daring me to do something about it, while Shantz limped behind him, one eye on me all the time. The deep, throaty engine roared into life as Rochford wound down his window with an arrogant grin. He looked straight at me and spat into the grass.

"Pretty big, eh? Goin' after a bunch of pickers with guns?" It was a lame thing to say but I felt I had to have the final word.

"Them's for woodchucks, man . . . but I guess there ain't much difference." The car started to move forward, then stopped, and he looked back. "Jus' don't think you're gonna get away with tonight mister. No way." Tires spinning in the grass, the Duster howled forward, headlights making ugly shadows on the track as it disappeared round some trees, until all I could hear was the Indy exhaust taking forever to fade away.

They'd done a good job on Alex's wagon. Not only the wheels, but the seats, battery, steering wheel, sun visors, radio, headlights, spark plugs, distributor, air filter, even the windshield wipers had gone. The glove compartment had been cleaned out and its contents thrown on the ground and trodden in. Hood up and doors open, the Coleman lamp behind it throwing eerie shafts of light, it looked like the skeleton of some prehistoric monster – a silent monster that had once been Alex's pride and joy.

I cleaned up the area, putting the empty bottles, the cooler and the garden chairs in the wagon, then sat down with the last bottle of beer. The only sound was from the Coleman lamp and a truck somewhere off in the distance going through its gears. Beside me were some charts of the Caribbean I'd found, an empty Montecristo cigar box and a cigarette lighter with "Ciao Alex" engraved on the side. It had been in the grass behind where the tent was and somehow had been missed by everyone who'd been there. It worked too, so I stuffed it in my pocket as a keepsake. From now on I wouldn't have to worry about damp matches.

I must have sat there for a couple of hours, moving on to the Canadian Club when I'd finished the beer. For some reason it reminded me of sitting on the snow plough up at the cut-off when it's all quiet and I'm the only one around. Except this year it was going to be different. I'd get something, goddamnit, something better than that.

You've always got to have something to aim for.

Right. All I've got to do is find it.

The liquor did nothing for me, and when I stood up to go back to the shed I felt completely sober and very clear-headed. I couldn't believe that people you worked with side by side, day after day, people you shared something with,

256

even if it was only the same reasons for coming in the first place, that these same people would come down like a flock of vultures, like the kid said, while the body was still warm.

Even if he didn't want all that stuff any more. I just didn't believe it.

It's true. They came here about seven-thirty – from the Shantz farm, the Carson place. I think the kids were up there first. Al Rochford did nothing to stop them, just laughed and said to go right ahead and that Alex was a troublemaker anyway and had it coming to him."

"And no one tried to stop them? Call the police?"

"No. Anyway, the only phone is in the Rochford house and he wasn't about to let anyone use it. It might have been different if she'd been there, but she took the car and went into town."

The walk home had been agony. Suddenly every muscle in my body was aching and I was shivering. When the moon went behind a cloud it became very black and I wished I'd brought the Coleman lamp with me. Connie was on the step waiting, and told me what had happened while she mixed up some skim milk powder and made me hot milk. I told her about my afternoon and evening, leaving out the bit about waiting for Rita, explaining that I got the new clothes because we couldn't afford to have me not working through a cold or something. I would have loved to have sat there with some more rye or rum and blot out the whole day. You never know, when a day starts, how it's going to end. This one started out just great – only inside Alex's body something was going on that, at a set time unknown to all of us, would snuff him out and turn everything around. And then what was good about the day became instant ratshit, a nightmare, turning reasonable people into animals, making them behave probably like they'd never behaved before or would again.

"There's something else."

"What?"

"Rochford came here right after we'd finished working and said we were to be outa here by the end of the week. And he doesn't want us working the fields again. He'll pay us off tomorrow."

It was like being kicked in the guts, then stomped on for good measure. There was nothing else that could happen, no surprises left. Memories of other times like this flooded through my head: getting fired from the mill; the Raiders closing down because of the war; being alone in France; my first days as a picker; searching Toronto for work; losing touch with my kids; realizing I was stuck in Black Rapids for life.

Connie sat and watched me. "I didn't want to tell you tonight, but . . . " Her voice trailed off.

"That's okay."

"I know what a terrible day it's been for you. I felt really proud the way you stood up to Rochford this afternoon, the way you got them all behind you. Really proud . . . " She took my hand and held it, tears in her eyes. "It's probably just as well. Being fired, I mean. We can go home early and have a few days just lying around the house, relaxing, doing what we want. You know something?" Her voice was a little higher than usual as she tried to lighten the blow, even though we both knew how tough it would make things. What it meant was that I was no further ahead, after all these years, than I was when I hit Caulfield Jr.

"No, what?"

"We haven't had a real holiday since our honeymoon, so a few days off 'll do us good. Anyway, this was going to be our last summer here so it doesn't really matter." She forced a smile and squeezed my hand. "I think you need a break, a change, something to take your mind off today."

"We all do, my love. You most of all."

"I . . . I didn't mean to be so bitchy to you out there today."

"It wasn't a good day for anyone."

"I was thinking that before we go back, you could maybe go to that reunion in Toronto."

"No . . . I don't think so. That kind of thing's not for me. For people like me." I wanted to say that those two years in the army, when they let me out of Black Rapids, were what did it, that I shouldve never come back, but there was no point.

Later, in bed, under the warm covers, we held each other very close for a while and I thought how great it would have been if we couldve made love, but with Janice sleeping across the room it was impossible. It wasn't sex that I want-ed, but comfort, something to reassure me that everything was going to be all right, at least until the morning. There are times, after bad days or bad moments, when that kind of closeness acts like a tranquillizer, but for some reason you say nothing, because it doesn't seem right to be thinking about making love when you're agonized or crushed by the

260

day's events. But that's just the very time you need it, not for its own sake, but for peace of mind and that closeness that it brings.

I think Connie must have sensed the way I felt, because she took my cock in her hand and brought it to life slowly and gently, then turned on her side with her back to me and guided it into the warmth and security of herself without saying a word. I put my arms around her, kissed the back of her neck, cupped a breast in my hand while we lay there, moving very slightly for a moment, and then drifted off to sleep.

They should put it in the family medical guides.

I was up early, before it was light, made some coffee with the aid of a small flashlight, threw on a heavy sweater and took a chair outside to enjoy the quiet and the sweet fresh air that only seems to exist at that time of day.

There were things to think about, plans to make, and it could only be done in this kind of solitude, with a clear head and the first cigarette of the day. I've always got a great charge out of beating the birds up in the morning or being lucky enough to see some late straggler on its way home after a night out as the sky starts to lighten; the owl flapping silently over to the pines to the north of us, or the raccoon that the sun revealed fast asleep in the crook of a tree, probably convinced that it was safe and no one could see it.

This morning there was just the beginnings of a red glow to the east, so I settled back and took in the smell of the coffee and its warmth as I drank it.

Connie had been great last night, trying to make it as easy as she could for me, letting me down gently as I'd

261

hoped to let Rita down if she had showed up. Last night, or was it the night before, two nights, ten, two years ago? Everything that had happened yesterday seemed distant, not quite real, like scenes from a movie that played in Black Rapids once and now I couldn't remember the name of it. And making love like that took me back to the first years of our marriage when we seemed to anticipate each other. Before we stopped working at it. I mean, it's reasonable to think that if it was good once it would stay that way, but it isn't like that. At least, not with us it wasn't. Sometimes I wonder if all those years ago she was really pretending all the time, conning me, and after we were married she felt she didn't need to pretend any more. With women there's no way of telling. They can con you out of the trees. It got to the point where I'd let her go to bed and fall asleep so's we wouldn't have to face it. But maybe now there's hope again. When the time's right I'll say something, get it out in the open. I mean, we've got a lot of years left yet. And I love her, I really do.

The red glow was starting to burn furiously as the sun forced its way up, causing the sky to change colour all the way from the night of the west through deep midnight blue to sapphire. Connie always wanted a sapphire ring and I used to say one day, my love, you'll have a sapphire ring, and I believed it. But now, if I said it, I wouldn't believe it and nor would she.

The first thing I should do is fix the brakes on the wagon. That'll take a couple of hours, no more. When I go and wash I should go over to Alex's place and check it in the daylight. Poor bastard, stretched out on a slab waiting for someone to come and claim him.

Okay, so you've fixed the wagon, got everything ready to head back to B.R. Then what? Wait for school to start?

Drift back into the way things were before, waiting for Janice to take off like the others did, drinking more and more until one day they say you're not fit to drive kids around in a school bus?

Last night you said you were going to look for something else.

Yeah, but I've got to give them notice so's they can replace me. Good bus drivers aren't that easy to find.

So you'll drive the bus until they find someone but it'll drag on and they never will and it'll be summer again and you'll be heading for the tomato fields like always, only to a different farm.

Not this time. Absolutely not this time. They didn't call me Ace Harris for nothing.

Eldon, baby, that was thirty-odd years ago. Forget it.

Jesus, time flies. Anyway, this time it'll be different.

Yeah, you said that the last time and the time before that and the time before that.

Yeah?

Yeah.

But this time it really will be different. I feel different about it, my . . .

Attitude is different?

Yeah, my attitude is different, goddamn that Caulfield. But see, I feel better in myself. I don't feel sorry for myself anymore. When you see someone die like that you realize . . . well, you realize. It puts things in perspective very quickly. Like Alex said, if I wanted to I could take the world by the balls and swing it around.

You really believe that?

Well, sure. Maybe. It's a pretty big world.

And there isn't much time left.

I'm not getting any younger. You shoulda seen the lines, the grey hair yesterday.

I did.

Oh yeah.

Maybe you should go out and do something for those tomato pick-ers, get them a better deal. Take advantage of your experience.

"I'd like to see the Prime Minister, please."

"You'd what?"

"Like to see the Prime Minister. It's about the pickers in south-western Ontario. You see, everyone says how great it is to live here and I thought he might have overlooked some things and I'm representing ..."

"Oh, he doesn't have time for that. There are far more impor-tant things like expressways, building government offices, scandals to look after. Anyway, he couldn't see you right now. He's down south on a much-needed vacation, and you must know how impor-tant a vacation is. Someone will show you out. By the way, if it will help, he does like tomato soup."

I'd thought of that. Problem is that no one gives a shit – and who would listen to Eldon Harris anyway? Like I said, I'm not getting any younger and I'm running out of time.

It's worth a shot.

Not for me it isn't. After what those motherfuckers did last night to Alex's things.

It's up to you.

Yeah, I know. Like, it's my last chance.

It probably is.

Yeah, thanks a lot.

Some lights came on in the Rochford house just before the sun burst over the ridge, throwing long shadows in front of it, lighting up the mist that lay in the lower ground. Just like that bloody Tang commercial, it's a brand new morn-ing. Or is it cornflakes?

Who cares?

A robin flew onto a fence post, fluffed itself up and flew on just as a wren appeared from nowhere, landed on a wire, and burst into its mighty song. I lit up another cigarette, using Alex's lighter. "Ciao Alex." Wonder what it means, why he never used it? Okay, start thinking, hard, because the whole world will be up soon, time's running out and if you blow your last chance that's it, baby, game over. You'll be able to sit back and watch everything go down the drain while you wait for your turn to be stretched out on a slab.

The roar of an engine starting over by the house shattered the silence. Grant Rochford was leaving for work. Even from where I was, I could hear the gravel flying as he spun the wheels, the car speeding down the narrow road leaving a rooster-tail of fine dust.

The door of the shed creaked open and Connie came out to join me in her dressing gown and slippers with a saucepan of coffee and a chair, sitting beside me and throwing her head back so that her loose hair fell over her shoulders.

"I thought you'd like some fresh."

"Thanks."

We sat quiet for a while, listening to the sounds of the birds, while my mind continued to toss over ideas, hoping desperately that I would have a brainwave that would solve everything, make everything all right again. Because I knew that great as Connie had been last night, she couldn't keep it up forever, I couldn't lean on her forever and we couldn't both hope the situation would just go away.

"I'm going to Toronto."

"When?"

"As soon as the car's fixed. Today, I hope."

We both lit a cigarette and turned to the warmth of the sun, which was now a crimson ball in the sky and climbing very quickly.

"To look for a job?"

"Yeah."

She seemed very calm about the whole thing, as though she'd been expecting it and knew that it was the right thing to do.

"That reunion is sometime this week. I've got the letter in my purse."

"I'll be too busy for that. Anyway, I don't have the right clothes. They wouldn't appreciate me showing up dressed like a tomato picker." We both laughed for the first time in a long while, sipping our coffee like two people under a gigantic sun lamp.

"You won't have much luck getting a job dressed like one, either. You'll have to buy something, and if you do you can go to the reunion. It'll do you good."

"We'll see."

"How long will you be gone?"

"We haveta be outa here by Saturday, so we have four days. Maybe I can be back sooner. It'll save money."

"Where will you stay?"

"Same place as before."

"D'you have to?"

"It'll be the last time."

"Yes." But she didn't sound too sure.

I took her hand, smiling at her to keep up her spirits. I also wanted to let her know how I felt about last night, but it wasn't easy to put into words. Those kind of things have always been difficult for me. Strange. When you think about it, it should be quite easy. All I could say was, "Connie . . . thanks for last night. It was good, special." I wanted to say a whole bunch more, but I couldn't get it out.

"It was good for me too. It's bin a long time."

"Yeah."

She smiled and her eyes were blinking as Janice's radio crashed its way into the morning.

I got a great feeling driving along the Queen Elizabeth Way and seeing Toronto unfold before me, the big tower sitting like a space rocket ready for launching, the Royal York Hotel dwarfed by the office buildings stretching up to the sky. Poor old Goodhead. If he could see it now, the Bank of Commerce building, a nothing blob of grey, hard to pick out across the rusty railroad tracks.

As I came over the Humber river onto the expressway the lake to my right was covered in sailboats and cruisers. Beyond them all, a gigantic freighter was inching its way toward the harbour. I don't see how anyone couldn't be impressed, want to live there, be a part of it. Further along the Exhibition was in full swing with the rides going, roller coaster hurtling down its steep ramps, and seemingly every hundred yards or so, a sign telling me the time and temperature as small aircraft took off from the island airport. To think that I'd never been up in a plane. Now that would be something, a challenge, learning to fly. Maybe I should've joined the air force instead of the army.

Then down a ramp near the ferry boat terminal, where

now there was a huge new hotel and a lineup of people, three deep, waiting for the next boat, and north to the city, the buildings crowded in by crappy signboards and neon on the sides of office blocks telling me where I could get my new glasses, what television set to buy, where to stay and who to insure my life with – all just as tacky as it was in '46.

Some things never change.

The brake job wouldn't have taken as long as it did except that Al Rochford came to pay us off, ignoring me throughout the whole transaction as we sat around the small table in the shed. The rat traps hadn't been cleared and the air was still stale from three people's sleep, mixed with the odour of breakfast, the first cooked one we'd had in three weeks. Finally he asked if we could move outside to tie things up, and I couldn't help smiling. So you finally got a short taste of what we had to endure all summer.

I counted the money, then stopped and counted it again.

"This isn't right."

"What d'you mean, it's not right?"

"You've shortchanged us."

"Horseshit. It's right! Your payment less shippin' costs to the cannin' factory."

"That wasn't part of the deal!" I was shouting. "That wasn't part of the goddamned deal, and you know it!"

"Costs have gone up all over. We ain't no different."

I grabbed him and slammed him across the hood of his truck, ready to murder him until Connie tried to separate us. Finally, slowly, I let him go. His face was white as he straightened up, fists clenched.

268

"He's very edgy, Mr. Rochford, what with yesterday and you firing us all." Connie tried to mend things while I lit up a cigarette, the flame from Alex's lighter shooting high. "He didn't mean to hurt you but he's right, you're cheatin' us and you know it. You never said anythin' about taking off shippin' charges. We worked all summer for this."

"Don't waste your breath. The sonofabitch shoulda lived in the south on a plantation workin' with all those coloured types. Bin right up his street!"

"Lookit, I had enough of your shit. You and Harpin were nothin' but troublemakers an' I'm running a business here an' I don't need your type upsettin' the other workers. You all got one big choice. You don't like it, fuck off and find somethin' else like you're about to! Let me tell you somat!" He was stabbing the air with his finger like my father used to. "You'll be walkin' the streets lookin' for work from now till hell freezes over, 'cause you ain't worth a pinch a coonshit! We get the dregs of the whole fuckin' country come out here to work 'cause that's all they're good for! And you're the worst of the lot, an' that's sayin' somethin' when you consider the shit that comes here every year. Losers every fuckin' one of them. Jerks who've screwed up so much they've hit rock bottom and they're gonna stay there 'cause they wouldn't know how to climb back up!" He brushed off his beige cotton pants, picked up his sweaty, dust-stained hat and put it on his head and lit up a half-smoked Colt. He blew out smoke and his voice went back to normal. "My family's bin workin' this land since 1860 and we was brought up Christian people. We respect our roots an' other people. It's only because of that I'm not throwing you all out on your asses right this minute even though I've a good mind to." As he got into his truck he went to say something else, but decided not to and drove away.

It was getting to be a habit, roughing up Rochfords. I was surprised that he hadn't mentioned his son.

After nearly three months of work we had, between us, nineteen hundred and forty three dollars, less than two hundred and twenty dollars a month each. As Christian Al would say, we also had room and board found, the most beautiful washroom facilities in the whole of southern Ontario, a natural, pure stream to wash in, and the rats thrown in for no extra charge. I bet they just love Al down at the church in his best suit on Decoration Sunday, when the whole family go to pay their respects to the relatives who've been working this land since 1860. Bullshit! Old Man Rochford must have turned in his grave a thousand times.

Connie cried and Janice even switched off her radio. For a moment I felt like Judas, as they looked at me and then at the money. There's nothing like reality to bring things into perspective. Trouble was, I'd ignored it for years. It didn't help having that sonofabitch tell me I'd hit rock bottom and didn't know how to climb back up. What would he know about it?

Before I left for Toronto there was one thing I had to do – find out what would happen to Alex. There was no way I could forget about him and hope that someone would take care of it. No one should go out that way, unnoticed, as though he'd never existed.

The problem was that the best price I could get locally was two hundred and fifty dollars, a package deal the mortician called it, that included a casket, cremation and burial without visitation. Visitation, for Chrissakes! Why don't they speak normal English? Under the new circumstances there was no way I could afford it, and anyway, I was sure that Connie wouldn't go along with spending all that money to bury someone she hardly knew and didn't like.

"He has no next-of-kin?" The mortician looked at me over his glasses in his plywood, phony oak office, obviously anxious to get rid of me.

"No." There was no point in mentioning his wife up in Pembroke. She'd made it clear she didn't want him.

"Then the City of Chatham will have to bury him. They do it quite often. Unidentified bodies pulled out of the Thames river."

"They pay for it all?"

"Yes."

The ultimate handout.

"I could phone the Clerk's office and see what's happening. The hospital will have been in touch by now."

"Thank you." Maybe I misjudged him. He didn't seem so bad now. Maybe he really cared.

It meant driving back to the farm to tell Connie that the funeral was to be held in two days' time and that I'd be back for it, but I felt better about the whole thing.

To be honest, the idea of staying at a hostel didn't grab me, so I found a room on Ontario Street for three dollars a night and went downtown to shop. New clothes, newspapers and some food. In Eaton's basement I found a goodlooking plain jacket, a couple of shirts and a tie. Then, at the last minute, I decided to get a pair of pants, and spent twenty minutes pleading with the salesman to get the cuffs turned up while I waited. Finally, I think to get rid of me, he said they'd be half an hour, so I wandered up Yonge Street, took a look at

Birks' window wondering how much sapphire rings would be, bought the papers and had a coffee in Kresge's while I pored over the Situations Vacant columns, then picked up my pants.

At College Street I ran into a whole bunch of people handing out leaflets telling me I shouldn't buy California grapes because of the way the pickers were being exploited and how great some guy called Cesar Chavez was who was trying to get them a better deal.

Crazy world.

My jobhunting went no better than the first time I'd tried to find work in this city. Oh, there were plenty of jobs advertised all right, but either I was too old, or I didn't have the experience, or I had to fill in ninety-five forms and they said they'd be in touch with me.

Sure.

It was a depressing day. I mean, I wasn't just trying for any old job like in a carwash or anything, but something respectable, so that Connie and Janice could be proud, and anyway, I had a point to prove and there wouldn't be another chance.

I bought a mickey of rye instead of dinner and stopped off at a bookstore for something to read. I'd chosen a thick paperback about the war and was about to leave when I was riveted to the spot. There, staring me in the face, was a display of books called *Letters to my Daughter* by Muriel Lobraico. Jesus H. Christ! It had to be the same one. I mean, how many people would have a name like that? On the back cover was a picture of her with the same black hair, only now she wore glasses, and to be truthful, if I hadn't known the name I might not have recognized her. Anyway, the back cover said she was born in a small northern Ontario town, went to U of T, was married with three children and this was her first book of short stories. Muriel Lobraico, for Godsakes! So I bought that too, and picked up a copy of the Toronto *Star* on the way back to my room.

There was an ad in the paper, bus drivers wanted by the TTC, good pay, uniform provided. Now there was something. And I had experience, admittedly not driving one of those big mothers that spewed fumes around Toronto, but hell, it was experience nonetheless. That perked me up and I planned to be at the employment office when they opened at eight the next morning. I celebrated the find with a stiff shot of rye and water. After the second drink I began to think the idea of dropping in on the reunion wasn't such a bad one. After all, there'd be free booze, probably some food, so what the hell. And like Connie said, the break would do me good. And why shouldn't I go? I earned the bloody medal and the only thing it's been good for is a job driving the school bus. Anyway, if I wanted to I could take the world by the balls and swing it around.

It was a mistake. A big mistake. Not only was there no free booze, you had to buy tickets. A dollar a drink, fifty cents for beer, and it cost twenty-five dollars to get in, including dinner and wine.

Standing back in the area outside the Ontario Room, I watched people arrive, check in at the door and move inside. So I waited for the right moment, when the man at the door was surrounded by new arrivals, then slipped inside when he wasn't looking. It was that easy. Jesus, I'dve hated to have him in our unit. I bought a beer ticket when I saw the size of the liquor shots and wandered around, feeling a little strange in my new jacket and pants among all the suits, vests and medal ribbons, much as I did at that party in Kirkland Lake years ago. The conversations were mixed. One very British type with a grey waxed moustache and face to match was talking about his horses up in King City, while others were going on about when they did this or that, laughing and slapping each other on the back, and over it all came the Brit loud and clear, going on about something that happened at Joker's Hill (I don't remember that battle) and how absolutely splendid Princess Anne had been at

274

the Olympics. Most of them sounded like they were sorry the war had come to an end, and it occurred to me that I might have been better off if I'dve signed on. I had one more beer and left.

I was going down the big staircase to the lobby where I heard running footsteps behind me and saw this bald-headed guy running along the corridor waving. I moved to let him go by, but he slowed up as he got close to me, panting, "Hey! Harris! Sergeant Eldon Harris DSM!" He rushed up to me, grabbed my hand and shook it heavily. "Harris, for Chrissakes! Don't you remember me? Redford!"

"Redford? My God! You old bastard. Howthehellare-you?" He stood there, getting his breath back.

"Out of shape, I think. Jesus, you're just as fast as you were in those days. Wheeeew! That's better. Listen, I saw you up there, thought it might be you, then I saw you leaving. God, I couldn't let a chance like that get by. You saved my life back there."

"I did?"

"Modest as ever. You know you did. I don't mind telling you now, I was scared shitless. Shitless! If you hadn't told me what to do I think we all would have had it. Let's go and have a quiet drink."

He led me to the Black Knight Room, where I felt better in the dim light, not so self-conscious in my clothes, which looked a little tacky against his grey suit with a vest and a handkerchief in the breast pocket.

"You haven't changed that much, eh? Me? I've lost my hair, put on weight, gone to seed, I'd say. That must be a tan from your cottage. The outdoor life. Me, I'm right out of condition. Too much time behind a desk."

"I thought you lived in Kamloops."

"I did. But everyone has to get out of Kamloops at some

time or another. I had the chance of a partnership in my father-in-law's firm here, so I grabbed it. What'll it be?"

A pretty waitress in a brief costume with a plunging neckline stood over us, waiting.

"Er . . . rye and water, please."

"J&B on the rocks." He looked at me, smiling broadly. "Well, for Chrissakes. I just can't get over meeting you. It's the first of these things I've ever been to, and the last I might add, and I just never thought . . . for Chrissakes! You still living up in . . . where was it?"

"Black Rapids."

"Yeh. Black Rapids. Sonofabitch. I mean, it seems crazy now. Here we are, two people who lived through that nightmare, sitting in a bar thirty-odd years later as though nothing happened. I'll never forget the way you took over and bluffed those Krauts right out of their drawers like you were born to it. And they gave *me* a medal, for Chrissakes. I was sure they'dve made you an officer." The waitress served the drinks. Her perfume and the shape of her arm took me back to Joyce. Why Joyce, after so long? Why Redford? All these memories?

"Listen, I'll be quite honest, when we were hiding there behind that rubble, shooting at them, I pissed my pants I was so scared, and that's the truth. And then when Gimby got it, d'you remember Gimby? Got it right through the head? Well, after that I figured it was just a matter of time and I as good as gave up. Only you took over like you were Monty or someone and I had no choice but to follow. I pissed in my pants, Harris. Cheers."

"Cheers."

"You still live in that place?"

"Yeah."

"You mean you came all that way just for this bash?"

276

"No. We were just . . . visiting. I wouldn't have come otherwise."

"What're you doing these days? I kept my eye on the paper to see if you ever made it with the Leafs, they could use someone, eh, but I never did see it."

"No . . . I gave up hockey. Family reasons."

"So what are you doing to look so healthy, prosperous?"

Dear Jesus, what do you tell a guy who thinks you're a fuckin' hero who saved his life and acted like Montgomery? An ex-tomato picker? School bus driver? Snow plough operator? An out-of-work guy looking for a job? A gemmologist? What do you tell a guy who's a lawyer, even if he did piss his pants once?

What d'you want to impress him for anyway? What's the point?

I don't know.

He's bin open with you. How many guys do you know who'd admit they were scared shitless and pissed their pants?

Not many.

Not many? None! So why the big deal? You ashamed or something?

Yeah. I guess so. No, just uncomfortable.

I thought you could take the world by the balls and swing it around your head?

I did too, before I walked into this hotel. Those guys intimidate. Make me feel worthless.

That's what your old man said you'd feel.

Yeah.

"I'm in carpentry. Do carpentry work."

"Well, if you're as good at that as you were with the Piat you must be pretty good."

Now what the hell d'you say that for? One lie leads to another lie. Remember that?

Yeah. But I got my pride. You remember that. Okay? Now shut up!

"Ever thought of moving to Toronto?"

"Yeah, lots of times. In fact that's why I'm down here now. Looking the scene over. I figured it's about time we saw something of the world." He laughed and signalled for the waitress and ordered the same again.

"Too bad you're not living here now. I could use you. We've just moved into a new place and we need some work done. You know the kind of stuff, new rec room, knock out a wall on the third floor to make two rooms into one for a studio for my wife. She's a painter. Does sculpture too. Do up the kitchen. Are you union?"

"No."

"That's the problem here, most of the guys you try to get are union, want an arm and a leg. Ten, twelve dollars an hour plus materials. Ridiculous. Think people are made of money. One guy wanted ten grand! Ten grand! Cheers."

"That's high."

"Goddamned right it is. Listen, if you're thinking of coming to Toronto anyway, why don't you take a look at it? Give me a quote. No harm done. Eh?"

"Well . . . "

"You're on. Let's forget that crap upstairs and go back to my place. Lisa'll make something for us. She's my second wife. Got divorced from the first. Bad scene. I came here for a convention and went to this art gallery opening and liked the work so much I wound up marrying the artist. It was cheaper than buying all her paintings." He laughed out loud and signalled for the check. "The first one was bad, though. One of those wartime things. You know, back from the army, a medal, a local hero and the girl next door? Of course you know. That's why I can't finish the inside of the house at union rates. Alimony."

"Let me get it."

278

"Are you kidding? This is on me. A kind of thankyou. Anyway, I want Lisa to meet you. I told her all about you and she appreciates what you did. You know something? It's taken me half a lifetime to be finally happy. Half a lifetime! And I wouldn't have had that if it hadn't been for you." He put a two-dollar tip down on the tray. Two dollars! That's almost six baskets. "It's a long time to wait, but it's been worth it. It can be a tough bloody world, don't you think?"

"Yeah."

We drove north, up University, in his silver-grey Thunderbird, moving effortlessly through the traffic, past the Parliament buildings and the office of the Prime Minister who liked tomato soup – and all the time my mind was whirring, trying to solve the situation I was getting myself into. I mean, here was a chance, but I hadn't done any carpentry work for years, I had no tools, no nothing, but Jesus, it could set us up, it would be a beginning.

You can bluff your way through like you did with those Germans.
Sure. Me bluff a lawyer? Come on!
Then forget it, quote high or tell him you've changed your mind.
But think of the chance.
You think of the chance. It's better than driving a TTC bus.
What would happen after this job?
You gotta gamble.
With someone else's money?
You built a greenhouse once.
Yeah, facing the wrong way.
Needum badlium, conquestium mondo.
Bullshit.

What do I ever aim for? That's what he said.

Sure, and all that crap about swinging the world by the balls. It's me that's goin' out on a limb.

I could feel myself sweating as I lit a cigarette. It would be madness. False pretences. And him a lawyer. He could really stick it to me. One thing was for sure, I was on my own with this one and I knew that if I went back to Black Rapids with nothing, they'd lock the doors and never let me out again. That would be it. Forever.

He lived in a large three-story house off Avenue Road, with garage doors he controlled from inside the car, large rooms with fancy furniture, thick broadloom, strange paintings on the walls and even stranger sculptures standing in corners – done by his wife, I guessed – a heated swimming pool out at the back and a long, narrow garden stretching off beyond the pool. It was without a doubt the richest house I'd been in since the night we won the cup in Kirkland Lake. Lisa was about his age, quite goodlooking with a good figure, wearing jeans (why would someone with all that money wear jeans?) with a loose top that reminded me of the choir-boys back at St. Mark's in B.R., only she looked much better in it, and it was obvious, especially when she stood against a window, that she wasn't wearing a bra.

Connie had had lots of arguments with Janice over not wearing a bra, saying it was cheap and would get her into trouble, especially in the fields. Connie won.

Lisa cooked us some steaks and Redford lent me a pair of shorts so that we could go swimming, and I must say, I felt much more relaxed sitting around in them with a beer than being dressed. We looked over the work to be done, making notes, and as the list got larger I got more nervous. On one hand I felt pretty sure I could do it, but that other voice kept telling me that I was going in over my head and with my record I was bound to screw it up. On top of which I didn't have the right tools and would need to spend a lot of money in order to do the work, didn't know the present costs of materials and really had no idea how long it would take, assuming I could do it in the first place.

"So what d'you think?" Redford lit a cigar as we stood in one of the rooms that he wanted extended to become a studio for Lisa.

"I don't know. I'd have to work things out and get back to you. There's also the question of when you want it done." I figured he'd say immediately and I'd have an out, using other unfinished work as the excuse.

"You can do it when you like. There's no hurry. I realize, if you plan to come to Toronto, you'll need time to make the move, settle in. Let's say by the end of next January."

"Can I phone you tomorrow?"

"Sure. Anytime. Let's go and have another drink."

The two of us sat in a room he called the library and drank until about midnight, yet for some reason I didn't feel the least bit pissed or even lightheaded, and I didn't even seem to be slurring my words. Redford, though, was sinking further into his chair with each drink.

"You know something, Harris? Everyone comes to Toronto eventually. I woulda come years ago only she wouldn't have any part of it. My first wife, that is." He shook his head and stared into his drink for a while. Then, shakily, he lit another cigar. "I mean, we had it made. Everything. I had a good job, we had a house, you name it and we had it. Except we weren't happy. Can you imagine? We weren't happy, for Chrissakes. It was like living in a vacuum, an icy, cold, silent vacuum. I even suggested going to Vancouver, but no way! I musta had rocks in my head for sticking it out so long. Fifteen years! Fifteen years of Goddamned purgatory. There I was during the day, in my office, advising people whose marriages were turning into ratshit, and I couldn't even set my own house in order. Now isn't that crazy? When it happened everyone was stunned. We were the ideal couple. She was beautiful, the perfect hostess. Everyone always said what a great cook she was. A gourmet cook, they all said, and she took it so seriously she started boiling eggs in wine!" He laughed for a moment, but it faded quickly as his head dropped and he stared into his glass. "Of course, there was no way I could get involved with anyone else in town. She'dve found out the next day. I tell you, Lisa was my salvation. Next to you, that is. I mean, if we hadn't got through that night none of it would have happened and some other poor bastard would have married the Ice Woman of Kamloops. The Ice Woman Cometh! Not very often let me tell you, not very often. She kept it sealed up for posterity. I told her she should donate it to medical science for a transplant. Be like new. Have another drink."

"I should be getting back."

"One for the road." He pulled himself out of his chair and lurched over to the bar, complete with small refrigerator, set in the bookshelves, and poured two more drinks. "Hey . . . d'you remember those women in Europe? Shall I tell you something? Never told a soul before. The only time I ever got laid was when I paid for it with a hooker. All that other stuff was pure bullshit! Ha! What d'you think of that?"

"I'll tell you somethin'. In Europe . . . it was the same for me. Didn't get to first base! But Christ, I was a good liar."

282

"You too? I don't believe it! Absolutely don't believe it! You're just saying that to make me feel good. I know you better'n that!"

The liquor must be getting to me after all. For the first time I admit something like that . . . and he doesn't believe me. For the first time I try to be normal about it all and –

"You know something, Eldon? It's a funny thing about that night in '45, that night and the next day, the things that stand out in my mind, apart from being scared. There you were, taking over like I said, as though you were born to it, but what I really remember was you sitting down after it was all over and nonchalantly drinking from a bottle of cognac. I thought that was real style. Like all you needed was a pair of pearl-handled revolvers. And then you started talking about some bloody bird. I mean, in the middle of the war, dead Germans lying around having only just survived ourselves, and you tell me about a bird."

I smiled, remembering myself. Jesus, that was a lifetime ago.

"Boy, you really impressed the hell out of me. Figured you could do just about what you pleased in life. And me? I was the dunderhead who knocked the rubble over and attracted their attention. It didn't feel very good, I can tell you."

"It worked out."

"Yeah, it did, thank God. It did. In more ways than one."

I took a cab back to my room, telling him I'd phone him the next day. It had been a funny evening, I guess mainly because I hadn't talked about the war for so long and it seemed strange to be discussing it in Redford's library. Like

283

we were talking about something that had happened to someone else, or discussing a movie or book that had been written about it and didn't actually involve us. Redford from Kamloops who used to hunt bear and figures everyone comes to Toronto eventually.

My mind was still very clear as I sat down on the bed with a drink from the mickey. There was one big decision to make, and not only was my mind clear, but I felt very calm about it. I'd taken over like I was born to it, he'd said, taken over like I was Monty. Thought I had real style and that they'd make me an officer. Me! Eldon Harris!

What it amounted to was that my whole life had been funnelled down to this one moment in a crappy room in Toronto, where one way or the other, I would decide not only my future, but Connie's and Janice's too.

And the most important person to consider was Janice. That's where the cycle had to be broken. For Connie and me it would mean making what time we have left more enjoyable. It would be a challenge, and that would be a good thing. But for Janice it would be a decision that would affect her whole future, her whole life, and it had to be the right one.

He made me this offer and I've decided to take it." There was a long silence while Connie and Janice just looked at me, not quite sure if I'd gone out of my mind or not.

After I'd got back from Redford's I'd sat up until about three-thirty in the morning going over figures, working out how much I could charge, how much I could make, approximately how much I would need to invest in tools, and how much we could save to carry us through until the next job.

Save!

Did you hear that?

Saving was something we hadn't done since Davie was born, and I almost had to look the word up to find out what it meant. I also tried to anticipate what Connie might say so that I would have good arguments to give her. One thing was for sure, for some reason I felt very good about it, and this was one chance I wasn't going to let slip past. Not this time.

I lay back on the bed with the last of the mickey, with a feeling I hadn't had since we won the cup way back when, a feeling that this one was really going to work.

I reached Redford at his office the next morning and told him that I would do it, then went to Simpsons and Canadian Tire to price the tools before heading back to the farm to tell Connie and Janice. I had it all figured out. I would buy the tools out of the tomato money and then rent a room in Toronto while I did the job and Connie tried to sell the house, which could be difficult because people weren't exactly fighting each other to live in Black Rapids. At the same time I would look for a place to rent for the three of us, preferably with a basement so that I could set up a workshop, and then she and Janice would come down to Toronto. I was going to make eight dollars an hour, three hundred and eighty four dollars for a forty-eight-hour week, and I figured the whole job would take about eight weeks, which would give us over three thousand dollars plus a small markup on the materials.

Connie was the first one to speak as we waited to leave for the funeral.

"But you haven't done carpentry for years. Supposing something goes wrong and he fires you?"

"That's a risk we've gotta take. Lookit, I know the responsibility I'm takin' on and that for eight dollars an hour I've gotta produce. It's . . . like comin' through with the decidin' goal in sudden-death overtime to win the biggest one of them all."

"What? What on earth has hockey got to do with it? Sometimes I wonder about you, Eldon."

Yeah. Well you wouldn't understand the way I see things now and again. "Forget it. I want you to realize that I'm not doing this just for myself but for all of us and for Janice in particular. It'll be a whole new life. A new world. No more tomato pickin' – "

"This was going to be the last summer anyway."

"I know, I know. What I mean is, I won't haveta bum for work any more. We'll be makin' real money for the first time in our life. It'll be like a new beginnin' for all of us. It's . . . well, it's somethin' I just feel I've gotta do. For once in my life I want to try somethin' to make good. It's very important to me . . . because I know I can do it. Finally make somethin' of my life, be someone . . . not live out of . . . well, not live outa some scrapbook that says what a great guy I used to be, what a goddamned hero I was . . . a collector of tie-pins and photographs on the wall . . . you know what I mean. I've got a lot of years left – we've got a lot of years left – and when I go I don't want to go like Alex where no one gives a shit, where the city picks up the tab and people say Eldon Who?"

There was another silence and I lit a cigarette and started to pace the shed, finally stopping at the window with my back to them while they thought about it. I was starting to get edgy, figuring that Connie would give me a hard time over it, throw up her parents at me and what would happen to them, how could I be so selfish, it was easy for me, I didn't have anyone to worry about. Well, if it came down to that . . . I didn't want to think about the alternative. The time had come to put up or shut up. There are some chances in life you just have to grab onto; this could be my last one, and I didn't intend to let it go.

The silence seemed to go on forever, so I gave them my final thoughts on the subject, pacing as I did so, stabbing the air with my finger to make a point, wishing to hell she'd say something. "It'll be good for Janice. She'll be able to finish her schoolin' there, better schoolin' I might add than she'd get up in B.R., and when she leaves, she'll have a better opportunity for jobs. There's things to do there. Lots of

287

movie houses, the islands, the museum, science centre . . . hell, we can even go out and have somethin' to eat in more than one restaurant. And if the worst comes to the worst, which it won't," I didn't want to say this because it would sound as though I wasn't sure of myself, but it would give Connie something less to worry about, something less to argue about, an option to hang on to, "I can always get a job with the TTC drivin' a bus or a subway train. Good money, uniform. And I can drive a bus pretty good. So we're covered in case of an emergency." I went right up to Connie and took her hand, looking right into her eyes. "But we won't need it, love. It's gonna work and in no time I'll be the best guy in town doin' that kind of work. Just like I am on the snowplough. I can see it now. Eldon Harris Remodeling. One day we'll even have our own truck. So whatdaya say?"

This was the moment, the crunch. Slowly she squeezed my hands, looking up at me with tears in her eyes, and nodded.

"Wow!" Janice leaped off her chair and flung her arms around me and kissed me, then hurled herself on Connie and did the same.

"You mean it? D'you really mean it? Eh mum?"

"Yes . . . I really mean it. We've got nothin' to lose, have we?" She looked around the room, dull and drab and revolting as ever. "I mean, when your dad says he's going to do somethin', doesn't matter what it is, he usually does it."

"Greato! Way to go!" She danced around as happy as I'd ever seen her. "When will you start?"

"Maybe in a couple of weeks. I'll drive you home, tell the Town I'm leavin', spend a week reading up and practising, then head down to Toronto. Start everything movin'." Connie blew her nose, then turned my wrist to see the time.

288

"We should be leaving for the funeral."

"Yeah."

"Do I look all right?"

"Just fine."

"The last funeral we went to was your mother's. I thought the Reverend Campbell gave a nice service."

"Yeah, he did." It was all he could do to hide his boredom. Probably couldn't wait to get back to Hilda Ecclestone's mother.

"I don't have a hat."

"You don't need a hat. It's bein' there that counts."

The funeral director smiled and said we had a nice day for it. Then he nodded to the United Church minister that everything was ready, and we picked up the grey, clothbound casket, three men from the funeral home and myself pressed into service as pallbearers, and walked slowly toward the grave site, followed by the minister, the funeral director, Connie and Janice. The funeral director who made the arrangements for the city had suggested getting the Salvation Army to officiate, but there was no way I'd go along with that. I mean they do good things and help a lot of people, but I knew that the last thing Alex would have wanted would have been someone from the Sally Ann having the last say as he was lowered to his final resting place. So we settled for the United Church as a saw-off, seeing that Alex hadn't belonged to any particular church.

We had driven from the farm in silence, each of us with our own thoughts about the speed with which everything had happened. It didn't seem the right time to be excited and enthused about what the future held. Or even worried. I still didn't quite believe that Connie hadn't given me an argument, and that unnerved me a little. It was going too smoothly; the whole business with Redford was all too good to be true. There had to be a pitfall somewhere along the line. There always was.

We turned off Park Avenue onto Cemetery Drive. Connie took my hand and gave me an encouraging smile as we pulled in behind the hearse parked under the trees. In the rear view mirror I could see Janice, tanned and looking more than ever like a younger version of Connie, still staring ahead, lost in another world. It was going to be a strange-looking funeral, with Janice in jeans and a sweater, Connie in slacks and a blouse and me in my new clothes from Toronto – the only things we had that came anywhere close to being right for the occasion. I switched the engine off and we sat for a second or two looking around at the quiet, deserted cemetery, the gravestones brilliant in the sun.

In the shadow under the trees stood the group from the funeral home, talking to the minister; they looked like a picture of death itself with their black jackets and grey pinstripe pants, big, black Cadillac gleaming behind them, and beyond that, the minister's black Volvo, all framed by the dark trunks and hanging leaves of the trees. Our engine spluttered slightly before it stopped, and five white faces turned and looked at us, then away, the funeral director breaking from the group and walking toward us, his hands clasped in front of him, his black shoes catching the sun as he stepped out from the shade. Connie squeezed my hand and picked up her purse. "It's very sad. Living all those years and only having three people who actually knew you coming to your funeral. It's very sad."

We were standing around the grave listening to the minister when I saw Al Rochford's wife standing about fifty feet away beside a gravestone, facing in our direction. She was wearing a flowered dress, a small dark blue hat and white gloves, holding a tiny purse in front of her. When the funeral director turned to where I was looking he waved her over to join us, but she shook her head a couple of times and then looked down at the ground, fidgeting with her purse. She looked very pretty in a subdued sort of way, and it was hard to believe that she was the mother of a kid the age of Grant Rochford.

That's four of us, Alex. I'm not too sure how well you knew each other, but she's here, paying her respects or whatever in her own sort of way.

The minister droned on, sometimes looking right over our heads as he spoke. Fifteen feet away a robin tugged at a worm. Janice shifted from foot to foot while the men from the funeral parlour looked properly solemn, one of them picking at a piece of skin on his finger. At a certain point the funeral director, who was standing at one corner of the grave next to the minister, carefully slid his foot onto a lever, partially hidden by the phony grass they'd put down over the newly-dug earth, and pressed it down. The casket started its slow descent to the bottom of the hole. Out of the corner of my eye I could see that Connie was crying and fumbling in her purse for some Kleenex while the minister said a prayer, the words blurring as I felt my throat tighten and my eyes fill. "We therefore commit his body to the ground" . . . it really was game over . . . "earth to earth, ashes to ashes" . . . really the end . . . "dust to dust" . . . poor bastard . . . "in sure and certain hope of the Resurrection to eternal life" . . . he had so much going for him . . . "through our Lord Jesus Christ" . . . so much to do . . . "Our

292

Father" . . . trouble was I didn't have a chance to say anything to him . . . "who art in heaven" . . . to thank him . . . "give us this day our daily bread" . . . why the hell should it please Almighty God to take to himself the soul of our dear brother? . . . "and lead us not into temptation but deliver us from evil" . . . what sort of God would stop him getting his boat, stop him doing the things he had to do? . . . "I am the resurrection and the life, he that believeth in me, though he were dead, yet shall he live" . . . it's all bullshit, they get you coming and going with doubletalk . . . "and whosoever liveth and believeth in me shall never die" . . . and blackmail, that's all it is, blackmail, so it's better to believe and make sure you've got your bases covered . . . "the grace of our Lord Jesus Christ and the love of God" . . . just in case . . . "and the fellowship of the Holy Ghost" . . . I haven't cried since I was a kid, since that day my father hit me and I decided to join the army . . . "be with us all evermore" . . . no, since Gimby got it. I've never felt anything at a funeral before until today – and now I'm crying.

Amen.

As I looked up, I could still hear the dull, sickening thud from when the minister threw the earth on top of the casket. By tonight it would all be filled in, and that would be that. One day, Alex, when I've got it made, I'll come back and put a gravestone up so that people will know. Then I realized that Al Rochford's wife was nowhere to be seen, like she'd vanished from the face of the earth. Moments later I saw their Buick moving toward the gate, flickering as it appeared and disappeared between the gravestones.

The minister gave us a nod, indicating that it was all over, then came and shook our hands, telling us how good it was of us to come and how he wished he'd known Alex Harpin and what a good man he must have been. How the hell would he know? Why the hell does he go through all this phony crap? Or is he programmed like some goddamned computer to spout that stuff? Jesus, I could have said some real things about him, made the whole service human, like there was someone in that box who really counted.

Behind us, Janice, who hadn't been sure what to do with the flowers she'd picked at the farm, or when, placed some wild michaelmas daisies and Queen Anne's lace at the head of the grave, the only flowers there were, and then we walked back to the wagon, Connie taking my hand. In the distance we could hear the wail of a train, and someone said that it was the 2:53 for Toronto from Windsor pulling out on time while someone else talked about getting the hearse washed and then going for a beer.

Business as usual.

Like he'd never died.

On the way from Toronto I'd bought a six-pack to celebrate, and when we got back to the farm we sat out under a tree and had a beer before starting the packing and making plans to drive back to Black Rapids the next day.

It was the first time we'd had together during the day, with nothing to do, since the early summer, and even if the beers were warm, it was a welcome change.

"Was that Al Rochford's wife at the funeral?" She knew damned well it was.

"Yeah, I think so." Now I was playing the game.

"I wonder why she was there?"

"I dunno. Maybe because he worked here – for Rochford."

"You'dve thought that he would have come. Out of respect. It was the least he could do."

"You should know better than that."

"I spose. Funny that she stood where she did, and then left so quickly."

"Maybe she's shy."

"Yes. I felt terrible when I saw her in a hat."

"Oh, come on."

"Strange she'd be there."

"Yeah."

The thing that surprised me was that the minister didn't have a beard. I'd done my own survey driving back and forth from B.R. to the farm and discovered that over fifty per cent of the men who drove Volvos wore beards, and I mentioned this to Alex over a beer one night. He thought about it for a moment and then broke into a grin. "You know what I think? I'd bet that most of them were either school teachers or social workers and all of them voted NDP. It's symbolic. I think, me old darlin', we've just made an important social observation! Let's drink to it." And he let out his deep belly laugh and burped.

We had just finished the packing and Connie was preparing dinner when she broke into a smile. She took aim and tossed a can of spaghetti into one of the cartons and a loaf of bread after it. "I've got it! Why don't we have steak for a really good last dinner here? A celebration dinner! I mean, it is a kind of occasion, getting that offer and all."

The way she tossed the spaghetti away told me that there'd be no arguing. And anyway, what the hell? We hadn't had anything to celebrate in years.

"Why not? I'll drive into town and get some – maybe another six-pack as well."

"I'll come with you." Janice was halfway out of the door and heading for the wagon when she said it. Connie stood there, her arms at her side, quite openly happy, the happiest I'd seen her in years.

"Eldon. I think it's the right thing. It's going to work. I can feel it."

"Me too."

"You'd better hurry. Before they close."

I gave her a kiss, checked my money, and went to the car. For some reason I had a lump in my throat, so I pretended to look for my keys until I could control it, then got in and started the engine.

"You know dad, maybe it was a lucky break, us gettin' fired like that."

"Yeah, maybe it was."

At the farm gate we were practically forced off the road by the Schantz kid in his pickup as he and Grant Rochford roared out ahead of us, leaving a choking trail of dust for us to drive through until we hit the county road.

We had planned to get T-bones, but when I saw the price we settled for wing steaks, the first real meat, aside from hamburger, that we'd had since leaving B.R. almost three months ago. This one I was going to enjoy.

To tell the truth, when I was eating at Redford's I felt a little guilty, knowing that Connie and Janice were probably having pork and beans or the canned spaghetti, while I was feeding my face with two-inch-thick sirloin, mushrooms and a French red wine. It was the same when I bought the mickey, knowing that Connie liked to have a drink the same as me. Even though I told myself it was stupid to feel that way, it took the edge off the dinner.

I bought the beer, filled up the wagon for the first part of the trip home, and we drove back to the farm with Janice very excited by the prospect of moving to Toronto.

Jesus, I've built her hopes right up now. There's no way

297

I can't deliver. If I don't that'll be it between us and, more than likely, between Connie and me.

"You know, dad, they have all those rock concerts in Toronto. Alice Cooper, Bachman-Turner Overdrive – "

"The what?"

"That's the name of a group, dummy."

"I shoulda known."

"Gordon Lightfoot."

Now there's someone I know. For some reason his songs mean something to me, because he manages to write things the way I'd like to be able to say them. He understands what human beings are all about. Now there was a guy who got out of a small town and did something.

"George Harrison. They hold them at the Gardens."

"Maple Leaf Gardens?"

"Yeah."

Lord Jesus, what's the world coming to?

"That's like playing hockey in a cathedral."

"They have concerts in those places too."

"Yeah?"

"Well, in churches anyway."

"There you are then."

"I wonder what the schools are like?"

"Big. Some have fifteen hundred kids to a school."

"Wow. Should be good for summer work."

"I was thinkin' that maybe you should have a summer off, the rest of your summers till you leave school. Enjoy doin' what you please." She looked at me for a moment, a little uncertain.

"You sure?"

"Sure I'm sure."

"I've . . . " She gave a small laugh, "I was thinkin' that I wouldn't know what to do with all that time in the summer

. . . but with all the things they've got there, the stores, the Ex, I'd be pretty busy. I've always wanted to go to a cottage and swim, water ski . . . have marshmallows over a fire. It's bin a dream of mine."

"Maybe we will. Who knows?"

"I think mum'll like it there once she gets used to it."

"I hope so."

"D'you think we'll have one of those fancy apartments with elevators and balconies, doormen, speakers down to the lobby and things like that? Like you see on TV?"

"Hold on, eh? I'm not Roy Thompson."

"Who's he?"

"He was a guy who made it. From nothing to millions. He proved that if you really want to, it can be done." Well, maybe I won't make millions, but at least something decent. "Anyway, I'd rather rent a house with a basement so's I can have a workshop."

"Oh, yeah. I forgot."

We drove in silence for a while and I lit a cigarette, pleased at her enthusiasm.

"Dad?"

"Yeah?"

"You know, all the kids in B.R. who took the bus? They really liked you." She went to say something else, stopped, smiled to herself, and then turned to me. "They said you were a good shit."

"Well . . . they did, eh?" I laughed with her as we swung onto the county road. "I guess I can't get a higher rating than that."

"Guess not. How come you never showed me your scrapbook?"

"There wasn't much point. It all happened in the past."

"I looked at it once."

"You did?"

"Yeah. You left it on your dresser and I was cleanin' the room. So I took a look. Pretty neat, eh? Your picture in the paper and things. All those nice things they said about you. Musta felt good."

"It did. But I was pretty young then."

"With a funny haircut."

"That was the style." Jesus, there was nothing wrong with a crewcut. Anyway, it saved going to the barbers.

"You're kiddin'. Those clothes too?"

"Those clothes too."

"I was over at Greg Inglis' before we came down here and his mother was sayin' you were quite a wow with the girls in those days."

"Ruth said that, eh?"

Dear old Ruth. She really did stay happy, and she obviously kept Harry Inglis happy too, because they had seven kids – and that was a sight when she waddled down the main drag eight months pregnant. But she was always smiling and invariably cracked a joke about my promise and how she was going to hold me to it one day. It's funny how the Inglises, with their seven kids, small house, struggling on Harry's money from the mill and having spent all their life in B.R. can be happy, yet Redford, with all his bread, his job and brains couldn't manage it until he was well over forty. Crazy.

"I think she likes you."

"Who?"

"Mrs. Inglis."

"We got along okay. I mean, we didn't know each other that well. Never have."

"She came to see you get married."

"She did?"

Janice sat up, very serious, and made like an actress.

300

"He left a string of broken hearts behind him when . . . when he went up the aisle with his new bride . . . The Harrises of White Pines. Tune in next week an' see what happens! Ta Ta!" She collapsed on the seat, laughing. "Pretty good, eh?"

"Yeah. Maybe you should take up acting when you get to Toronto."

"Maybe I will . . . there's a truck up there pullin' out – "

"Yeah."

"And you can come to my opening nights free of charge. An' I'll have my own television special with long, super gowns, a Cadillac, and when I'm interviewed they'll ask me where I came from, and I'll say, 'Black Rapids of course, doesn't everyone come from there? I'm the daughter of Rennie White Pine, my dear man.' "

She collapsed into laughter again as we slowed to let the pickup pull out of a field. I wound down my window to let in some fresh air.

"Steak and pilsner's gonna taste good."

"It sounds like one of those commercials on the hockey game. Can I have a beer with my dinner?"

"We'll see. You're a bit young for that."

"I bet you drank when you were sixteen."

Yeah, but that was a little different. Kids were more mature then. I think. I couldn't stop myself from smiling. "Maybe the odd one." She smiled back, knowing she had me.

I thought I saw an animal move in the ditch, maybe a rabbit out and about early, or a racoon, and then, suddenly, I was staring down the barrel of a .22 rifle held by the Shantz kid.

"What the – "

"Out!"

Janice screamed as Grant Rochford jumped down from the truck, which was parked right across the road, ran to the passenger side of the wagon, opened the door and grabbed hold of her, dragging her out as she continued to scream. Moving across the seat to help her, I was stopped dead in my tracks by the sound of the bolt going on the .22, a rapid, three-stage movement of steel on steel that gave its own warning. Turning slowly, I saw the muzzle sticking through the window, levelled right at my head, and behind it the acned, downy-moustached face of Shantz, eyes wide and excited.

"Don't move mister, 'cause we ain't foolin'. Now you just get out on this side nice and easy, okay? Now!"

Sliding back across the seat, I started to get out. Rochford slapped Janice across the face a couple of times while he held one of her arms behind her back.

"Cut out the noise, eh? Quit it!" He hit her again and her screams turned to silent, frightened sobs. He looked over the top of the wagon at me, smiling.

"You didn't really think I was gonna let you go and leave this place without settlin' up the score, did you? Listen, no one makes an asshole outa me and gets away with it, especially some fuckin', scummy picker! You motherfuckers haveta be taught a lesson, an' it's gonna be one hell of a lesson. And in case you think the .22 is along for the ride, remember your old lady waitin' back at the farm. She jus' might be wondering tomorrow why the two of youse took off and never came back."

They led us into a field and made us lie on our stomachs, like some prisoners you used to see on the TV news in Vietnam, with the Shantz kid standing over us with the rifle, far enough away to be safe if I tried to rush him, while Rochford backed the truck into the field and then drove my wagon in and parked it behind a clump of young maples.

302

"Hey man, they gotta six-pack in here. We can have a party too." He got out with the beer and my cigarettes from the dash and placed the package on the roof of the wagon before walking over to us. "Jus' to make sure you realize we know what we're doin', we'll give you a little demonstration." He nodded to Shantz, who quickly brought the .22 to his eye and fired, knocking the cigarettes flying from at least forty feet, and then, just as quickly, had the chamber reloaded and the gun pointing at us again. He'd made his point.

"When you go out scoopin' up groundhogs, man, you gotta be fast 'cause those sonsabitches can move pretty quick when they wanna." He nodded to where the cigarette package had been. "Jus' wanted you to understand. Okay? Now get up and start walkin' to those trees over there."

There was a small woods across the field that had just recently had a crop taken off it. We started to walk, the Shantz kid limping about twenty feet behind us. Behind him came Rochford driving the pickup, blocking the view from the road.

Janice stumbled slightly, looking across at me with tears pouring down her cheeks, her eyes pleading and frightened.

"D-a-d . . . do something!"

"Honey, I will . . . when I can."

"But when?" She was nearly hysterical.

"When the right time comes."

"You ain't gonna do nothin', mister. Nothin'!"

"They're gonna . . . kill us!"

"They won't kill us. Don't worry . . . I'll do somethin'. Trust me." I said it pleading with her, trying to comfort her at the same time.

Don't worry!

Christ, what a thing to tell a sixteen-year-old kid with a gun at her back.

Don't worry.

You took over like you were born to it.

Okay, so do it now.

Give me half a chance.

You might not get even that.

Christ, I never once got in a position like this with the whole of the German army out there.

That was thirty-odd years ago, you're not getting any younger.

Trust me, I said.

Trust me.

I wasn't sure whose field we were in. It could be the back of the Shantz property, in which case the chances of someone coming along at this time of the evening were about nil. The sun was starting to go down straight ahead of us, so we were going away from the Rochford farm, which was about five miles from here. In this part of the country, by the time the sun has finally disappeared the locals are closing the drapes and getting ready for bed. I figured that was about forty-five minutes away.

We stumbled deeper into the field and a flock of cowbirds and grackles took off in a gigantic, chattering cloud. I took advantage of the noise to talk to Janice.

"It's gonna be okay, luv, believe me. We gotta get to Toronto and these little bastards aren't gonna stop us. Okay?"

She forced a smile of sorts, her face stained with tears and a red mark where she'd been hit.

Sonsofbitches! I'll kill em if I get the chance.

At the edge of the woods we stopped while Rochford parked the truck and came out with two open beers. He left one on the hood for Shantz, who stood beside it with the .22 at the ready, his eyes still very wide and excited. I knew he was itching to squeeze that trigger just to see what hap-

304

pened when a bullet smashed into someone's head. And he wouldn't miss. Like Rochford said, no way.

At that point Janice tried to run, and Shantz raised the gun toward me as Rochford caught her and threw her to the ground.

"Now that's stoopid, bitch! You do that again and your daddy over there's gonna have a bullet go right into his mushy brain. An' then we got no choice but to kill you too! All right?" Her whole body heaved with her sobs. He grabbed her by an arm and hauled her to her feet.

"All right? You understand?"

She nodded her head, petrified, still sobbing.

"Shutup!" Rochford slapped her again, then again, snapping her head from side to side. When she didn't stop, he threw her to the ground, grabbed her by the hair and hauled her back up.

"All right?"

I don't know if it was shock setting in or if she realized that she'd be better off not sobbing, but she quietened down, her arms and face scratched from when she hit the ground.

Inside I was almost at bursting point, but I had no choice other than to watch. Sure I couldve gone to help her, but I'dve never made it more than three feet and being dead wasn't gonna help her one little bit.

As though to prove a point the Shantz kid in one smooth movement raised the .22, picked off a small bird sitting in a tree about forty feet away, and had it back, levelled right at me, with another bullet ready to go.

"How's it feel, Mister Scummy Picker, to have the boot on the other foot? To have your little girl slapped around a bit, eh?" He strutted around, drinking his beer, perspiring a little, with a broad grin on his face, loving every minute of it. "Well, man, let me tell you. This is jus' the beginnin' of the show."

"Okay, lookit, you wanna get even with me, go ahead. But leave her alone. She's nothin' to do with it. Let her go. She's done nothin' to you!"

"Oh, but she has, man. She's given me the biggest hard-on I've had in years. As for lettin' her go, that would be dumb, 'cause if we jus' happen to kill you, and there's a good chance we will, it wouldn't be very smart to have her runnin' around tellin' the cops all about it, now would it? And anyway, man, you tell me a better way to get back at you than with your pretty little girl here. You tell me."

"For Chrissakes, she's only a kid. Let her go!" I hoped the anger, and possibly fear, that I felt didn't show in my voice, but he just smiled and nodded to Shantz, who moved up to within three feet of me with the gun trained on my head.

"Sit down!" I sat, and now he lowered the gun to a comfortable position with my head still the target, only this way it was a dead cert he wouldn't miss.

Rochford finished his beer and walked over to Janice, who backed up slightly, frightened. He took her arm and turned to me.

"I've thought about this a lot since the other night, man, and I finally decided the first part of gettin' back at you was gonna be with your precious little daughter. She's gonna put on a show for us and then the two of us is gonna put on a show. Just for daddy there. Isn't that right, kid?" He pulled her face to his and kissed her roughly and then stood back, looking at her. "Okay, gorgeous, take off that blouse."

She didn't move, holding her arms in front of her, shaking, looking to me to help her. But Rochford moved over to her and forced her arms apart, took the blouse and ripped it

306

off. I turned away. I had to wait for the right moment. Not do anything stupid, however heroic it might seem. That would kill us both.

"Hey, make him watch, for Chrissakes. That's the whole point."

Shantz moved around to the side of me so that he could see my eyes, moving the gun closer to my head.

"Watch! Otherwise you're not gonna have any eyes to watch from again."

The sound of the .22 going off so close was like a clap of thunder, and I felt the movement of air as the bullet sped past my head. Janice screamed and Rochford hit her.

"Next one, man! The next one! It'll splatter your brains all over the place. That's the final warning." Rochford seemed jumpy, his breathing quicker as he paced to and fro. "Okay, now let's get it on!"

My heart was pounding in my head, my body soaked with cold sweat as Rochford came over to me, leaning in so that our faces were inches apart.

"Now you watch every fuckin' thing, man! You hear?" He screamed it at me, suddenly gripping my shoulders. "Cause I've just changed the whole game plan! Any more foolin' and she's the one who'll go first! Right in front of your eyes! Then it'll be your turn!"

"She's fainted, man."

Janice was on the ground, out of it. Rochford hurried over to her, then took two empty beer bottles to a small stream just inside the woods, filled them and poured them over Janice's head. I figured we had about half-an-hour of daylight left; the sun was sitting just above the trees at the back of the woods. On the other hand, that was dumb, because the daylight had nothing to do with what was going on. Darkness wouldn't stop them.

Janice got up by herself, looking over to me, not believing that I was still alive, shivering from the cold stream water and the evening air. Rochford nervously lit a cigarette, went behind Janice and unclipped her bra, came round the front and pulled it off. She stood, looking down, her arms at her side, as though she had decided to accept whatever was going to happen.

"Hey dad! What d'you think of them tits, eh? Is it the first time you've seen them? Little beauties, I'd say." Shantz stole a look as Rochford moved behind her and put his arms around her, cupping her breasts in his hands and rubbing them.

"Are you watchin', dad? Hey, make sure he's watchin'. Beautiful little nips here are all hard, standin' out jus' like she was hot to trot."

I stared past them, focussing my eyes on the sun that was flashing brilliantly through the trees. Even though she had no way of knowing I wasn't watching the horror that he was putting her through, I still felt that I should do it. Then it occurred to me that if a chance did present itself, I wouldn't be in very good shape to see what I was doing if I continued to look at the sun, so I shifted my look lower but still way past what was going on, occasionally coming back to glance at Shantz who was always ready, waiting for the chance to be a hero.

Rochford started to undo the belt of her jeans and then unzipped the fly.

"All right, blue eyes, take em off."

She hesitated and I moved forward, almost by reflex, to go and help her, but the stock of the .22 smashed behind my ear and the ground came up at me. I guess I must have been out for a couple of minutes, but when I finally came around, Janice was kneeling over me, crying, holding her blouse to the back of my head, with Rochford standing over her.

"What a touchin' scene. Little daughter helping daddy. Well, well, well. He'll be okay, jus' another warning. Now dad, before we carry on, show us how much you appreciate what she did for you, eh? Give her a nice kiss on the tits!" My head was aching and pounding. Shantz was standing there, rifle ready, grinning.

"Way to go, dad."

"Shantzy, the man doesn't hear us. Maybe you should get his ears workin' again like you did just then." He grabbed Janice and forced her down to me. "Kiss em, I said!"

I raised my head slightly and Janice moved so that her breast brushed my lips and then moved away. "That's better, now let's get on with it. From now on, Shantzy, no bullshit. This is where it gets interesting and the man might object again." Pulling Janice about thirty feet away from us, he slapped her across the face and then smiled at her. "Okay, now this time, take em off!" My eyes were watering and through the blur I could see her going through the motions as she took off her jeans. Got to keep the eyes clear, focus again, on the trees. There's got to be a chance.

"And the pants!"

Slowly my eyes began to clear, and I could feel blood trickling down my neck to my shirt as the pain seemed to come and go in waves, at times making me want to throw up. There's got to be a chance.

"Well, look at that! Hey, dad, you ever seen such a neat little cunt? Eh? Nice tits, neat, soft cunt, daddy's pride and joy. His little girl. An' me standin' here with this hard-on, man, so big it aches. An' old Shantzy there. He's got a hard-on just waitin' for his first time. Ain't that right, Shantzy?" Shantz looked at me for a moment, a little embarrassed, even blushing slightly. "A little bit of revenge, man, cause I don't like bein' made a fool of, like I said. I don't like scabby little pickers tellin' me what to do or shovin' my old man around. Okay, Shantzy, now's the time. Stick that gun right against his head, an' if he moves a muscle, pow!"

I felt the steel of the barrel against my head. By rolling my eyes almost into the top of my skull, I could see Shantz looking down at me, still grinning.

Rochford took hold of Janice and tried to force her to the ground. She resisted and he hit her, then picked up a tree branch and hit her again across the back until she finally lay down on the ground and he stood over her, breathing very hard, the sweat rolling down his face.

"Hey dad? You got a hard-on for your own daughter?" He laughed and undid his jeans, took them off, and then his shorts. "Look at that, man . . . jus' throbbing and waitin' to go. You watch him now, Shantzy. Open your legs! Wider! Jesus Christ, wish you could see this. It's beautiful, man. Like a picture in Penthouse." He knelt down in front of Janice and moved toward her.

"No. Please. Don't do it. Please."

"Are you watchin', dad?"

I heard her gasp and sob as he entered her. Through the blur I could see his violent motions. He was calling out between breaths.

"Christ, Shantzy . . . you're gonna love it man. Tight as a drum . . . Jesus . . . you watchin' dad? This little whore is really gettin' it. She's really gettin' it Shantzy. She's gonna be really ready for you man . . ."

I forced my eyeballs up again, past the bulge in Shantz's jeans, to look at him, just as he turned to steal a quick glance at his buddy. I had a feeling he wouldn't be able to resist just one look – after all, it's not every day you get the

310

chance to watch your best friend raping a girl, especially when you know you'll be next and for the first time in your life. With all the strength I could muster I hit the barrel of the rifle with the side of my arm, knocking it away from me as he pulled the trigger, the noise of the shot and the whine of the bullet echoing in my ears.

"What the fuck—"

The sound of Rochford's voice blended into the echo as I threw myself at Shantz's legs, knocking him off balance, grabbing the rifle as he fell, twisting it out of his hands and smashing the stock in his face. I unloaded it and threw it as far as I could into the woods, then hurled myself across the thirty feet between me and Janice. And Rochford.

One chance. That's all you've got.

He was already on his knees, looking helplessly toward me as the distance between us shrank at incredible speed. Even as he knelt there, frozen to the ground but trying to back off, I could see that he had reached that point of no return and had no control over himself, spurting white, creamy liquid in jerky motions into the grass and onto his legs, my hand reaching out for him as I sidestepped him at the last minute, grabbed his hair, and pulled him away from Janice onto his back.

I took time only to make sure that Janice had been able to roll away to safety and that Shantz was still where I'd left him. Then I turned to Rochford.

He was trying to get up and I let him reach the right height before I smashed him in the face, sending him staggering into a tree, then I caught him again and he fell to his knees and bounced back with his fists swinging wildly, spitting out blood as he rushed at me with the same kind of anger I'd seen in his eyes the night he came at me with the beer bottle. For a moment he tried to make a fight of it, until I caught him with the most vicious blow I could manage right into his guts, and he staggered back toward the stream, the red glow of the sun shining off his sweat-covered face as he stumbled and finally fell, blood pouring from his nose and mouth.

I paused for a moment and tried to catch my breath, looking at him, hating him, with more rage still to come out when I thought of what he'd done to Janice.

"Open your legs! Wider! Jesus Christ, wish you could see this. Like a picture in Penthouse."

"No. Please. Don't do it. Please."

"Are you watchin' dad? Tight as a drum. This little whore is really gettin' it."

My hand was grabbing his medallion and twisting the leather, lifting him to his feet, holding him by the shoulders, inches away from me, my voice calm and quiet.

"You're never gonna forget tonight! Never! I jus' want you to understand that. Understand what you did to her, because you're the one who's gonna regret it for the rest of your life! D'you understand?"

"Y-e-s." He coughed the word out.

"For the rest of your fuckin', miserable life, you're gonna regret it!"

And I brought my knee up into his balls with all the momentum and power I could. His face went blank, then changed, the redness from the fighting fading to white, then ash grey, his eyes bulging as a silence fell for a brief moment before his scream split the air right open, bouncing off the

312

trees in the woods. A few crows took to the air with their noisy, grating call; weird black monsters flapping and circling in the red, glowing sky. Again I brought my knee up, even harder this time, so that I felt his balls crush through my pants and there was nowhere for them to go except back up into his body.

This time there was no scream.

Lowering his limp, unconscious body to the ground, I realized I was just one step away from killing him. Only the sun, now almost at ground level, blazing through the trees, had stopped me. If I'd gone any further everything that I had been striving for these past couple of days would have been for nothing. It still might be. But it stopped me from killing him.

The crows disappeared, and the sudden silence was a great relief. I stood up, exhausted, my mouth dry and raw, my head swimming from the rifle blow, sweat pouring down. Janice was kneeling where I'd left her. She hadn't moved, shivering and staring at the ground, the redness of the light making her look like an old world painting. I picked up her clothes and took them to her, put the torn blouse over her shoulders.

"Put your clothes on, love, and I'll get you out of here. Take you to the hospital." Still she didn't move, her eyes wide and glazed. "Janice, love. It's all right. They're not going to hurt you any more." No reaction. I took off my shirt and buttoned it around her, checked to see that the two kids were still breathing and went to start the truck, but the keys weren't there. I went through their pockets but I still couldn't find them, so I picked Janice up and started the long walk back across the field. By the time we'd reached the halfway point her arms were around my neck and she was clinging to me like a baby, sobbing onto my shoulder, shaking with the cold, while my head felt as though it would burst open any minute.

It was another of those nightmares. I'd wake up and it wouldn't be true. Just a bad dream.

But the pain and the wetness from Janice's tears on my shoulder made me realize that like the others, this one was for real.

It was the light that woke me up. Bright light coming through the window onto the yellow walls, causing a shadow to fall across the picture of what looked like Georgian Bay, grey and mauve rocks with the water and a pine tree standing alone on the rocks, the kind of picture they have hanging in Black Rapids railroad station, only this one seemed to have a cardboard frame.

Then there was the smell, a funny smell of antiseptic, and the smell of bandages that reminded me of when my mother used to wrap them around my legs after I'd done something stupid like fall out of a tree or off my bicycle.

I closed my eyes for a moment and then tried again, but nothing had changed, only now I was aware of the dull ache behind my ear. My fingers moved slowly up the pillow to feel the thick gauze at the back of my head, following it round to the front, across the top of my head and back round the other side. Then I saw the tubes in my other arm and the bottles hanging from a chrome stand and it all came back with a sickening lurch and I wanted to leap out of bed, tear off the tubes and go and find Janice.

"You're awake, then?"

Turning, I found myself looking up at these gorgeous eyes, beautiful lips, rolls of blonde hair sticking out from the front of her cap over her forehead, and a gentle smile. Maybe I was in heaven.

Before I could ask her she put a thermometer into my mouth and took my wrist. Then the next wave of remembering hit me, coming like some of those commercials you see on television, jerky, fast, no sooner seeing one picture and it's gone and another is there, getting faster and faster.

The car. No keys. Back across the field. On the seat of the truck. Running back. Weird lights in front of my eyes. The car. Driving fast. Heater full blast. Janice sobbing. Mosquito bites. Head throbbing. The hospital. Carrying Janice in. Man in white. Nurses.

Janice sobbing.

Tired, very tired.

Tired.

The nurse's hand felt my forehead. "Just relax. Your pulse really started moving then."

Relax. Sure.

I remember staying with Janice as long as I could before they took her away, talking to nurses, then the police, my head being bathed, then X-rayed, stitched, the bandage going on, Connie off in the distance looking worried, voices echoing louder and louder and louder until they were booming around inside my head.

Connie holding my hand, trying to smile at me.

Going to the washroom where my legs suddenly went to rubber as I leaned over the bowl, throwing up and crying as

I saw the fear on Janice's face, heaving and heaving until nothing more would come except tears.

"That's better. We'll bring you something for those bites. D'you feel like breakfast?" She was taking the plaster off my arm and removing the tubes, young and beautiful and wearing something that reminded me of Joyce back in London.

Joyce? Why do strange, beautiful women always remind me of Joyce? That was almost thirty years ago.

I can't imagine her getting old. Wonder what happened to her?

"The doctor will be in to see you in about an hour."

"Oh. Thanks."

"Breakfast?"

"No thanks. No breakfast. How's . . . my daughter?"

"She's doing fine. They sedated her. The sleep will help."

"Take it away . . . the memory?"

"Er . . . no. But it'll help."

"Yeah. What . . . what happened to me?"

"You passed out in the Emergency washroom."

"Oh."

"Why don't you rest until the doctor comes?"

"Yes. What about my wife?"

"She stayed in town."

"We can't afford . . . is there a washroom here?"

"Right over there. Can I help you?"

"No. Thanks. I can manage."

"Your wife should be in to see you soon."

In the washroom mirror I saw that old man staring back at me again, his lifeless, grey, lined face in need of a shave, the hollow, blank eyes staring into nowhere.

I wanted to see Janice. But not like this. Like one of those monsters who flew over the woods. Jesus, they sounded like they were laughing at me. Waiting for me to die, probably.

You look half dead already.

Yeah, like that Rochford kid.

Fuckin' bastard!

"Lousy, rotten, fuckin' bastard!"

The nurse and a guy in white took me back to bed.

"There's an old man in there."

"We'll get rid of him."

"You won't. He'll still be there when I go back."

"Just rest for a while."

"He's old, dyin' . . . washed up."

"I'll see he doesn't come back."

"But he will. He looks like he's come from a wreckin' yard . . . no, maybe that's where he's going."

"Maybe. Your wife'll be here soon."

"I did my best."

"You did fantastic."

"But it wasn't enough! It wasn't soon enough!"

"You did what you could and that was more than enough."

"But she won't know that. She'll never believe that I did my best. She knows me . . . knows I haven't done my best for years."

"Shall I call a doctor?"

"No. He's falling asleep."

"I was on my way down when – "

"I'm sorry."

" – I heard him yell. The language!"

318

"These things happen."

"It's a misplaced meal break, you know. I can't not – "

"Don't tell me your problems."

I woke up after lunch and Connie was sitting there, coming in and out of focus, trying again to smile. When my head started to clear, I saw that she was crying.

"Hey, it's okay. Nothin' to cry about. It's gonna be okay."

"It was such a shock . . . seein' the both of you. Hearing what had happened." She took a Kleenex and wiped her eyes.

"Yeah." We didn't say anything for a while and I stared at the picture which was now caught by the sun and looked better for it.

"I brought your razor and things."

"Thanks, love."

My mind started to churn with a mixture of thoughts tumbling over each other. I mean, I've read about rape and things in magazines and how it affects the victim. How it takes them years to get over it sometimes and how, in some cases, they never do. It screws them up for ever. Puts them off men, off sex, makes 'em nervous wrecks.

It wouldve never happened if I hadn't lost my temper and belted the Rochford kid when I caught them drinking Alex's beer, found his tent gone and his car stripped.

It wouldn't have happened if we hadn't come to work in the tomato fields in the first place, if I hadn't hit Caulfield Jr. at the mill Christmas party.

Funny thing is, I don't really have a temper. It's just that sometimes in my life I've got to let go, like a safety valve lettin' off steam.

I mean, playin' hockey I very rarely got into fights, nor at school either, nor in the army. It's since I got back.

But it was belting Caulfield that started the whole chain of events that led up to it. If we hadn't gone for steak it wouldn't have happened. But then, on the other hand, maybe it wouldve. Only someplace else. They had it planned, that was for sure.

Dear Jesus, she was so helpless, standin' there, waitin' for me to do somethin', I wanted to cry out then and there, rush over and comfort her, tell her it would be all right.

But would she have believed me?

I dunno.

I do know that I loved her like I never loved her before when I was carryin' her back across that field, so help me I loved her. I mean, she's my daughter. She's gotta know that I did somethin' as soon as I could.

That I didn't let them go through with it because I was scared.

"What you thinking?" Connie's voice came out of nowhere, snapping me back to that yellow room with the funny smell and the picture on the wall.

"Oh, lots of things. A mish-mash. Last night, today, what's gonna happen in the future. What it's gonna be like for her, after she gets outa here."

"It would have never happened if we hadn't come here to work. I always said it was no place to bring her – "

Christ! Why did she have to say that? Doesn't she think I know it!? How does she think I feel about it? Goddamnit!

"I'm sorry. I shouldn't have said that. It was stupid."

"Yes, it was."

"I didn't mean to hurt you. I guess it just came out."

"If it was in there waiting to come out I spose it's better that it does."

At that moment the doctor came in, and after his examination I went to the washroom to shave.

The old man was still there like I said he'd be, but he looked a little better with the stubble gone, and his face wasn't so grey. He looked a little more alive, as though he might make it after all. Hanging behind the door were my pants and shorts. On the knee of the right pant leg I could see the stain of dry, caked semen, my new pants I'd bought in Toronto and would probably never wear again. But then who the hell can afford to throw away a pair of brand new pants when a good cleaning job would fix them up?

Apart from the head wound and the mosquito bites, they said I was also suffering from malnutrition. Now, if I ever heard a crock of shit, that was it! Me? In my physical condition, and they tell me that? On the other hand, Alex was in pretty good shape and look what happened to him. Anyway, they started giving me pills and feeding me good meals, and they decided to keep me in for another day for observation, which was the way they told it. When all the examinations were over and they told me my head was fine, no fractures, and they'd put on a new dressing, Connie came back in and we stood there, just holding each other for a long time, until I started to laugh, and then Connie, at the sight of me in this little white gown, and although both of us were forcing the laughter because we both had Janice on our minds, it eased the tension. Connie had been to see Janice briefly and said she was quiet and withdrawn, so I told her I would go down and see her later.

"I stayed at a nice hotel last light. Only ten-fifty for a single room."

"Which one?"

"The William Pitt. D'you know it?"

"No. Well, I've seen it." I must have shown some reaction, but there was no point in going into that now.

"I had a lot of conversations with myself in that room. I was going to leave you for good, take Janice back home, I didn't give a damn what happened to you. It was you that caused it and it was me that had gone along with all your crazy, lazy ideas all these years, and I decided not to any more. That was it! I couldn't take any more and I hated you for it. Then, after I'd said it this morning, about how it wouldn't have happened if we hadn't come here to work, I realized that it was me that I was . . . feeling sorry for. Me that had been hurt. It was me who stopped us from coming to Toronto all these years."

"Honey, that's all in the past. Like that goddamned scrapbook."

"Will you let me finish? This isn't easy. I realized that it was Janice who'd been hurt, raped, made to do those things. That you were hurt and in hospital too – that it was you who had the gun to his head. Not me. It was . . . well, very selfish. But then, it's easy when you've having a conversation with yourself to win the argument. We've . . . we've both got to help her and the doctors say it won't be easy. I know now . . . what you meant about a person having his pride . . . and I just wanted you to know that." I wanted to pull her to me, hold her very tight and say a lot of things, but all that came out was that it takes two to make things work. Why couldn't I say the right thing when I needed it most?

"I know . . . and I haven't always helped by being . . . " She shrugged and there were tears in her eyes again. This time it was her that had to search for something to say.

"You know?" I held her close and very tight, not only comforting her, but feeling it myself. "That's a lousy picture they've got on the wall."

"Maybe that's why it's there. So's people can talk about it." She smiled and wiped her eyes again and took the keys to the wagon to go back and pack the last few items so that we could leave once and for all. It was when she went through my things that I discovered I'd lost Alex's lighter somewhere in the field where it happened.

The police came in later and I went over the previous evening with them step by step. They told me that both kids were in another ward on the next floor down, the Shantz boy with a broken nose and cheek bone and Rochford with contusions and hematoma of the testicles, severe they called it, and they said that he'd probably be sterile for the rest of his life.

"Thing is, will he ever be able to get it up again?"

"You'd have to ask the doctor that."

I did, later, and he told me that there was a chance that he wouldn't but it was hard to tell at this stage.

In the afternoon I went down to see Janice.

It wasn't a moment I'd been looking forward to. That is, I wanted to see her, but I didn't want her to get upset by my being there. She'd had time to think about it too, have conversations with herself, and the doctor warned me that she was still having crying spells and felt very ashamed about the whole thing. There was also a good chance that she would resent me, but that with luck, time would sort that out in her head.

The drapes were pulled, throwing a soft, strange light in the room, and Janice was lying in her bed staring at the ceiling, not seeming to be aware that I was there. I crossed the room slowly and sat down gently on the edge of the bed and took her hand, seeing her swollen, bruised face for the first time. As I moved my hand to touch her cheek, she turned away toward the window and I could see the tears forcing their way through her closed eyelids and rolling slowly down her cheek to her neck. I was thankful for the moment of silence as I mopped up the tears with tissue, because I didn't know what to say. I'd gone over it in my head, rehearsed it on the way down, but now none of it seemed right.

The door opened and a hospital volunteer came in with a trolley and placed a glass of ginger ale on the bedside table and I resented her for interrupting something that was between Janice and me. Something that was as important as any moment I had ever spent, and this woman barges in like she owned the joint, staring at Janice as though she'd never seen a patient before.

Janice turned and looked at me, her eyes red and raw from crying, and I smiled, picked up the ginger ale and helped her up so that she could drink it, and then we sat for a moment looking at each other until a nurse came in with a tray of pills in small plastic containers, all bright and breezy.

"Well, how are we today? One red one, one red and yellow and a green one. Oh, you've got something to take it with. Don't you find it dark in here?" But Janice was lying down again with her head turned away.

When the nurse had gone I took the container with the pills and the ginger ale round to the other side of the bed and held them out for her, sitting beside her again to help her up, and then passing the pills one by one as she took them.

I suppose I sat with her for about half an hour, wiping away the tears, holding her hand, neither of us speaking, until she finally sat up and put her hand out to touch, very gently, the dressing on the back of my head, the bites on my arms, which were a mess of swollen blotches. Then she leaned forward and put her arms around me and clung to me, as she had the night before, only this time there were no tears, while I held her tightly, not wanting to let go. Her voice was a whisper.

"You . . . were very brave, dad."

Sweet Jesus, here she's telling me *I* was brave? An even greater surge of warmth moved through me, and I pulled her closer.

"Are . . . are you ashamed of . . . me?" She looked right into my eyes.

"My darlin', why would I be ashamed of you?"

"What I did."

"You had no choice."

"I know. It . . . it was better than being killed. I thought they'd shot you. I was sure you were dead."

"It's all over now. I shoulda never brought you pickin' in the first place."

"It wasn't your fault. It was no one's fault except theirs. Anyway, it happened. We can't change it, can we? I just didn't want you to be ashamed or embarrassed . . . seein' me do it and when they made you . . . kiss me."

There was another silence and this time I had to turn away from her.

"I've never seen you cry before. Except I thought you did at Alex's funeral. I didn't think men cried." She smiled for the first time and gave me a Kleenex.

It's taken me years, but yes, men do cry. We have all sorts of emotions we're not supposed to have.

"Dad."

"Yes, my love?"

"You won't . . . well, tell anyone about it, eh? Not any-one?"

325

"No, my love . . . I won't tell a soul . . . ever."

I took some more Kleenex and blew my nose, then lit a cigarette.

"Can I have one?"

"Sure, why not?"

I wound the back of her bed up, made her pillows comfortable, and we sat there quietly smoking. Occasionally I'd smile, watching her smoke like every other teenager who hasn't been doing it for very long, taking deep breaths in and then blowing the smoke everywhere with quick, frantic puffs.

"Would you like some more light in here?"

"No thanks . . . my face looks better with the drapes closed."

"Okay."

There was another silence, and Janice stubbed out her cigarette half-smoked, pulling the bedclothes tightly around herself until just part of her face was showing.

"Dad? The doctor said he didn't think I'd get pregnant. He didn't find any . . . stuff inside me."

"Yeah, I know. Mum was talking to him."

"What did he say?"

"Well . . . it might take a little while to get over it, but you will."

"Anything else?"

"He said . . . you were very determined, very brave, someone we should be proud of." I couldn't remember what Connie had told me, but it sounded right and it was a way of getting things I wanted to say, but somehow couldn't, across.

"The funny thing was . . . I didn't really know what was goin' on at the end, after he kept hittin' me. I mean . . . I didn't feel anythin'. I don't remember him . . . well, you know."

God, I hope she never remembers it, but things like that are usually too good to be true.

"I remember hearing the gun go off again . . . an' a lot of shouting . . . and a scream . . . an' then you carrying me."

"Try not to think about it if you can. I know that sounds dumb, but . . ."

It was too.

"Are you sure . . . you weren't ashamed . . . or disgusted?"

I leaned in and kissed her cheek, taking her hand again.

"My darlin' . . . how could I be?"

That night after dinner, Connie came and visited me again before going back to the hotel, and we sat and drank some take-out coffee she'd brought with her.

"How was it at the farm?"

"Same as usual. No one spoke to me."

"See Rochford?"

"Nope. I got the things ready, set the traps and came here."

"What d'you set the traps for?"

"Habit, I spose."

The conversation was strained and there were many silences, with both of us not crazy about talking about the future. How all this might have changed things. Finally I brought it up.

"I think the move to Toronto has come at the right time. It'll be a new start for Janice, give her new interests, get her mind off things."

"You still plan to go through with it?"

"Of course. I said I would. Don't you want to now?"

"Yes. I just wanted to make sure that you did. I know how important it is for you . . . but you might have changed your mind and not wanted to say so. Pride is a big thing, you know."

"I know."

"I wanted you to have . . . well, the chance to back out of it if you wanted."

"You know somethin'? We've bin married for twenty-eight years and we're not doin' bad. It coulda bin better but we got through . . . an' now we're gonna start something completely new. Not bad, eh?"

"Not bad." She smiled and started to put her coat on.

"After you've gone I'm gonna have a big, deep, hot bath an' just lay there and soak."

"Me too. They got tubs at the hotel."

"Stay here and share mine. We haven't done that for years."

"Herr Kapitan! Periscope up! Somehow I don't think the nurses would approve if they came in."

"I guess not. We'll take a rain check."

"Sure."

"And if a nurse comes in in the meantime, I'll be sociable and ask her to join me. They say they're very good with periscopes."

"Yeah? Well, lotsa luck."

She gave me a kiss and left, placing some of my books she'd brought on the table for me.

Later I lay back in bed and opened *Letters to my Daughter* by Muriel Lobraico. I saw that Connie had marked a short story called "*First Love.*" It was about this girl in a small town who was in love with the boy who sat behind her in school, only he never knew it and she was too shy to say anything. Even though she knew that once he spied on her from a tree when she went skinnydipping it didn't make any difference, and she never let him know that she saw him.

It seems that this kid was something of a hockey hero in the town and she went faithfully to his home games, but he ignored her as though she didn't exist. She still loved him, knowing that one day he'd leave the town and become famous in the big city. The problem was that she was a Catholic and he was an Anglican, and her parents forbade her to have anything to do with him. Then came the day when the local team won the championship and had a parade and presentation in the local arena and Don – that was his name – got a standing ovation from the crowd when he was introduced while she stood proudly in the background – at the same time sad and lonely, because it was something she wanted to share with him. Then he got down from the platform:

He walked through the crowd, humble but, because of that, magnificent in his glory, sometimes lost from sight as he accepted the adulation. And then, to my horror, I realized that he was walking straight toward me. I felt myself colour, the warm flush moving through my body with a sudden swiftness that was suffocating. A feeling of uncertainty gripped me as I looked around, searching for somewhere to flee. Filled with panic, I found myself the prisoner of hundreds of grotesque, laughing faces, all pressing closer and closer, hemming me in, forcing me back toward him, mocking, ridiculing; devils whose distorted images and sounds told me that this was the penance I would have to endure, the pain I would have to suffer if they were to free me.

Then we were face to face and I found myself saying, "Hello, Don."

He seemed surprised, a little puzzled, as though he was trying to remember who I was, where he'd seen me before.

"Oh . . . hi. Howya doin'?"

"Fine. Congratulations." My tongue was tied, my mind a swirl-

ing blank, and I prayed for the floor to open up beneath me and swallow me forever to purge my gaucheness once and for all. But the prayer went unanswered and my feet remained firmly planted on the floor. I could see that he wanted to move on. Caring about fluttering, childlike, teenage girls was something he'd grown far beyond.

"Nice seein' you. Take care." And he was gone, absorbed by all the well-wishers, the knight returned from the crusade receiving the homage of the adoring hordes. If only we had met somewhere else, the two of us, where I could have said the things I'd always wanted to say. All those years and he never knew, never realized how I felt about him.

It had been my cherished ambition, ever since I found out about such things, that I would give myself first to him. That despite the teachings and threats of the church, despite my parents, he would be the one to take my sacred virginity from me. He never knew that I was his for the asking and I was too shy to say or do anything about it. I've kept his photograph all these years in memory of something that never was and never could be again. He was killed in France in 1945, killed in the bloom of his fragrant youth.

Never knowing my love for him.

Sonofabitch. For Chrissakes! She didn't have to kill me off, though. Wouldn't you know it? Wouldn't you goddamned well know it? The knight returned from the crusades! Sonofabitch. It would have been good for my scrapbook, only I don't keep it any more.

We left for Black Rapids a few days late, speeding up Highway 400 to Highway Eleven, putting as much distance as we could between us and the farm, the memories, the implement shed, where we'd left all six traps and their victims for Rochford to clean up. Leaving the stink of piss and tomatoes, the whole degrading process, hidden behind the neat fences and painted barns of southwestern Ontario, that grinds human beings into nothing; fuckin' scummy pickers, like the Rochford kid said, while everyone else looks the other way, not wanting to know about it. Not even us any more.

They've got a new guy on the snow plough now, a young kid about twenty-five, and although he's having trouble cutting a nice, straight, clean line, they say he's going to be all right even if he does leave the driveways blocked. It takes time. It's not something you can learn overnight.

I saw what he could do when I drove back up to Black Rapids for Christmas—a celebration that would include Connie's parents because it was the last we'd spend there. Two days later we were handing over the keys of the house to the new owners, a husband and wife from Toronto who were coming to teach at the school. We didn't get as much as we wanted, but seeing as it was the only offer in three months, we were only too happy to accept. He didn't have a beard, but goddamnit, he drove a blue Volvo station wagon, the first ever in B.R.

This meant that we had to spend New Year's with Connie's folks, which was kind of nice in a way. They gave us their bedroom and at night we made sure the door was closed to keep out the new poodle her father had bought for her mother, complete with a red bow round its neck, so that she would be occupied now that she was losing her daughter. But it all worked out. We saw the new year in with champagne and Connie and her mother cried while her father told me that things weren't as good as they used to be in the town hall.

I was a couple of days late getting back from Toronto because I had to complete a kitchen I was doing for one of Redford's friends and they wanted it finished in time for Christmas. They'd been to a party at the Redfords' just before I'd finished the job there, and she thought that Lisa's studio was just darling and when would I be free? Now they want their bathroom done and when I suggested putting a skylight in its sloping roof, she thought that was the end of the world. What with that and friends of theirs who want their rec room redone, things are pretty hectic. Redford even suggested I form a company for tax reasons. He offered to handle it free of charge, but I told him there was no way. He'd be paid, like all the other people I deal with.

Connie and Janice like the name, Eldon Harris Remodeling, so I guess we'll call it that. It'll look good on the side of the truck I'm going to need pretty soon. I mean, it's nice to see your name in print.

The worst part of those first few months was going back to an empty room at night, but it was there that I was able to put everything in perspective, realizing that I'd been lucky and that I was going to have to work my ass off to make sure it stayed that way. Realizing also that when you've got something to aim for, it makes a difference. The only mad thing I did during that whole period was two days before I went back up north.

I was on Yonge Street looking for Christmas presents to take back when I got this wild idea, and without giving it a second thought, went to McTamney's on Church Street and bought Connie a two-hundred-dollar sapphire ring, including tax. There are some things you just do, and that was one of them.

Considering everything, Janice has made good progress. For a long time she was quiet and withdrawn, occasionally coming out of it for brief periods, but lately, Connie says, she's been much better and actually talks about it, but always as though it happened to someone else. When the case comes up for trial they're hoping that the kids will plead guilty and that Janice won't have to give evidence – but I set them straight on that. There's no way that memory is going to be reopened for her. She's doing good, and nothing is going to upset the new beginning.

The day before we left, Connie and me took a walk through town, holding hands like we used to years ago, the snow crunching and snapping under our feet, our nostrils seizing up as we breathed. She stopped at the window of Black Rapids Credit Jewellers and took off her glove, looked at the ring, smiled at me, then took my arm and led us to Wong's for some hot chocolate. Then we went to get the car, at her suggestion, so that we could drive to the cut-off for old times' sake. By the Lions Club seat we met Bert Powell walking his dog, both wrapped up against the cold, Bert in a heavy coat and fur hat, the dog with an old blanket tied around it.

"Eldon. Connie."

"Bert."

"Bit fresh."

"Gonna be warmer tomorrow."

"So they say. I tell you, Eldon, what this town needs is a good snow plough operator."

"The kid 'll do alright."

"I suppose. Kids don't seem to care though. Like they used to. Well, take care."

"Take care. Say hello to Agnes."

"Will do."

The windshield still froze over in ten minutes, the patterns of frost changing rapidly until the view faded away into white. We sat and had a cigarette, taking turns sipping from a mickey of rye, and when I put my arm around her, she took the glove from my other hand, undid a couple of buttons on her topcoat, and slid my hand inside, holding it there tightly where it was warm and loving.

"That's nice," she whispered, and rested her head on my shoulder.

"You're . . . you're not wearing a bra!"

"I know."

I thought I saw her blush slightly as I tipped her head and kissed her gently. "You, of all people. I don't believe it."

She gave a little shrug and a smile. "There's a lot of catching up to do." She looked down and snuggled closer. "My folks have gone to the Senior Citizens' Club and Janice is out with her friends . . . the house is empty . . ."

"And if we stay here . . ."

"We'll freeze to death."